The Invocation

Carl Alves

End of Days Publishing

ISBN: 9781090153029

Cover art and design by Kealan Patrick Burke

Created in the United States of America

DEDICATION

I would like to dedicate *The Invocation* to my wife, Michelle, and my two boys, Max and Alex, who continue to support me with life and writing and everything in between.

ACKNOWLEDGEMENT

Thank you to my readers, who continue to support my writing career. Thanks to Mort Castle and all of the writers who have given me sage advice over the years. A special thanks to Kealan Patrick Burke for the great job he did on the cover, and Tim Marquitz, for helping me whip this book into shape. Beyond all, I would like to thank my two sons, Alex and Max, who give me daily inspiration, and my wife, Michelle, for continuing to make my life complete.

Chapter I

"You're moving it," Kenna said.

Ben's face turned white. "I swear, it's not me."

"If neither of you is doing it, then how's it moving?" Carlos asked in a small voice.

Kenna bit her lip. Using her brother's Ouija board had been a bad idea. She wasn't sure whose idea it was to try the board. Probably Cordy. She always thought they were mature enough to handle grown-up things even though they were still in the fourth grade. "I don't know."

Cordy brushed her curly blonde hair back. She folded her hands and leaned forward. "Ask their name?"

The poor lighting in the basement did nothing to help the apprehension she felt. Kenna took a deep breath and stared at Ben. He looked as scared as she felt. Her voice trembled. "What's your name?"

Kenna's heart thumped as the planchette moved across the board. Her eyes went wide as she stared at Ben.

The first letter was M, the second I, the third A. Kenna waited, but no longer felt resistance on the planchette. "Is your name Mia?"

The planchette moved to the word Yes.

"Um, are you dead?" Ben asked.

How could he ask that? Kenna gasped when she felt resistance on the planchette as it moved to Yes. Her fingers were lightly pressed on the top of the planchette, barely holding it. The same with Ben. Neither of them was moving it.

Kenna took a deep breath. "When did you die?"

1975.

"Wow," Carlos said. "That was, like, a long time ago."

"Find out how she died?" Cordy moved in closer to them.

It blew away Kenna's mind that they were actually talking to a spirit beyond the grave. She had always believed in ghosts, but this proved it beyond any doubt. Now that they were actually communicating with a spirit, couldn't they ask Mia happier questions? Her friends spent way too much time watching scary movies.

A damp chill ran across the basement. Although the floors were carpeted, it was just used for storage. There were boxes of junk everywhere. The two lights that were on didn't provide much illumination.

"How did you die?" Kenna asked.

A shiver ran through Kenna's body as the planchette abruptly moved, spelling LAKE. Nobody spoke. Kenna barely breathed. DROWNED.

"Oh my God," Carlos said. "She drowned in a lake."

"How did you drown?" Kenna asked.

ACCIDENT. Kenna thought this was all they would get, then the planchette moved, spelling FRIENDS DRINKING.

Kenna shivered. Her father had died in a drunk driving accident when she was five. Mom forbade alcohol in the house. The couple of times she had caught her older brother Jake drinking, he had caught hell for it. After Jake had been released from prison, he told Mom he wasn't going to drink again. Kenna thought he said it to make their mom feel better. No matter what anyone said about Jake, she believed her brother to be a great person. He always made her feel safe.

"Where are you?" Kenna asked.

There was no movement from the planchette. Then it spelled BEYOND.

Carlos folded his arms. "How come she ain't in Heaven?"

Cordy's eyes widened. "Because she was drinking. Drinking's a sin."

"No, it's not," Carlos said. "My daddy drinks every night."

Kenna took her hands off the planchette and put them on her hips. She gave the others a stern look. "Focus, guys."

"Right," Ben said. "Where were you from?"

TRAPPE.

"Freaky," Kenna said. "That's just up the road. How old were you when you died?"

18.

"That's how old Jake is." The thought saddened Kenna. She could barely remember her dad anymore. If Jake died, her whole world would shatter. "Are you alone?"

The planchette went to No.

Carlos' eyes narrowed. "Who do you think's with her?"

Cordy shrugged. "I don't know. Let's ask."

As each moment passed, Kenna felt less freaked out about talking to a dead person. It was no longer so mind-numbing. In fact, it almost seemed normal. Even her friends didn't look as spooked as they had been when the planchette first started moving. "Mia, who's there with you?"

OTHERS.

"Are they like ghosts or something?" Ben asked.

No.

"What are they?" Kenna asked.

SPIRITS.

"I don't get it," Carlos said. "What's the difference?"

"Aren't ghosts and spirits the same thing?" Ben asked.

The planchette went to No.

Kenna didn't fully understand the difference between ghosts and spirits either, but she figured the explanation would be long and complicated. A Ouija board probably wouldn't be the best thing for that kind of explanation. "Let's move on. There's so much I want to find out about."

Cordy stood and began walking around the basement. "What else should we ask?"

Ben took his hands off the disc. "Let's find out what Mia did before she died." He put his hands back on it.

"Ooh, maybe she knows famous dead people like Kurt Cobain," Carlos said.

The planchette jerked. It spelled MUST GO before moving to Good Bye.

A wave of claustrophobia hit Kenna. She had the distinct feeling this was somehow coming from Mia. It was hard to explain, but since they started speaking with her, she had felt Mia's presence. It had been as if she was in the room with them. While they were communicating with her, it felt sunny, light and breezy, like an afternoon down the shore. What she felt now was cold and dark, like an oncoming storm. She wondered if the others felt it as well.

Ben let go of the planchette as if it was a hot coal. He looked spooked.

"What was that all about?" Kenna asked.

"No idea," Ben replied

Carlos shook his head, staring at the board. "I can't believe Mia would just hang up like that."

Kenna rolled her eyes. "She didn't hang up. It's not like we were on the phone."

"I can't believe we actually talked to a ghost." Cordy twirled her blonde hair. In the dim light, she looked more like a little girl and less of the mature pre-teen she always strove to be.

"Spirit," Kenna corrected.

"Whatever. You two really weren't moving it?" Cordy asked.

"I swear it was going on its own," Ben said.

Cordy's face tightened. "Swear on your mom that you didn't move it."

In a low tone, Ben said, "I swear on my mom."

Cordy turned to Kenna. "What about you?"

"I didn't move it either."

"Swear on Jake,"

Kenna's upper lip flared. "I'm not going to swear on Jake."

"Then how do we know you're telling the truth?"

When Kenna crossed her arms, the planchette moved on its own.

Carlos shrieked.

Kenna stared wide-eyed as the planchette moved across the board slowly as if at a crawl. With shaky movements, it spelled out HELP ME.

It was Mia. That feeling of despair must have been coming from her. Now she was reaching out to them. But how could it be moving on its own?

"Quick. Grab it," Kenna said.

Ben held the other end of the planchette.

"Is that you, Mia?" Kenna asked.

It went to Yes.

The lights went out. The next few seconds were a jumble of yelling and screaming as they tried to scramble out of the basement. Someone's knee collided with Kenna's back, and she grunted. She had to reach the door and get outside. Behind her came a crash, followed by a loud thud. She turned, and her heart nearly stopped. In the darkness was a glowing figure of a tall man with short hair glaring at her. She screamed at the top of her lungs as the silhouette approached her.

Moments later, the lights came back on and the silhouette was gone.

Kenna screamed at the sight of Cordy lying face down on the floor, blood surrounding her.

Chapter II

Jake Trigg put the applications on his desk. It felt good to be home. Anything was better than being in the pen. Still, he wasn't looking forward to filling out these applications after completing several online already. He had been turned down for a half-dozen jobs in his short time back. In the couple of interviews he'd had, the prospective employers showed blatant consternation regarding his prison record. He tried what he could: dressing professionally, being as respectful as he could with the interviewer. He even pleaded with one woman that he would bust his ass for them if they gave him a chance, but who wanted to hire an ex-con?

He couldn't blame them. Attempted robbery. Assault. It didn't matter that they didn't know the full story. When he got convicted, Jake knew this would be difficult to overcome. He was a fighter, and he was damn sure not going to quit. Someone had to be willing to take a chance on him.

The phone rang.

"My man, Jake. It's good to hear your voice again."

Jake closed his eyes and nearly groaned. Adam Fallon, the last person he wanted to speak with. Adam was the reason Jake had spent six months in jail.

"Yeah. What do you want?"

"I meant to stop by, but things have been hectic. I've got this high paying gig."

Jake scowled. Adam had some nerve calling like this and boasting. "Whatever it is, I don't want to hear about it."

"No problem, my man. Hey, I'm not going to get you involved in anything you don't want to do."

Jake had nothing to say to Adam. They may have been best of friends once, but six months of hard time could destroy a friendship.

"You know I hate asking favors and wouldn't ask unless it was necessary."

Jake ground his teeth. "Favor?"

"Yeah, you see, I have to make this delivery to some not so friendly folks, and I might be in a tight spot. They think I took something that belonged to them, which I didn't, so I could use some backup."

Jake clenched his fist. "Adam, I don't want to hear about this. I don't want to know anything about it. I am not doing anything that might get me back in jail."

Adam spoke in a low tone. "Look, I really need your help. This delivery might be a setup, and I can't get out of it. I think they might hurt me. That's why I need you. They won't do anything if you're there. Everyone around here knows you're a legit tough guy."

"If you think something bad might happen, then back away."

"I can't, Jake. They'll erase me if I don't do this delivery. I'm in a no-win situation. I need your help. Come on, you've always been there for me since kindergarten."

"If you cared about our friendship, you wouldn't put me in this situation again."

"You have to help me, Jake. It's going down next week."

"I have to go."

"Think about it at least."

Jake hung up the phone. He slammed his fist on the desk, knocking over the applications. Less than a month out of jail, Adam was already asking him to do something that might put him back in prison.

He sat, put his palm to his forehead, and sighed. If Adam really was in trouble, he would have a hard time just leaving him hanging. For as long as they had known each other, Adam had always done stupid things that pissed people off, and Jake would have to bail him out, often with his fists.

Jake sighed. He had to fill out these forms. One of these places would hire him. He needed to work. Besides much needed cash, it would give him purpose and direction. He hadn't even been to the gym to train since getting out of prison.

Jake propped up a picture of him and Kenna taken at a park prior to his incarceration, having inadvertently knocked it down when he smashed his fist on the desk. The picture brought a smile to his face. Kenna wore a pink tank in the picture. She had an angelic smile. Her hair had been blonde back then, but it was steadily getting darker, and now it was light brown like his. In the picture, he had her hoisted on his shoulders, and she was picking leaves from a tree.

She was the best little sister a guy could ask for. Kenna's faith in him never wavered. She and his mom had visited him every weekend during his six-month prison stint. Her letters and hand-made cards got him through those dark hours when he felt lower than the dirt encrusted against the walls of his cell.

He would die before letting Kenna down again.

He leafed through the applications. Bus boy at a restaurant, working in the stockroom at Target, landscaping. None of the prospects thrilled him, but it was honest work, and he would gladly take any of the jobs if they were willing to hire him.

Jake's head shot up when a loud bang came from downstairs. Someone screamed.

He bolted out of the bedroom and ran into the kitchen. More screams and shouting came from downstairs. He opened the door leading to the basement. What the hell were they doing with the lights off? He felt the side of the wall until he found the light switch, then flicked it on.

"Kenna, what's going on?" He ran down the stairs, turned the corner, and found the faces of three terrified children. He followed their gaze to Cordy, who was lying on the floor, blood streaming from her nose and from a cut above her eye.

He clenched his fists and got into a front stance, his eyes darting around the room, not sure what had happened but ready to fight if there was an attacker present. "What the hell happened, Kenna?"

***

A surge of relief flooded through Kenna when Jake arrived. She had no idea what that silhouette was, but she felt safe now. Her brother would protect her.

"What the hell happened, Kenna?"

"I, um, don't know. We were playing with your, um, Ouija board, and the lights went out and…" Kenna trailed off, not sure what to say.

Jake stared at her, his face etched with concern. He cradled Cordy into his arms.

"Aww, my head." Cordy touched her forehead and screamed. "I'm bleeding."

"Let's take her upstairs." Jake carried her as Kenna and her friends followed. "Kenna, get me a towel. I'm taking her to the bathroom."

Once they reached the kitchen, Kenna opened a drawer. She picked the oldest towel she could fine. Her mother would be pissed if she used one of her good towels.

She followed Jake into the bathroom where he sat Cordy on the toilet.

"My head hurts." Cordy's eyes filled with tears.

"It's okay," Jake said. "You're going to be fine. Now tilt your head back."

Cordy tilted her head, and Jake took the towel from Kenna's hands. He wiped the blood off her face and forehead. He then took a tissue, rolled it tightly, and put it in her nostril to stop the bleeding. He reached into the medicine cabinet and took out cotton balls, swabs, and a bottle of hydrogen peroxide. "This is going to sting." When he cleaned the cut on her forehead with the peroxide, Cordy cringed. "Now that wasn't so bad. I'm going to apply pressure to stop the bleeding."

Jake pressed the swab against Cordy's forehead and held it tight. "Get me a bandage, Kenna."

She found one with dinosaurs. She wasn't a kid anymore, but her mom didn't always realize that.

Jake continued to apply pressure on the cut, and then put on the bandage. "You okay?"

Cordy nodded.

"All right," Jake said. "Let's give her room to breathe."

They exited into the living room. Kenna glanced back at Cordy, who still seemed dazed.

Jake sat Cordy on the sofa. "So, what happened downstairs?"

All at once, they started talking until it became a loud, jumbled mess.

Jake stood. "We're getting nowhere. Kenna, tell me what happened."

She recounted everything as best she could.

Part way through, Jake interrupted. "Wait, you're telling me it moved on its own."

Kenna nodded. "We were talking, and the planchette started moving."

"Is this some kind of joke?" Jake asked.

Kenna shook her head. "It really happened."

Jake folded his arms. "All right. Then what?"

Kenna couldn't stay still as she relayed the events. A bundle of nervous energy, she bounced from foot to foot and looked at her friends for support. Kenna told Jake everything except the part about the silhouette. She didn't want to mention it out loud. Doing that might bring it back.

"How did you get banged up, Cordy?" Jake asked.

Cordy shook her head. "I don't know. When the lights went out, I tried to reach the door. Then something hit me in the head. I tripped and landed face first on the table. I don't remember much after that."

"It probably happened because you guys were running over each other trying to get out. You gotta watch out with these Ouija boards. You start messing with these things and your mind starts to play tricks on you."

"But the planchette was really moving," Kenna said.

Jake took a deep breath, not knowing what to make of this situation. Although his sister was not the type to make up stories, the alternative was too much for him to believe. The most likely scenario is that she and her friends were spooked and thought they saw something that wasn't there. "All I know is that you guys had a little scare. Fortunately, nobody got hurt too bad. Is your mom home?"

Cordy nodded.

"Okay, I'm taking you home. I don't think it's going to help matters if you start talking about Ouija boards and stuff like that. I'll tell your mom you guys were rough housing and it got out of control. You got a little nick on your head when you tripped and fell, so I patched you up. How's that sound?"

"Yeah," Cordy said. "Mom will buy that."

Jake followed his sister and friends out the door. He saw the haunted look on Kenna's face and wondered just what she saw in the basement.

Chapter III

Jake looked up while doing crunches in his bedroom to find Kenna staring at him. He had worked out like a maniac in the pen, not wanting to lose his conditioning. After getting out of jail, he figured his home would feel alien to him, but Kenna's presence made it where he belonged.

When he finished, Kenna jumped onto his chest. He groaned as she knocked the wind out of him. She giggled and stood.

Jake held out his hand. "Now you have to help me up."

"I'll try." Kenna acted like she was trying to lift him but wasn't giving much effort.

Jake sprang to his feet. "Thanks for the assist."

She sat on his bed. His room was sparse with a desk and a bookcase. The only thing that adorned his wall was his black belt in Tae Kwon Do and his brown belt in Brazilian jiu-jitsu. "I watched that DVD you have of your last fight yesterday."

Jake sat next to her. "Did you?"

"It was in a drawer in the living room. You crushed your opponent in like under a minute. Why haven't you been back to the gym?"

"I'm just trying to get my life back together."

Kenna looked up at him with her big brown eyes. "But, Jake, that's part of who you are. Fighting is what you do."

Jake stared at his sister, taken aback by a nine-year-old's insight. "You might be right."

Kenna smiled. "I'm glad you agree. I knew you would, so I went ahead and called Joe Renken. He's coming over tomorrow."

Joe Renken owned the gym Jake had trained at and had been his head trainer and manager prior to his incarceration. In many ways, Joe was a father figure after Jake's father had died. Joe had visited him several times in jail, but they had not spoken since Jake's release.

"Why did you do that?"

Kenna wrapped her small arms around his waist. "Because I can't have you moping around the house all day. It's not like anyone's hired you. Plus, I love watching you fight. You rock out there."

"Thanks."

There was no question he had been feeling a void in his life. He wanted a new start, but he had been training in martial arts since he was a kid and wrestling since high school. Even before becoming a professional fighter, the mental discipline, the respect, and the grueling physical training had molded him into the person he was. To deny this was pointless. More than anything, he was ashamed of being an ex-con. Forever more, people would look down on him.

Kenna jumped off the bed. "I'm going over Cordy's house."

Jake looked at the clock. It was almost eight. Her bedtime was nine-thirty. "Did you ask Mom?"

Kenna nodded. "She said I can go. Can you walk me over? It's dark out."

Kenna had never asked him to accompany her to her friend's house. She was probably spooked by what had happened that afternoon. "Sure, I'll go."

She grabbed Jake's hand and led him out of the room. "Let's go."

"Hey, Mom, I'm taking Kenna to Cordy's house."

Their mother looked up from the television set. She was watching one of those silly entertainment news shows. "She has to be back by nine."

"No problem."

His mother went back to watching her program.

Jake sighed. He was worried about his mom. She had been through a rough patch with his dad's death and Jake's imprisonment. Those two events had sucked the life out of her. Before, their house used to be filled with her laughter. He missed her jokes, even though he never found them funny. She used to play silly games with him and Kenna. These days, she seemed to be going through the motions instead of actually living. Kenna had told him that, sometimes, it was like she wasn't there at all. She would come home and stare at the television with a blank look on her face, forgetting about dinner until Kenna reminded her. She acted like a drunk, without actually drinking.

Once outside, Kenna said, "So, Cordy's parents aren't home. They went to a restaurant, something about entertaining clients."

Jake furrowed his brow. "She's home alone."

"No way. Cordy's mom doesn't trust her. She has a sitter over."

Jake held Kenna's hand as they crossed the busy street. Even though it was only a few blocks away, Cordy lived in the more upscale part of town in a new development.

When they arrived at Cordy's house, Jake stood in the background as Kenna knocked. Jake's eyes lit up as the door opened. He stared, probably looking like an idiot, almost not believing what he was seeing. Standing in the doorway was June Fisher. He had not seen her in a while, but he certainly had not forgotten her.

June had a broad smile. "Jake Trigg. I wasn't expecting you to come over."

Kenna ran past June. Inside, she and Cordy giggled. This was a setup from the start.

Jake stepped closer to the door. He tried to control his racing heart. Why was he so nervous? It's not like they had never spoken before. Somehow, he sensed things were different now. At least, he was a different person. "I'm Kenna's older brother."

"Small world, huh? Well, don't just stand there. Come inside." Before he could enter the house, June gave him a big hug. "How long's it been?"

"It's been a while."

He knew exactly how long it had been. The last time he had seen June was high school graduation. They always had good chemistry, frequently talking to each other in the hallways, before, during, and after school. She was pretty, not quite beautiful, with long auburn hair, a slightly freckled face, and enchanting green eyes. Glancing at her body, Jake realized she had developed nicely since high school.

He had always wanted to ask her out, but never had the guts to do it. She ran with the popular crowd and the smart kids. He had tended to hang with the outcasts, those who couldn't fit in with any crowd. Plus, she had been going out with Chad Garrett, who was rich, privileged, and made sure everyone knew about it. For his seventeenth birthday, Chad's parents bought him a new Corvette. Jake had a nice laugh when, two months later, Chad had smashed up the car. People like Chad never had the time of day for someone like Jake.

"So, what have you been up to?" June had a gleam in her eye. Her smile was filled was mischief.

Kenna ran across the room with a look of alarm. "Jake's a professional fighter."

Cordy ran beside Kenna. "Yeah, he's really good."

June frowned. "A fighter? Like a boxer."

"No. I'm a mixed martial artist."

Kenna beamed. "Jake's undefeated."

"I've only had four professional fights."

June's eyes went wide. "Really? That's so cool."

It was more than obvious that Kenna and Cordy were steering the conversation away from the fact that he had been incarcerated. He wasn't keen on bringing up the subject either.

"It's nothing really," Jake said. "I haven't fought in a while."

"That's because he's been helping mom and me, but he's going to be back in the cage real soon."

Cordy grabbed Kenna's hand and led her downstairs. "Come on. I want to show you my new bike."

"Cute kids," June said.

"They sure are. I didn't expect you to be around. I thought you went away to Boston College."

"Come inside. Let's sit down."

Jake followed June into the house, which was spacious and filled with modern furniture. The living room housed a large grandfather clock. The floors were all hardwood. She sat on the sofa, and he sat on an adjacent couch.

"I just transferred to Ursinus last fall."

"Ursinus? That's just down the road." Jake still felt wildly attracted to June, and now they didn't have the trappings of high school to pin them down.

"I wanted to be closer to home because my dad had a heart attack last year. Plus, I wanted to get away from Chad."

Jake's heart skipped a beat learning about her availability. "I'm sorry to hear about your dad."

"He's getting better. Anyway, I don't know if you remember, but Chad and I had been going out."

Jake nodded. Of course, he remembered.

"I thought it would be a good idea when I enrolled at BC. It was a foregone conclusion he would go to Harvard. His family has a legacy there, so even though his grades didn't merit it, he had no problem getting in. The president of the university personally called his father to let him know he had been accepted."

Jake rolled his eyes. "It must be nice to have connections."

"Yeah, I guess so. I couldn't take being near him anymore. He was so involved with his frat brothers and mingling with New England high society. I just wanted to study, get good grades, and get a degree that would land me a good job. He became arrogant and obnoxious."

"Became?" Jake grinned. "You may not have noticed, but he's always been that way."

"Maybe. I didn't realize it until we were a few hundred miles from home. Worst of all, he became possessive, convinced we were going to get married and have three point two kids even though I never gave him any overtures to suggest that. He would check in on me at all hours of the day, questioning where I went, who I was with, what I was doing. I couldn't take it."

He had to play it cool. If she were no longer with Chad, then he just might have a chance with her. He casually leaned back and spoke in an even tone. "Don't blame you. Who would want to be with someone like that?"

"I broke up with him a few months ago. Unfortunately, Chad refuses to accept that. He still calls and texts, acting like we're together. I've told him it's over, but he doesn't take no easily."

"Sounds like a stalker."

June waved her hand. "He's harmless. He just has this feeling of entitlement. What about you, Jake? Any serious girlfriend?"

"Um, no. I was with someone for about a year, but that ended."

"Why's that?"

Jake folded his arms. "Nothing I want to talk about."

"I just laid out my whole life story, and you won't even tell me about your last girlfriend."

"What can I say? My life isn't interesting."

"Hmm. If you say so." June frowned.

The conversation died just like that. Jake felt compelled to keep speaking with her after having sensed some sparks earlier.

"You really want to know what happened with my last girlfriend?"

June nodded. "I wouldn't have asked otherwise."

"You sure about this?"

"Yes, I'm sure."

"Well, you see, her family wasn't too fond of her dating a convict. If she continued dating me, they threatened to disown her. At least that was what the letter she wrote to me in prison said."

June's face went white. "A convict?"

Jake looked down. "I'm afraid so." After a moment, he raised his head. Reluctantly, he gave the highlights of what had happened that fateful night that led to his incarceration.

"That's terrible. But you didn't really do what they accused you of."

Jake tilted his head back. "I did what I felt I had to in that situation, and I paid the price for my actions."

June leaned in close. "What was prison like?"

"What? Are you trying to be Oprah or something?"

"I didn't mean it like that. I'm just concerned. I've always liked you."

Jake looked into her eyes and found genuine empathy. He didn't want to tell her about his prison stint, but he was in too deep.

"What's there to say? Prison isn't fun. For the most part, it was lonely. There were gangs and factions in the pen, but I didn't belong to any of them. I purposely didn't have any friends. Spoke to maybe two or three guys the whole time I was there. The other inmates knew I could fight, so they didn't mess with me. I did a lot of reading. I worked out every chance I had and took a few computer classes. If anyone was willing to hire me, I've developed some good computer skills." Jake sighed.

"Kenna's the one who got me through. She never gave up on me."

"I can tell she really cares about you. Look, Jake, I realize spending six months in prison is a pretty significant setback."

Jake smirked. "I wouldn't recommend it."

"But it shouldn't define your life. You're a good person. What happened was a bump in the road, but you can overcome it. You have inner strength. Take this opportunity to focus on what's important in your life and grow from it. If you do that, then those six months won't be a complete waste."

Jake continued to chat with June, surprised at how easily their conversation flowed after his revelation. He had never thought about his prison term in that light before. Somehow, June had a way of making everything make sense. Not to mention, her penetrating green eyes captivated him. They seemed to twinkle in the soft lights.

Jake looked at the Grandfather clock. "Kenna needs to head back, and since I walked her over here, I'm responsible for taking her home."

He rose to call Kenna, but June grabbed his hand. "Look, Jake, I really enjoyed talking to you. I'd like to see you again."

Jake's eyes widened. "Really?"

June smiled. "Yeah. I wish we had gotten to know each other better in high school, but it's not too late. We've all made mistakes. Mine was wasting so much time with Chad thinking it was going somewhere."

"You don't have a problem with me having been in prison?"

"I'm convinced you're not a hardened criminal."

"Thanks. I appreciate that."

Jake walked Kenna home with a big smile on his face as he answered her rapid-fire questions about how he hit it off with June.

Chapter IV

Kenna and Cordy approached Carlos, who was playing freeze tag in the school playground.

Kenna grabbed his arm. "Hey, we need to talk to you."

"I'm in the middle of a game," Carlos said. "Can't this wait until later?"

Cordy dragged him away from the game. "No, this can't wait. This is important."

Carlos gave an exasperated sigh. "All right. What's going on?"

"First, get Ben," Kenna said. "That way we can tell both of you at the same time."

A minute later, Carlos returned with Ben, who had been playing basketball. Ben was taller than almost all the other boys in their grade, but he wasn't very coordinated. Still, his height made him popular when picking sides.

Ben's eyes went wide with alarm. "What's going on? Did something happen? This is about the whole Ouija board thing, isn't it?"

"Let's go to the other end of the yard where nobody can hear us," Kenna said.

The playground had a basketball hoop on one end of the paved area as well as space to play hopscotch and foursquare. The edges of the yard were covered with mulch. There was a swing set and a large play set with multiple slides. They walked toward a gazebo at the far edge of the yard, where nobody was congregating at the moment. Kenna sat on the bench inside of the gazebo and looked around just to be sure nobody could hear them.

"Cordy and I've been thinking about this." Kenna paused and looked at each of her friends in turn. "We should contact Mia again."

Ben looked at Kenna as if she had suggested mugging the Easter Bunny. "Are you crazy?"

"Mia sounded like she was in trouble the last time we talked to her. I'm worried." Kenna folded her arms.

Carlos furrowed his brow. "But she's dead."

"I know she's dead. That doesn't mean she can't get hurt. Something was going on that had her real scared. I don't know how to describe it in words, but it was like I could feel her fear."

"What are you talking about?" Carlos said. "I didn't feel anything. Maybe you were just cold."

"This isn't a good idea," Ben said. "Look what happened last time with the lights going out and Cordy getting hurt. What if we try it again and something even worse happens?"

Cordy rolled her eyes. "Why are you always so scared? I'm the one who got my head busted, and I'll do it again, so why won't you?"

Ben looked at the ground. "I never said I wouldn't do it. I'm just not sure this is a good idea. We should think about it."

"Kenna and I already have thought about it, and we decided we're going to talk to Mia again."

"We want you two to be there, since we were all together the first time," Kenna said. "Are you in?"

Carlos shrugged. "You can count me in. Especially if it means I can get out of soccer practice."

Ben gave a long sigh. "I don't know."

"If Mia's in trouble, and I think she is, then we should help her," Kenna said.

Cordy's face tightened. "You can't chicken out on us."

"All right," Ben said. "I just hope you know what you're doing."

Kenna also hoped they knew what they were doing.

***

Jake sunk into the sofa and stared at an empty television screen. "Damn." He had just come back from an interview at an auto body shop after they called him that morning and told him to stop by. He had spoken to the head mechanic. Everything went great until the man's eyes narrowed as he looked over the job application.

"I see you have a criminal record," the mechanic had said.

Jake went into his rehearsed explanation. The mechanic just nodded. They had continued talking for a few minutes, but the man's attitude had cooled. He told Jake he would call in a few days, but he knew the man wasn't going to hire him.

Jake sighed. No sense fretting about it. He would just apply to more places. Somebody would eventually hire him.

As he read through the ads in the jobs section of the newspaper, the doorbell rang. Joe Renken stood at the door. Jake was startled at first, until he remembered that Kenna had told him Joe would stop by.

Joe stepped inside and gave Jake a half-hug. "It's good to see you again. I would have stopped by sooner, but I wanted to give you some space. How have you been holding up?"

Jake tilted his head. "Trying to manage. Can I get you something to drink? I was about to eat lunch. How `bout I fix you a sandwich?"

"No, I'm good. To be honest with you, I'm a little disappointed you haven't been to the dojo since your release."

Jake sighed. "I wasn't sure if I wanted to continue training. After all that happened, I thought I needed a fresh start, but— "

Joe interrupted him. "But you're not happy with the way things are going."

Jake nodded.

Joe picked up the newspaper. "I see you're looking for a job."

"I had an interview today. Auto mechanic shop."

Joe sat down on the sofa. He hadn't changed since they had last seen each other. The man was short but all muscle. His cardio conditioning was astounding. Even though Joe was getting older—his actual age was a mystery, but Jake figured he was in his mid-forties even though his hair was mostly grey—he made the younger guys at the gym look silly when they were huffing and puffing, and he hardly broke a sweat.

"Any luck so far?"

Jake shook his head.

"Look, Jake, it's great that you're trying to get a job, and I'm sure working in an auto body shop or something like that would be good, honest work, but I can't let you do that." Jake crinkled his forehead.

Joe gazed at him with fierce concentration. "You got too much damn talent to waste in some ordinary nine to five. I've worked with some good fighters before, but no one I've trained has your potential. You're only nineteen and your skills are off the chart. That alone doesn't make you a great fighter, but you have the determination and the dedication to match. I want you to work for me."

Jake stammered. He felt humbled and touched. "Really?"

"I'm opening a new dojo in Jersey, and I have plans for one near Harrisburg the following year. This is going to spread me thin, so I need someone I have absolute trust and confidence in to work as the head trainer. I need someone who's going to train the students the right way. I trust you, Jake, more than anyone."

"You trust me? Even after being in jail?"

"You never told me what went down." Joe gripped his shoulder with a strong hand. "But I know it wasn't you who did those things. I know what's in your heart, what kind of person you are."

Jake fought back tears. "I let you down. I let everyone down."

"I was there at the trial and I don't think it went down the way the prosecutor suggested. You never let your lawyer put up a proper defense."

Jake shrugged. "She did what she could."

"Maybe. But she was frustrated you weren't helping. Why did you hold back?"

Jake lowered his gaze.

"I'm sorry but I don't believe for one second you broke into that liquor store, robbed them, and assaulted the storeowner. I've known you since you were a kid, and that ain't you. I don't know how you got involved, but there's no way you did those things."

Jake looked away from him.

"You can tell me about everything in your own time. Bottom line, Jake, I want you to be my head trainer. I'll pay you a good wage, and we can get your career back on track. I've got connections with fight leagues, and I want to get you back in the cage soon. I know helping out your mom is a big priority, and this will allow you to do that. You don't have to make any decisions now. Think about it."

"I don't have to think about it. I'd love to be your head trainer. I haven't been back to the dojo because I didn't feel like I was worthy after what happened, but yesterday, Kenna kind of snapped me back in reality. Fighting is what I do."

Joe patted him on the back. "That's what I want to hear. We can get your life back together."

Jake stared into his mentor's eyes. Joe trusted him. Now he had to trust Joe.

"I didn't know a robbery was going down. Adam Fallon asked me to come with him and his friend, that there might be some trouble and he needed me to back him up."

Joe shook his head. "That guy's bad news. I told you that."

Jake shrugged. "He was my friend, and if he was in trouble, I had to help him. We drove into Norristown, supposedly to a party. Pulled up to a side street, and I asked what's going on. The next thing I know, Adam and the other guy are putting on ski masks."

Joe grunted. "You gotta be kidding me. Why didn't you leave?"

"I was going to bail, but Adam said I didn't have to do anything except keep lookout. Something went wrong. The owner of the store grabbed a nightstick from under the counter and smashed Adam's face."

"Served him right," Joe said.

"Adam's gun went sprawling. Anyway, the owner was about to nail Adam again, so I ran inside, grabbed his arm, punched him twice in the ribs, got Adam, and ran the hell out of there.

"Should have left the son of a bitch there," Joe said. "If that was me, I would have twisted him into a pretzel and left him there for the cops."

Knowing Joe, he would have done just that.

"Adam and the other guy bolted to the car."

"And you were left holding the bag," Joe said.

Jake nodded. "I wanted nothing to do with them anymore. Bad move. I walked home, and by that point, the storeowner had called the police and gave them my description. Adam and the other guy wore ski masks, so he couldn't identify them. The police picked me up as I walked home."

Joe stood, shook his head, and paced around the room.

"They wanted me to give up Adam and the other guy, but I took full responsibility."

Joe clenched his hands into fists. "What the hell were you thinking, Jake? You're not a dumb guy, but that was really stupid. Those two did the crime, they should have done the time. They deserved to go to jail, not you."

Jake buried his hands in his face. "Adam had been arrested a couple times. If he got nailed again, he would be looking at a long prison stint."

"That's his problem, not yours!"

"I know. It was stupid. Doing time made me realize that."

"You have to look out for your family. Stay the hell away from Adam Fallon. You did your time. Now you need to keep your nose clean. Fortunately, going to jail doesn't hurt you as far as working at the dojo. If anything, the wannabe tough guys will be impressed."

"I don't need that kind of rep."

"No, you don't. Your fighting speaks for itself. You wasted enough time in jail. I want you to get started right away. I expect you to be at the gym tomorrow morning. I'll introduce you to your new students, and we're going to get you ready for your next fight. I'm going to start you on an intense training regimen. I see you've stayed in shape, but you're not in fighting shape. We have our work cut out, and don't expect me to go easy on you."

Joe made his way to the door.

Jake grabbed his arm. "Thanks for everything. I'm not one to ask favors, but what you've done for me means a lot."

"Welcome back, Jake."

Chapter V

They gathered in Kenna's basement. Kenna and Ben sat on the floor on opposite ends of the Ouija board. Carlos stood directly behind Kenna. Cordy stood off to the side, in between Kenna and Ben. Kenna wasn't sure they needed to recreate the conditions from the first time they had contacted Mia, but it couldn't hurt.

After the incident, Jake told her they should stay away from the Ouija board, but he hadn't taken it away from her. Even if he had, she would have found a way to get it back. Anything short of destroying the board wouldn't stop her. She had felt this amazing connection with Mia.

Ben asked, "Why don't we go to my place and play with my PS3? I borrowed Grand Theft Auto from my cousin. My mom's not home, so we can play it."

Carlos' face lit up. "Really? Let's go."

Cordy's blue eyes burned holes into him. "No way. You can play later."

"I just don't want you to get hurt again," Carlos said.

Cordy rolled her eyes. "Thanks for your concern."

"All right." Carlos ran his fingers through his wavy black hair, which he actually combed today, a welcome change. "If you really want to do this, then let's do it. We probably won't even reach Mia this time."

"Do I have to hold the planchette again?" Ben asked. "It was kind of scary."

"We should do everything the same way." Kenna put her hand on his shoulder. "Don't worry. I'll be holding the planchette, too."

Cordy put her long blonde hair into a ponytail. "Come on, let's talk to Mia."

Kenna stared at each of her friends. "You guys ready?"

Ben stood and shook his head.

Cordy grabbed him by the arm and sat him down next to the Ouija board. "Well, we're doing it anyway. Come on, Ben. You promised."

Kenna put her fingers lightly on the planchette and waited for Ben to do the same. Everyone stared at him. With shaky hands, he reached for it.

"It's okay." Kenna hoped she sounded reassuring. As they got closer to actually doing this, she had developed an empty feeling in the pit of her stomach.

"I have to go to the bathroom," Ben said.

Cordy glared at him.

"Okay." Ben grimaced and put his hands on the disc. Slowly, Kenna and Ben moved it across the board.

"Mia, are you out there?" Kenna asked. There were no tugs of resistance. A minute passed. "Mia, we're trying to reach you. If you're out there, please let us know."

"Maybe she's watching TV," Ben said.

Cordy frowned. "How can she watch TV? She's a spirit."

Ben shrugged. "They probably have cable."

Carlos shook his head. "No way. If they got anything, it's satellite."

Kenna stared at them. "Please focus." Suddenly, the planchette jerked. "Mia, is that you?"

Kenna watched in wide-eyed amazement as it moved to Yes. For a moment, she thought their overactive imaginations had conjured up the previous encounter.

"Mia, are you okay?"

The planchette moved to Yes.

"What happened the last time we were talking to you?" Ben asked. "It ended like all of a sudden."

It spelled out HAD TO GO.

"Was there anything wrong?" Kenna asked.

Mia answered Yes.

Icy fear gripped Kenna. She looked around. The others seemed fine. Why couldn't they feel it? It was like Mia was passing down these bad vibes to her. "What was it?"

HE WAS HERE.

Ben took a big gulp. "Who's he?"

COTTER.

"Is Cotter bad?" Kenna asked.

The planchette went to Yes.

Carlos frowned. "I don't like this Cotter guy."

"Me either." Kenna looked around the room. Could that have been the silhouette she had seen? She shuddered, not wanting to think about it. "Mia, tell us about Cotter."

There was a strong tug on the planchette. HURTS ME.

Ben's voice trembled. "Is Cotter there now?"

The planchette circled around No.

"Thank God." Kenna gave a sigh of relief. She knew there had been something wrong at the end of their last conversation. It hadn't felt right. "Mia, where are you?"

OTHER SIDE.

Ben took his hands off the planchette. "This is getting a little too spooky. Maybe we should stop."

Kenna gazed into his green eyes. "It's okay. Mia's our friend." She nodded toward the planchette, and he put his hands back on it. At least he was coachable. Most boys weren't.

"Is that where all the spirits are?" Ben asked.

No.

"This place you're at, what's it like?" Kenna asked.

LIKE UR WORLD BUT DIFFERENT.

Cordy frowned. "Can't she be a little more specific?"

"Tell us more," Kenna said.

TO LONG TO EXPLAIN.

Kenna wanted to ask Mia a million things, but this wasn't like talking on a phone or texting. "Do you like talking to us?"

She answered Yes.

"How do you know when we're trying to reach you?"

For a while there was no resistance on the planchette. It was like Mia was thinking about her answer. IN TOUCH WITH YOU.

Cordy folded her arms. "What does that mean? Does she have like a psychic connection with us, or does she mean she's going to reach us again?"

Kenna shrugged. "Beats me. Mia, can you explain that?"

SENSE YOU. After a slight pause, the planchette spelled STRONG PULL.

"Do you like where you're at? I mean, when Cotter's not around and stuff."

She answered Yes.

"Do you miss being in our world?" Kenna asked

SOMETIMES.

That got Kenna thinking about Mia's life before she died. "Did you have a boyfriend?"

Yes.

Ben's nose curled, and his forehead scrunched. "He didn't, um, die in that accident you had?"

The planchette went to No.

"Well, that's good."

Kenna took her hands off the planchette and glanced at Cordy. "Are you thinking what I'm thinking?"

Cordy nodded.

Kenna put her hands back on the planchette. "Mia, what was the name of your boyfriend?"

MARK SALESKI.

"Can you remember that?" Kenna asked.

"No problem," Cordy replied.

MUST GO.

"Is it Cotter?" Ben asked.

The planchette went to Good Bye.

Kenna waited, but there was no resistance on the planchette. "I guess that's it."

"Well, at least Cotter wasn't around," Carlos said.

"But why did she leave so quickly?" Ben asked.

"Maybe talking about her old boyfriend brought back bad memories." Kenna brushed her hair out of her eyes.

"Maybe," Cordy said.

"What was her boyfriend's name?" Kenna asked.

"Mark Saleski," Cordy replied.

Carlos eyed Kenna and Cordy warily. "What are you two up to?"

Kenna said, "Let's contact Mark."

Ben's eyes went wide. "What? Are you crazy? Why would you want to do something like that? Maybe he's like an axe-murderer or something."

"I think that's a good idea. It might be kinda fun," Carlos said.

Ben shook his head. "Fun? This is a bad idea."

"Why?" Kenna asked.

Ben stammered. "It's just...it's a bad idea."

Kenna ignored Ben's protests. If they listened to him, they would never have any fun. "So, how do we find Mark?"

"Well, she told us she was from Trappe," Carlos replied. "She probably went out with someone who lives nearby. Maybe he still lives here."

"Maybe," Kenna agreed. "But let's say we found his number, what would we do, just call him?"

Cordy's face tightened. "He probably wouldn't talk to a bunch of kids."

"What if he didn't know who he was talking to?" Kenna asked.

Ben's eyes lit up. "We can send him an email."

"Good thinking. We need to find out more about him. What do you say, Carlos?"

"I can get his information." Carlos spent entirely too much time on the Net. He even had his own Facebook account.

Ben folded his arms. "What if Mia doesn't want us to talk to this Mark Saleski guy?"

"Of course, Mia wants us to talk to him," Kenna replied. "If she didn't, then she wouldn't have told us, right?"

Ben didn't respond.

"Good. It's settled. We'll contact Mark."

This was much better than the last time they had chatted with Mia. She wasn't in danger. Nothing crazy had happened at the end of their conversation, and they had a chance to help her.

Then why did Kenna feel this tugging inside of her, suggesting everything was all wrong?

Chapter VI

Jake never realized how frustrating it could be to teach new students how to fight. Maybe it was because fighting came easy to him, or perhaps his students didn't have his dedication. He had been a gym rat growing up. Every day after school, he used to hang around Joe Renken, trying to absorb his knowledge. Whenever someone needed a sparring partner, he volunteered, no matter how overmatched he was. He pumped iron, worked on his cardio, whatever he could do to get better. Fighting was in his blood. His grandfather had boxed professionally in his youth, and his father had made his mark in the Golden Gloves scene but had never gone any further than that. For as long as he could remember, Jake had been driven to develop his fighting skills and learn all he could about the art of combat.

His students wanted to become black belt level fighters without putting in the time training. Lawrence Crawford was the biggest pain in the ass in the bunch. A businessman who worked as a financial planner, he came to the gym wearing a three-piece suit before changing into expensive, designer gym wear. Lawrence dominated Jake's time, insisting he teach him advanced techniques like a triangle choke, even though he couldn't do something simple like throw a proper front kick.

Lawrence had about six inches and fifty pounds on Jake. The first time they had worked together, he got the impression that Lawrence thought he could use his size advantage to dominate Jake, but his attitude quickly changed after Jake repeatedly put him on his ass with judo throws.

He tried to explain to Lawrence that the best way to learn was to start with the basics, but the man wouldn't listen. Jake had suggested he sign up for private lessons. At least that way, he wouldn't commandeer everyone's time. "Listen, we'll work on this during our next session. This is a process. You can't build a house before you lay a foundation. In order for you to advance and improve, you need to get your fundamentals down first. Practice kicking on the heavy bag. That way you can leave with something positive from today's class." Before Lawrence could put up an argument, Jake walked away.

Later that evening, Jake was scheduled to train with a highly skilled Muay Thai fighter Renken had brought in to help him with his first match after his incarceration-induced layoff. Jake had five regular training partners, but Renken wanted to bring in someone specialized to help prepare for his fight. His choice puzzled Jake, who had expected him to bring in a strong wrestler since his opponent had been a standout collegiate wrestler and the captain of his wrestling team, but Renken had told him his ground skills were already strong, and he needed to work on his striking, defying conventional wisdom in not training with someone who would mirror his opponent. The fight was three weeks away, and he had to bust his ass to prepare for it.

Jake put the students in groups of two and three, so they could spar. The floor of the classroom was lined with red and black mats. Mirrors covered one wall. At each of the corners were heavy bags. In another room was the cage Jake used to train for his mixed martial arts bouts. There was also a room in the facility with weights and cardio machines. Generally, he did his fight preparation in some of the smaller rooms in a more intimate setting as opposed to the large studio this class was being held at.

A loud cry echoed across the dojo. He turned around to find Robin, a petite red head who didn't weigh more than a hundred pounds, on the floor clutching her chin. Tim Wingate stood above her wearing a big smile.

Lawrence might be a pain in the ass, but Wingate was a total asshole. He was a typical ex-jock and bully who came into the gym thinking he was a tough guy and picked on the smallest, weakest person he could find. In this case, it was Robin, who had spunk but was about half his size.

Jake made his way over to her, knelt, and lifted her head off the mat. "You okay?"

Robin nodded. She had a busted lip but otherwise looked fine.

"Why don't you get some ice for your lip. We'll work on some defensive techniques at the end of class."

"Okay." Robin groaned when Jake helped her to her feet. She wore knee high sweats and had welts on the exposed parts of her legs. Wingate had been kicking her way harder than he needed to for a sparring session. Robin had showed her toughness by not complaining about it.

Jake folded his arms and stared at Wingate.

Wingate laughed. "I guess she's not tough enough to hang here."

It was time he taught Wingate a lesson. "I guess not. You know, I think you're a little too good for the rest of the class. You need a new sparring partner. How about you try me on for size?"

Wingate's smile faded. "Um, yeah sure."

Jake raised his hands in a defensive posture. Wingate did the same. Normally, he avoided stretching out his students, but this asshole needed to learn an important life lesson.

He shot in at Wingate, used a double leg takedown, hoisted him in the air, and slammed him to the mat as hard as he could in the blink of an eye. He got into the mount position, swung his hips, and hooked him into an arm bar.

The other students stopped sparring and gathered around. Today, he would give them a clinic on submission grappling using Wingate as his test dummy.

After Wingate tapped out, Jake helped him to his feet.

Wingate tightened his face. "I wasn't ready for that."

Jake nodded. "All right. You shoot in on me this time."

Jake put up his fists. Wingate shot in with no technique. Jake sprawled to stop the takedown attempt, landed a short knee to his chest, and kicked him sharply below the ribs. When Wingate bent down from the blow, Jake sunk in a guillotine choke. Within seconds Wingate tapped.

The students clapped.

Lawrence shouted, "That was awesome."

They continued sparring with similar outcomes. Jake took him down with ease, landed a few strikes that didn't do any real damage, and put him into a submission. Jake made sure he locked it in for an extra few seconds after Wingate tapped, just to increase his pain level.

Standing in front of the class, Robin smiled when Wingate squealed in pain.

After Jake made him tap out a dozen times, Wingate said, "I've had enough."

Jake doubted he would see him again at the gym.

The students disbursed, with the class about over. When they cleared, he was stunned to find June Fischer standing at the back of the crowd.

She walked toward him and clapped. "That was impressive."

Jake couldn't stop himself from grinning. "Thanks. Um, what are you doing here?"

"I've always wanted to take a self-defense class. You never know who you're going to run into. Plus, I figure if Chad doesn't learn the meaning of no, I can give him a beatdown. Did I say that right?"

Jake nodded, still grinning. "You said that perfectly well."

"So, anyway, I figured I'd check out this whole ultimate fighting thing and I signed up for your class."

Jake folded his arms, trying to think of something to say that wouldn't sound stupid. "How did you find out I was instructing here?"

"Cordy and Kenna told me all about it yesterday. It sounded intriguing, so I called and talked to some guy named Joe, and he enrolled me."

"That's Joe Renken. He's my trainer."

June looked around, surveying the gym. "My first class is next week."

"This isn't for the faint of heart, you know. It gets pretty rough when we roll on the mats."

June smiled. "Ooh, rolling around on the mats. I like the sound of that."

"It's not like that. You're guaranteed to go home with some bumps and bruises."

June's face tightened. "That's okay. I'm tough."

"I just want to warn you. We get a lot of people who sign up and quit after the first session. And I'm not going to go easy on you just because were, um, friends."

"I wouldn't want you to. You should treat me like the rest of the students, even though we're, um, friends."

Jake pointed to her dress slacks and pink sweater. "That's not proper gym attire."

"Of course not. I just wanted to say hi to my new teacher."

Jake smiled. This class just got a whole lot more interesting.

Chapter VII

Carlos had a beaming smile as he approached Kenna and Cordy. Meanwhile, Ben trudged behind him with his hands in his pocket, looking like someone had stolen his favorite comic book.

Just like before, they gathered near the gazebo at the rear of the schoolyard by the fence. The spring air was crisp and cool. Kenna could smell the bloom of flowers nearby. She felt like an international spy having a clandestine meeting. While all the other kids were playing some silly game or hanging out, they were doing something important.

Carlos took a sheet of paper from his pocket and handed it to Kenna. Before she could read it, Cordy snatched it from her hands.

"I got everything: his email address, where he lives, his phone number, the works," Carlos said. "It was all just a few clicks away."

Kenna peeked over Cordy's shoulder at his chicken scratch handwriting.

"How did you find this?" Kenna asked.

Carlos pretended to wipe something off his shirt, milking this moment for all it was worth. "Can't tell you. Top secret."

Ben rolled his eyes. "Carlos couldn't figure it out, so his cousin, Alex, came over. The guy's like some kinda computer genius or something."

Cordy rumpled Carlos' shaggy black hair. "Good job. I knew you would come through."

Ben looked down at the ground. "So, we're actually going to do this?"

Kenna nodded. Yesterday, she and Cordy had contacted Mia. They hadn't mentioned Mark, but after they finished, Kenna was convinced it was the right thing to do. Mia had seemed tense. The air around them seemed heavy, as if the atmosphere was dragging her down. Mia's physical presence had become more palpable since they had first spoken, like it was extending into their own world.

Mia had once again mentioned that Cotter had hurt her. When Kenna tried to get more information, Mia clammed up. The vibe Kenna got suggested that Cotter both mentally and physically abused her. Maybe reaching out to Mark Saleski would somehow help.

"So, now what do we do?" Carlos asked.

"We shouldn't do anything," Ben said. "We'll hold onto this information in case we need it."

Ignoring Ben, Cordy said, "We should email him and pass along a message from Mia, you know something only they would know about. That way he would know it was really her."

Kenna frowned. "I don't know. I'm not sure we should let Mia know what we're up to. She might not go for it."

Ben waived his hands. "If she's won't go for it, then why are we doing this?"

"Sometimes people don't know what's best for them," Kenna said.

"You sound like my mom," Carlos said. "Why don't we just ask Mia what she thinks? Even if she says no, it's not like she can stop us. She is dead, you know."

Kenna felt like smacking Carlos. "I know she's dead. But if she specifically told us not to talk to him, then I wouldn't do it."

Ben shook his head. "I'll never understand girls."

Carlos's face lit up. "We can IM him and say we're Mia. That would freak him out."

Cordy punched his shoulder. "We're not trying to scare the guy."

"That hurt." Carlos rubbed his shoulder. "It was just an idea."

"A bad idea." Cordy stuck out her tongue.

"We're getting off topic," Kenna said. "How about we pry something out of Mia but don't tell her what we're doing. Then we email him, so he'll know we really talk to her."

Cordy's eyes opened wide. "I have an idea. He probably had a nickname for her like honeybunch or sweet cheeks or, I don't know, muffin."

"Why?" Ben asked.

Cordy shrugged. "Boyfriends and girlfriends do that."

"Remind me never to have a girlfriend," Ben said.

"With your attitude, it won't be a problem. Anyway, if we could find out his nickname for her, or her nickname for him, then he'll know it's from Mia."

Kenna rubbed her palms together. "That might work. Now we have to get that from Mia without her finding out about our plans."

"Yeah, good luck with that," Carlos said.

"Well, it doesn't hurt to try," Kenna said. "How about we meet at my house after school? Ben and I will try to reach her."

Ben sulked. "Do I have to?"

Kenna patted his shoulder. "Don't worry. I'm sure that thing that happened the first time with the lights going off and Cordy getting her nose busted won't happen again."

Kenna failed to mention the apparition she had seen. Since it had not reoccurred, she had tried to convince herself she had imagined it, but that didn't stop the twinge of fear she felt each time they took out the Ouija board.

***

Kenna hung her head and tried to control her breathing. The mysterious apparition had invaded her nightmares, haunting her. Although she would have liked to believe her imagination had run wild, inside, she knew that wasn't true. She had seen this thing with perfect clarity, and it had frightened her more than the scariest horror movie ever had.

What if it came back? What would she do?

She doubted the others had seen it, or they would have said something. They weren't as good at keeping things inside as she was. She held back a lot, like the emptiness she felt after her father's death. Her memory of him was disappearing more and more each day. If it wasn't for pictures of him, she would hardly remember what he looked like. She also held back the hurt from her mother's neglect. She didn't even share that with Cordy. While Jake was in prison, she felt so alone. Even her friends couldn't make that go away. She had been terrified of what might happen to Jake in prison, even though Jake was the toughest person she had ever known. Other kids had told her stories about bad things that happened in prison.

She wiped back tears thinking back on those times. When she had visited Jake, she always tried to hide how much it hurt seeing him locked away like that since he had enough to worry about.

Kenna took a deep breath, walked up the stairs, and entered Jake's bedroom.

He sat on his bed, his head resting against the headboard, reading a book. He must have been really into it, since he only looked up when she shook his right foot.

Jake put down the Gillian Flynn novel he was reading. He scooted over, and Kenna sat next to him.

"Since when do you read?"

Jake shrugged. "I picked it up in the pen. I had a lot of time on my hands, so I read."

"Cool. Say, do you believe in ghosts?"

Jake stared at her. "No. Why do you ask?"

Kenna closed her eyes. She had to tell someone and she trusted Jake more than anyone else in the world. She ran through what had happened on the first day they had contacted Mia. He nodded as she spoke, but his face showed no emotion.

Jake folded his hands. "Listen, I don't think you actually saw a ghost. The lights had gone out, and you were scared. I remember once when I was your age, these kids at school kept saying there was a witch in an abandoned house in our old neighborhood. On a dare, I went to the house one night. It was dark and misty. I got myself so psyched up that when I looked into a window of the house, I nearly wet myself when I saw a witch on the top floor."

Kenna's eyes went wide. "Really?"

"It wasn't an actual witch. I went back a couple weeks later, this time during the day. I looked up at the same window and saw a soapy outline. That was the witch. I got so worked up that my mind played tricks on me. Just to be sure, I went back again at night, and this time I could clearly tell it wasn't a witch. You see what I'm saying?"

"I guess."

"Has this ghost shown up since that day?" Jake asked.

Kenna shook her head.

"If it was real, it would have come back."

"Are you sure?"

Jake put his arm around her shoulder. "Listen if it shows up again, I'll put that ghost in a rear naked choke and make it tap out."

Kenna giggled. "That would be funny. So, are you ready for your fight?" Kenna threw punches at him, and Jake blocked them.

"Getting there. I'm nervous. It's been almost a year since I last fought, and this guy has some serious wrestling credentials. He was the captain of his wrestling team at Penn State, and they have one of the top programs in the country."

Kenna looked at him incredulously. "Come on. A wrestler can't beat you. You have mad skills."

"I don't want to be overconfident, but I'll be ready come fight night. You gonna get Mom to take you to see the fight?"

Kenna looked down at the floor. "Mom won't go for it. She gets all afraid and stuff, like you're going to get hurt out there. Plus, she doesn't want to expose me to violence. She needs to keep it real."

"Well, I'd like you to be there. You're my rock. I need you for support. I can't do this without you."

Tears welled in Kenna's eyes. After hearing that, nothing in Heaven or Earth would stop her from being in Atlantic City next week to see her brother fight.

Kenna went back to her room, waiting for her friends to arrive. She was too distracted to do homework, even though she knew she had to get it done.

Five minutes later, the doorbell rang. She ran out of her room and told Jake she would get the door. At the front door, she found her three partners in crime.

"Anyone home?" Carlos asked.

"Just Jake. He's heading to the dojo soon. My mom won't be back for at least an hour."

Ben approached the door leading to the basement. "Then we should do this now."

"I thought you were against this," Kenna said.

"I am, but if we're going to talk to Mia, I'd rather do it before your mom comes home."

"All right," Kenna said. "Let's go."

As they walked downstairs, Kenna's heart thumped with a mixture of excitement and healthy fear. Talking to a dead person had gotten far from old, even though they had spoken to Mia several times.

Kenna got the Ouija board from its hiding spot, put the board on the floor, and sat at one end. Ben sat at the other. His fingers trembled as he gripped the planchette. Cordy and Carlos sat to either side of them.

Kenna glanced at Ben. Their eyes met for a brief moment. They rotated the planchette around the board. An electric vibe coursed through the air, which had a pungent odor. The short hair on her forearms stood on end. This never happened until they started speaking to Mia.

"Mia, this is Kenna. Are you here?"

Without hesitation, the disc went to Yes.

Ben's eyes went wide. "Whoa. How did she know we would be here?"

The planchette spelled YOUR PRESENCE STRONG.

"How are you today?" Kenna asked.

HAPPY.

"That's cool," Carlos said. "Sometimes she seems so down."

"You would be too if you were dead," Cordy said.

They asked a few softball questions about life on the other side.

The door leading to the basement opened. Jake yelled out, "Hey, Kenna, I'm rolling. Let Mom know I'll be back around eight. Tell her not to make any food for me. I'm cutting weight."

"Okay. Mia, that was my brother, Jake. He's going to see his girlfriend."

Cordy gave her a thumbs-up.

"You told us about your boyfriend," Kenna said. "His name was Mark, right?"

The planchette moved to Yes.

"How long did you go out with him?" Kenna asked.

2 YEARS.

"Do you think about him still?"

ALL THE TIME.

"Did you go to your senior prom with him?"

Mia answered Yes.

"Can you see him?" Kenna asked.

The planchette moved to No. Then it spelled NEED MEDIUM.

"Like what we're using now?" Ben asked.

Yes.

Ben's brow furrowed. "You said that when you died in your drowning accident, Mark wasn't there. How come?"

There was a long pause. Kenna and Ben circled with the planchette for a while. Maybe Mia had gone away, although she usually told them when she was exiting the conversation.

"Mia?" Kenna asked.

The planchette tugged and spelled out STUPID FIGHT JEALOUS TOLD HIM NEED TIME APART.

Kenna took her hands off the planchette. "That's horrible. They got into a fight before she died. He must have been really broken up about it." Kenna touched the disc. "Mia, do you wish you could let him know how you felt about him?"

There was a pause before the planchette went to No. A few more seconds passed, and then it went to Yes.

"Do you love him?" Kenna asked.

She answered Yes.

Kenna had been so wrapped up with the conversation that she forgot about the whole point of this contact. As if to remind her, Cordy pointed at the Ouija board.

"Did Mark have a nickname for you?"

There was another long pause before the planchette spelled SUNSHINE.

Carlos smirked. "Sunshine? That's dumb."

Cordy elbowed him in the ribs, which caused Carlos to groan. "No, it isn't. She was around in the seventies. It was like the whole Hippie generation and stuff."

Kenna ignored the bickering. "Did you have a nickname for him?"

No.

Kenna was tempted to tell Mia they were going to email Mark, but she wouldn't know what email was. She was thinking about what to ask next when a force knocked her backward. Her arms flew up and her body lifted off the floor. Her back landed hard against the carpet. For a moment, she couldn't breathe. She flipped onto her belly and took two shallow breaths. Her head spun, and she closed her eyes. What was that all about? She propped herself on her elbows and looked up.

Ben was on the floor. Cordy and Carlos hovered over him. He must have gotten it worse than she did because he looked out of it. She crawled over to the board and found the planchette moving on its own, spelling COTTER.

Kenna's entire body shook with fear. Dreading what she would see but knowing she had to do it, she turned and stared at the spot against the wall where the silhouette had appeared the last time. She braced herself, ready to see the silhouette, but this was worse. Two red eyes stared daggers at her.

Kenna screamed.

Chapter VIII

Carlos grabbed Kenna's shoulders. "What is it?"

Kenna caught her breath. She pointed at those horrible red eyes, but they were gone. Could she have imagined it?

"I, um, I was scared." Kenna turned around. "Is Ben all right?"

Ben sat up, touching his forehead. Thankfully, he wasn't bleeding.

Kenna gazed into his dazed eyes. "You okay, Ben?"

"I think so."

Cordy glanced at the Ouija board. "What happened? It was like the two of you were hit by something."

Kenna rubbed a swelling bump on her head. "Something hit us, but I have no idea what it was."

"It was like a blast," Ben said.

Kenna nodded. "Yeah, kinda like that. It lifted me off my feet."

Carlos folded his arms and paced around the room. "It was freaky. I ain't never seen anything that scary."

He must not have seen the board spell out Cotter on its own.

"I don't get it," Cordy said. "Did the blast come from the board?"

"No way," Carlos said. "That's impossible."

Cordy glared at him. "You would have said talking to a dead person was impossible, but we've been doing that."

Carlos shoved his hands into his pockets.

Kenna helped Ben to his feet. "It must have come from the board. I don't think anything's impossible anymore. Not after what we've seen. But it wasn't the board that did it. It was Cotter."

Ben's voice trembled. "Whaddaya mean Cotter?"

Everyone stared at Kenna.

She looked down. "When I got up, you guys were hovering over Ben. I looked at the board. Nobody was touching it, but it spelled out Cotter's name on its own."

"Now you're freakin' me out," Ben said.

"It gets worse. There were two red eyes on the wall." Kenna pointed to where she had seen them earlier.

Carlos's hands trembled. "You're not making this up, are you?"

"I wish I was."

Cordy shivered and wrapped her arms around herself. "That's creepy. You think they were Cotter's eyes?"

"I have no idea. It's not like I've seen him before." Kenna paused. After what had happened today, her friends deserved to know the rest of it. "There's more." She told them about the silhouette from their first contact with Mia.

Cordy scowled. "Why didn't you say something? We're your friends."

"I just thought, you know, maybe I had imagined it."

Ben threw his hands in the air. "Okay, that's it. We're not using that Ouija board ever again.

In fact, we're throwing it away."

In unison, Cordy and Kenna shouted, "No way."

Carlos nodded. "Yeah, man. We can't give up now. We have to find out what this is all about."

Ben folded his arms. "Then you can do it without me."

Cordy batted her eyelashes and leaned in toward him. "Ben, we need your help. We're all in it together."

Kenna patted his shoulder. "Yeah, we're a team. We need to stick together and do whatever we can to help Mia. The first thing we need to do is get in touch with Mark Saleski. Then we can figure out what to do about Cotter."

Carlos raised his hands. "Back up. I'm on board with contacting Mark, but I want no part of Cotter. That dude's bad news."

"We'll worry about him later. First, we'll talk to Mark." In her mind, Kenna was already formulating what she wanted to say to him.

***

Three days after Kenna had seen the red eyes that had scared her senseless, they gathered in Carlos' house.

"So, did you find out anything more about Mark?" Kenna asked.

"I Googled him, but there were a dozen Mark Saleskis," Carlos replied. "One lives in Pennsylvania. He's a lawyer. He might be our guy."

Kenna tilted her head. "Maybe. There could be another Mark Saleski in the state, or he could have moved out."

"I don't like lawyers. We could get in big trouble," Ben said.

"We're not going to get into any trouble." Carlos led the others upstairs to his bedroom and turned on his computer. "Make yourselves comfortable."

Kenna moved a pile of clothes from the bed so she could sit. His room was a mess. Video games, toys, clothes, and books lay scattered throughout the room. She never realized Carlos was such a slob. The rest of the house was neat, probably because they had a cleaning lady.

"What if he's not at his computer or phone right now?" Ben asked.

"Then he'll reply later," Kenna said.

"That's if he replies at all," Ben said.

Cordy shrugged. "If he doesn't, then there's nothing we can do about it. All we can do is try, for Mia's sake."

Carlos logged into his email account. He started an email message and typed in Mark's address. "What should we put in the subject line?"

"How about something like "Hi Mark," Cordy suggested.

"Nah, that might look like spam," Carlos said. "Or he might not pay attention to it. How about greetings from Mia?"

Kenna chewed her fingernails. They had to get this right. This might be the only chance they had to communicate with Mark. "That might freak him out."

"Then how about we try, your friend Mia," Cordy said.

Kenna pumped her fist. "Yeah that will work."

Carlos typed. "Now what?"

"Write this isn't a joke, so please don't delete this message," Kenna said.

"That'll make him want to delete it faster," Ben said.

They haggled back and forth to get the exact wording. Cordy argued she knew better what to say since she sort of had a boyfriend last summer at camp, although when Kenna pressed her, she admitted they had only held hands twice. In the end, the email read:

Mark,

We're friends of Mia. You went out with her just before she died in that drowning accident and you used to call her Sunshine. Just wanted to let you know that Mia is a-ok. Still thinks about you lots. Mia loved you back then, still does. If there's anything you want to pass on to her on the other side, let us know.

Friends of Mia.

Carlos rubbed his hands together. "So that's it. No more changes. Once I hit send, there ain't no turning back."

Kenna fretted about tweaking the message but decided this was as good as they could make it. "I think it's good."

Ben looked up from the Captain America comic book he was reading on Carlos' bed. "That's if you call a train wreck good."

Cordy yanked the comic book away from him. "If you're not going to contribute, then you shouldn't say anything bad."

Ben put his hands in the air. "You shot down everything I suggested."

"So, you just gave up?"

"Yeah."

Ben stuck his tongue out, and Cordy returned the gesture.

Kenna ignored the bickering and stared at the screen. "This is as good as we can make it. Let's send it."

Carlos glanced at Cordy, and she gave him a thumbs-up. "Bet ya he doesn't respond."

"He'll respond," Cordy said.

"What makes you so confident?" Carlos asked.

"Because this was the love of his life. Of course, he's going to respond. He's probably had this emptiness inside him since she died, and now he's finally going to be fulfilled."

Carlos rolled his eyes. "You've been watching too many chick flicks. That stuff don't happen in real life."

"And you spend too much time watching scary movies."

Kenna didn't know what to expect. This might not even be the right Mark Saleski. Maybe Mark would think they were trying to mess with him. Maybe this would devastate him. There was nothing to do but sit and wait. The others engaged in idle conversation, but she couldn't.

Ten minutes later, the computer chimed with the voice of Sponge Bob.

"Looks like I got mail," Carlos said.

They all huddled around the computer. Kenna nearly stopped breathing. It was a reply from Mark Saleski. It read, "Who the hell are you? This shit isn't funny. Mia died thirty-five years ago. If this is your idea of a sick joke, I'm not laughing." He didn't even sign the email.

Kenna closed her eyes. This wasn't the response she had hoped for.

Ben paced around the room. "I told you this was a bad idea. But does anyone listen to me? No. Ben's just trying to keep us from having fun. Maybe next time you ought to listen."

"Will you just chill," Cordy said. "You're making my head hurt."

Kenna sat on a chair next to the computer. "All right. Tell him know we're not messing with him."

Ben frowned. "After his email, you still want to do this?"

Kenna nodded.

Carlos said, "It's not like it can get any worse."

Ben stared out the window at the dreary fall afternoon. "Sure it can."

Kenna took a deep breath. "Write this isn't a joke, and we didn't mean to make you angry. We really are friends with Mia. We know she's dead, but we talk to her almost every day."

"Yeah, yeah," Cordy said. "And write that we can prove we talk to Mia."

"Like how?" Kenna asked.

Without turning around, Ben said, "We can have him ask Mia a question, something only Mia could know. Then we email him back with her response."

"But we would have to let Mia know we talked to Mark," Kenna said.

Ben folded his arms. "You wanna fix this mess?"

Cordy ran her fingers through her long, curly blonde locks. "He's right. We have to let Mia know what we're doing."

Kenna stared at the screen. "Fine, Write that down."

Carlos finished typing. "Anything else?"

Kenna shook her head. "Send it."

They waited a half hour and received no response.

"So, what's this guy up to?" Carlos asked. "I thought we'd hear back from him."

Kenna shrugged. "Maybe he wants to wait and see if we're legit. I don't think he believed us."

Cordy said, "That's the problem with grown-ups. They have a hard time believing in things. The first time we made contact with Mia, I was like, yep, that's a ghost."

"She's a spirit," Ben said.

"Whatever."

Kenna stretched her arms. "Well, I don't think he's going to respond. He would have done so already, so we might as well do something else."

She stared at the computer screen. They could get Mark to believe if Mia would cooperate. The only problem was Cotter's looming specter. She wanted to talk to Mia, but Cotter scared the hell out of her.

Chapter IX

Sitting on the bench in the locker room, Jake took a deep breath. His fight was next. The locker room was hot and humid. He typically liked to warm up and break a sweat before a fight. Tonight, it took little effort. He wasn't sure if the room was cramped or if it was just his mind playing tricks with him, but he felt claustrophobic. He even had to step out of the locker room and walk around the hallways outside in the arena.

He had never been this nervous before. His first professional fight had been in front of a hundred drunken idiots who wouldn't know an arm bar from a side kick. Tonight, three thousand people were in attendance at Boardwalk Hall in Atlantic City. More importantly, representatives from major fighting organizations were in the stands. Tonight would be his chance to shine…or wilt under the pressure.

Earlier on, his nerves had been so bad he had vomited his dinner. His normal walk-around weight was one hundred and eighty-five pounds. Yesterday, he had made weight at the contracted one hundred seventy pounds. By fight night, he was usually rehydrated and close to his normal weight, but he had barely been able to eat or drink anything today.

His stomach felt queasy, and his head ached. Because of the drug testing administered by the state athletic commission, he had not taken anything for his headache, not wanting to chance failing his drug test.

A half hour earlier, Joe Renken had sat him down. "What's wrong, Jake? You don't look so good."

"I don't feel so good."

Joe put a strong hand on his shoulder. "There's nothing wrong with being nervous before a fight, but you can't let it get the better of you."

Jake stared at him, saying nothing.

"Listen, you're a good fighter, a damn good fighter. You trained your ass off for this fight. Win or lose, I'm damn proud of you. The crowd don't mean nothing. All that matters is the guy in front of you. You've worked hard to develop your skills, and we've come up with a good game plan. Go out there, execute, and have fun. You may not be a physician, or an accountant or a finance expert, but very few people in the world are as good at fighting as you are. Relax and enjoy yourself out there."

He was at ease for about ten minutes. When the announcer introduced the fighters for the bout preceding his, he became petrified. It was easy for Joe to tell him to relax. He wasn't going against someone looking to take off his head.

A guy from the athletic commission stepped into the dressing room and told Jake it was time for him make his way to the cage.

A few seconds later, *Enter Sandman* by Metallica played on the speakers in the arena. Jake had requested the song for his entrance. It always pumped him up when he worked out in the dojo.

Joe squeezed his shoulder. "You ready?"

Jake took a deep breath and nodded.

Joe smiled. "Look at it this way, fighting in the cage certainly beats being in prison."

Jake froze for a moment, then realized Joe was trying to make a joke to loosen him up. All at once, Jake let out a loud laugh. It certainly did beat being in prison.

Joe followed him to the cage to a small cheer from the crowd. He was an unknown fighter, and this was the biggest venue he had ever fought in. He stepped into the cage and circled around, then came to a sudden stop as he stared into the audience. He broke out into a big grin as he spotted June and Kenna in the crowd. He didn't think they would be here. Kenna had told him their mom wouldn't let her attend the fight, and June had told him she had other plans.

Not only was June in attendance, but so was his entire class. Lawrence Crawford, wearing an Armani suit, had his hands in the air. Robin waved at him. The other students stood cheering. They had all come to support him. He raised his fist to salute them.

His opponent, Blake Witman, came out next. Kenna stood on her chair booing him. The guy was clean cut with a good build. He looked like a typical college athlete, contrasting with

Jake's longer locks and tattoos, which made him look more like a surfer than a jock.

After the ring announcer made the introductions for each fighter, the ref brought them to the middle of the cage and gave last minute instructions.

He looked into Witman's eyes and saw complete confidence, like he had this fight won before the bell sounded. Jake was going to ruin his plans.

Jake walked back to his corner.

Joe Renken shouted, "He's going to shoot in from the outside. Sprawl and brawl. Sprawl and brawl."

Jake nodded. He closed his eyes and clenched his fists. The bell sounded and, instantly, he felt relaxed.

For the first thirty seconds, they stood at the center of the cage exchanging jabs, then Witman made his move. Just as Joe had predicted, Witman shot in from the outside trying to take him down with a double-legged takedown. He was a freestyle wrestler, so this was his specialty.

Jake met the charge with a sprawl, driving his opponent to the mat. He got back to his feet, connected with two punches followed by a roundhouse kick to the ribs.

Witman winced and staggered back. Undaunted, he shot in again.

"He comes in, you give him a receipt on the way out," Renken yelled.

Jake sprawled. This time he followed it up with a knee to the abdomen and two right hooks. He got into his boxing stance, landing jabs and body punches that sent Witman against the cage. They got in a clinch, and Jake employed his dirty boxing, landing three short elbows to the head followed by a knee to the abdomen.

Jake's face tightened when he realized a second too late that Witman had lured him into a trap. Since he couldn't take Jake down by shooting in, he was trying to trip him to the mat.

Instead of expending energy unnecessarily, he let Witman take him down. Jake was perfectly comfortable fighting off his back. Immediately, he wrapped his legs around his opponent's body in a full guard position, reducing his ability to land strikes. Witman threw a series of elbows to Jake's face, but he partially blocked them. Witman tried to punch him, but Jake grabbed his arm, twisting it around his back in a kimura.

Witman grimaced. If Jake could bend his arm back further, he could get his opponent to tap out, but that would be tough off his back. Another option would be to use his leverage and sweep his opponent. This way Jake would be on top. Witman rolled his body to the right and landed two punches to Jake's head. So hyped on adrenaline, he hardly felt them.

Jake released the kimura and scrambled to his feet. Witman was a step slow, and by the time he had gotten to his feet, Jake landed two punches to his face. Witman staggered, giving Jake the opening he needed. He took two steps and leaped in the air, landing a flying knee to the top of Witman's forehead.

Witman slammed against the cage and rebounded forward. Jake wasn't sure if he had knocked out his opponent with the blow, but Witman's eyes were glazed. Since the referee didn't stop the fight, Jake charged after him, slipped his right arm underneath Witman's windpipe, and applied a guillotine choke. The end of the fight came seconds later when Witman tapped out.

After releasing the choke hold, Jake pumped his fists in the air, filled with elation. He felt an explosion of energy ripple through his body. He released it with a primal and savage roar. Not only had he beaten his opponent, but he had done so in spectacular fashion. He felt more alive at that moment than he had ever felt in his life. The crowd roared its approval. The sound was almost deafening. Throughout the fight, he had completely tuned out the thousands of people in attendance, so focused on his opponent. Now that the fight was over, the noise came at him like a rush.

He climbed to the top of the cage and searched for Kenna. Their eyes met, and he gave her a thumbs-up. He raised his fist and saluted June and his other students, feeling touched in a way he could hardly describe that they had come out here to support him.

He dropped from the top of the cage and walked toward his opponent. Witman looked dazed but otherwise seemed fine.

Jake shook his hand. "Good fight, man. You have nothing to be ashamed of."

Witman congratulated him, and they embraced. Jake acknowledged the crowd once more.

He felt on top of the world when the announcer declared him the victor.

Jake paused for photos before Joe Renken led him out of the cage. Joe patted him on the back. "Now, did you have fun out there?"

Jake smiled. "I sure did."

"Just like I told you. You did the hard work in training. The fight's the fun part."

Back in the dressing room, Jake removed his fighting gloves and stared at himself in the mirror. Other than a slight abrasion over his left eye, he looked untouched. He had worst bruises after tough sparring sessions in the dojo.

Joe stood behind him with a wide smile. "You did great out there, Jake. You made me proud. That whole time you were in prison, I never stopped believing in you. You validated my belief in you tonight."

"Thanks, Joe. Thanks for helping me pick up the pieces. If you didn't offer me a spot at your dojo after I got out, man, I don't even know what I'd be doing now. I know I wouldn't be here, and for that, I owe you more than I can ever pay you back." Tears welled in his eyes. He hugged his trainer in an unusual display of affection for him.

"All you have to do is keep yourself clean and fulfill your potential. I ain't blowing smoke up your ass when I tell you that you can be a great fighter." Joe turned around. "Looks like you have company."

Kenna's gleaming smile lit up the locker room as she stepped inside. Jake opened his arms, and she ran to him. He lifted her into a big bear hug.

"You rocked out there. You were awesome. I told you that you would handle that wrestler."

"It wasn't easy." Jake ran his fingers through her hair. "Thanks so much for coming. I didn't think you would make it."

Kenna frowned. "You think I'd miss this for anything? I had to beg Mom to let me go. She still wasn't going to let me, so I called June and asked her to help."

June stood at the edge of the room and stepped inside. She waved to Jake, and he waved back.

"I got June to sweet talk Mom. She volunteered to take me here and promised she wouldn't let me out of her sight all night."

June took a seat on the bench near Jake. "We wanted to keep it a surprise. All of us at the school were planning on coming, so we bought tickets a few days ago and we had an extra one for Kenna."

Jake had a wide grin on his face. "You sure had me fooled." On Tuesday, he had asked June if she wanted to come to see his fight, but she had told him it was her friend's birthday, and she had already made plans to get together with her. Jake hadn't been sure if the story was legit or if she had been blown him off. Being a pessimist by nature, he had come to the conclusion that he had overestimated June's interest him. Why would a woman with as much going on for her as June ever want to go out with an ex-con?

Jake held June's hand. "I appreciate it. This means so much to me."

Kenna nodded eagerly. "If you want to kiss her now, I'll leave the room."

Jake glared at his little sister. The last thing he needed was her giving him relationship advice. "That's all right. I gotta, um, shower and get changed."

June put her hands on Kenna's shoulders. "Sure thing. We'll be heading out. Lawrence has invited everyone from class back to his place for drinks and food. He was so confident you'd win, he arranged for catering for a victory celebration. Are you going to be able to make it?"

Jake raised his brows. "Really? He didn't have to do that. That's so cool. Yeah, of course I'll go."

June smiled. "Well, I'm going to take Kenna home. I told your mom I'd get her back at a reasonable time. I'll meet you there."

"Sounds great."

Jake walked June and Kenna out of the locker room. Just as she reached the doorway, June pulled him close and gave him a full kiss on the lips.

Jake went wide-eyed but said nothing.

"Nice work out there." June winked. "I'll see you later."

Chapter X

Jake was hoping his nervousness would subside, but he couldn't shake it. Damn, this was almost as bad as his last fight. He had been like this since June had told him about the celebration Lawrence was holding for him. Ever since June had kissed him back at the locker room, his heart had been racing into overdrive. He was sure to find some alone time with her and didn't know how he should respond. He could have something truly special with June, and the last thing he wanted was to blow it.

He knew Lawrence was well off by the way he dressed and carried himself, but he didn't realize he was this loaded. He lived in a mansion. Besides the Mercedes Lawrence usually drove, he also owned an Escalade and a Maserati. At the gym, he seemed like an obnoxious bastard, but after spending time with him at his house, Jake came to realize he was a really cool guy. He gave Jake a tour of his place and even showed him a picture of him at the top of Mount Everest, as well as one of him white-water rafting near the Grand Canyon. As it turned out, he was not only the CEO of the company he started almost a decade ago, but he was also a thrill seeker.

The party was a pretty sweet affair. Lawrence had arranged catering, and there was plenty of food and beverage to go around. All of Jake's students attended the party. They made him the center of attention, wanting a blow-by-blow description of what he had been thinking and doing inside the cage. The attention made him feel uneasy.

Ordinarily, he would have crawled into his shell, but these were his students, and it would be a good learning experience for them to know what happens in a real combat situation. He promised to break down the video of the fight for their next class. He would have been at a loss explaining it right now since everything he had done was instinctual and he hardly remembered it a couple hours later.

June arrived later since she had to drop Kenna off. He wanted to spend time with her, but it was difficult with everyone trying to talk to him.

At one in the morning, people started leaving, giving him a chance to speak to June alone.

He was stammering, trying to make interesting conversation, when June said, "How would you like to go out with me? It doesn't have to be a big deal. Something casual. Maybe we can catch a movie. Get some coffee or a bite to eat afterward. What do you think?"

Jake tried to play it cool, but his heart was doing flip flops. He was starting to sweat. Despite her assertions, this was a big deal for him. A huge, massive deal. He was crazy about her. He had never been a lady's man and invariably said and did the wrong thing around members of the opposite sex. June was special. He didn't want to do anything to jeopardize their budding relationship.

"Um, yeah. I'd love to."

***

He let her pick the movie since he had no idea what was playing and didn't want to pick something she might find stupid. He tended to favor juvenile comedies and superhero movies. She continued to surprise him by picking a horror movie.

Everything had gone well for the first half of the date. He picked her up and met her parents, who seemed wary of him. His mother didn't seem to know what to say and busied herself with other activities, while her father stared at him the whole time. Undoubtedly, they did not find him up to par with Chad Garret, June's wealthy ex-boyfriend. He wondered if she had mentioned that Jake had served time in jail.

Driving to the theater, he actually managed to make witty comments. Fortunately, he didn't have to talk during the movie. Even better, they held hands and she snuggled next to him during the scary parts.

As they walked to his car after the movie, she pulled him aside and gave him a deep kiss. He felt like he was walking on clouds. He had been thinking that nothing could spoil this evening. That was until they arrived at Starbucks.

He wasn't much of a coffee drinker, especially the designer coffee they served there, so he ordered a plain black coffee. She ordered a Mocha Latte something or other, and they settled into a good, comfortable conversation.

"So, what are you thinking about long term now that you're no longer in Boston?"

"I plan on becoming a financial analyst. My idea was to settle in New York or Chicago or some other big city, but things change. I didn't plan on going to Ursinus. It's hard to predict what's going to happen." June smiled. "Sometimes you meet someone, and it changes everything."

It took him a few moments to realize that the somebody she was referring to might be him. His eyes went wide. "Well, you know, I'm pretty flexible about location. There are lots of places where I can get a good training camp for my fights. Of course, I'm loyal to Joe Renken. If it wasn't for him, I wouldn't be back on my feet right now."

June looked down. "But we're getting way ahead of ourselves."

"Of course, I'm just saying…" Jake wasn't sure what he was saying. He wished he could speak more eloquently around June.

They didn't talk for a while. Then June looked up and frowned. "Oh shit."

Jake looked around. "What is it?"

June groaned and covered her eyes with her fingertips.

Jake turned in time to see Chad Garrett and his posse of suburban tough guys approach their table. He tensed. Things had been going so well.

Chad stood next to their table with his hands on his hips. He wore a turtle neck and jeans. On his wrist, he had a Rolex. No college kid should have a Rolex. The bastard hadn't done anything to earn one. Chad shook his head and glared at Jake. "What the hell are you doing here with…*him*?" Chad said it like he was pond scum. People like Jake didn't exist to him. "I know you're trying to make me jealous, but come on, this is pathetic. You can do better than Jerry."

June's face tightened. "It's Jake."

Chad tilted his head and grimaced. "Whatever. Like it really matters what his name is."

In the background, Chad's friends snickered.

Despite his anger rising, Jake tried to remain calm.

"The point is, I know I didn't always appreciate you and pay you the proper attention, but we were good together. Forget about this loser. He's a nobody. He's not worth your time. Let's get back together. All that bad stuff will be water under the bridge."

Jake clenched his fists. He felt like thrashing Chad. Despite the restraint he was trying to show, he couldn't let this creep continue. He could deal with personal insults, but June didn't deserve this. He spoke in the calmest voice he could manage. "Listen, Chad, I think it would be best if you leave."

Chad had about five inches and thirty pounds on Jake. He had been a star baseball player in high school. He had a tall, athletic build, and no doubt thought he could intimidate Jake. He turned to his friends. "Excuse me. Did any of you hear something? Maybe it was just background noise."

Chad's friends roared with laughter. This guy was a regular comedian.

June shook her head. "Chad, you're an asshole. I don't know why I ever went out with you. Jake's ten times more of a man than you could ever dream of being."

Chad's friends erupted with catcalls and exaggerated facial expressions. Jake couldn't figure out who annoyed him more, Chad or these clowns.

This had gone on long enough. Jake stood. "Why don't you get lost?"

Chad wore a pompous smile. "That was so witty. Did you come up with that on your own, or do you have a team of writers working for you?"

"Let's get out of here," June said.

Jake shook his head. "We're not going anywhere. He's leaving."

Chad glanced at his friends. "You talk tough, but the last time I checked, there are five of us and one of you. I know math probably isn't your strong suit, so let me spell it out for you. You're way outnumbered."

"You're right," Jake said. "You should probably get a few more of your friends over here if you want to even up the sides."

Chad narrowed his eyes and pushed him.

Jake took a step backward. He could probably take on all five of them if it came to that, but that would cause a ruckus. He preferred not to fight, but if he was going to, he would make it quick and decisive.

Jake went face to face with Chad. "I'm giving you one chance to leave. I don't want to embarrass you in front of your buddies."

Chad mimicked his words and made monkey sounds. "What do you say? Should we teach him a lesson? Normally, I wouldn't waste my time with trash like you, but we need to make an example out of you."

June sighed. "You're making a big mistake."

Chad waved his hands, pretending to cower in fright. He buried his finger deep into Jake's chest. "I don't want to see you with June ever again."

Jake waited for Chad to make the first move. The pompous bastard didn't disappoint him. Chad swung wide with his right fist. Jake blocked his punch and threw a short right to his ribs. Chad gasped. With no wasted motion, he shot in for a single leg takedown that sent Chad to the floor. As quick as a pistol, he twisted around so he was at Chad's side. Jake grabbed his right arm, flipped his left leg so that it was tightly wrapped under Chad's chin and looped his right leg over Chad's forehead. He wrenched down on Chad's right arm in a textbook arm bar, hyperextending his ligaments and muscles, just the way he demonstrated to his students.

Chad shrieked so loud that Jake's eardrums popped.

Jake knew that this position left him vulnerable for an attack by Chad's friends, but he was convinced that they would not intervene. They were all talk and no action. Even if they did, in his current mood he wouldn't mind thrashing them as well. He stared at them from the floor, almost daring them to jump in. He held onto the armbar for about ten seconds before letting go. He then pinned Chad's shoulders with his knees and rammed his forearm against Chad's chin. He bent down so his mouth was near Chad's ear. "You damn well better stay away from June, or next time I might have to hurt you."

He stood and glared at Chad's friends. As expected, they did nothing.

Chad stood like a little boy who had just had his favorite toy taken from him. He was holding onto his arm. He turned to his friends, his hands trembling. "Don't stand there. Do something."

A tall guy with closely shaved hair pulled Chad back. "It's not worth beating up this loser. We might get into trouble."

A short guy with a thick goatee spoke softly into Chad's ear. "Yeah, he's not worth our time. Let's roll."

Chad didn't put up an argument. As he and his friends walked out of the Starbucks, he yelled, "I'll be looking for you. You better watch your back."

Jake gazed at him with cold, steady eyes, but said nothing. After they left, he paid for the bill and apologized to the store manager.

As he drove June back in his rusty Hyundai, she had a wild-eyed look on her face. "That was so cool what you did back there."

Jake frowned. "No, it wasn't."

"You were great. That was an awesome arm bar."

Jake kept his eyes on the road, wishing the whole episode had never taken place. "It was stupid, senseless. What I do in a cage is a contest between trained athletes. I don't like to fight people who don't know how to fight back."

June's brow furrowed. "But Chad had it coming. He's a jerk."

Jake shrugged.

"Thanks for standing up for me. I appreciate it."

Jake felt his spine tingle. He glanced at June. She looked radiant, even in the dimly lit car. "I wasn't about to let him treat you like that. You deserve better. I just wish I didn't have to do what I did. When you know how to fight, you have a responsibility not to abuse your skills."

When they stopped at a red light, June leaned over and kissed his cheek. "You're my knight in shining armor."

Jake couldn't help smiling. "Well, he is an asshole."

"You're damn right he is. Plus, you didn't actually hurt him. The only injury he sustained was to his massive ego. He deserved it."

"I don't think we'll have to deal with him again."

"Thank God."

When they arrived at June's home, he walked her up to the front steps.

"Do you want to come inside?"

Jake took a long breath. "I'd love to, but I have a class to teach at seven in the morning. I'm filling in for one of the other instructors."

"Oh," June said in a low tone.

As much as he would like to spend more quality time with her, he took his job seriously. Joe Renken showed faith in him, continuing to give Jake more responsibilities. He didn't want to do anything to jeopardize Joe's trust.

It took him a few moments to realize she might have taken this the wrong way. He held her hands. "You know, I had a great time tonight. Even with Chad stopping by."

"Me too."

"I'd love to this again. Soon."

"So would I."

Jake leaned in and gave her a long kiss, something to remember her by until the next time. He walked her to her door and gave her another kiss. When he left, Chad Garrett was a distant memory.

***

When he got home, he was floating in air with fanciful thoughts of June dancing in his head. That was his best first date ever. Hopefully the sequel would be just as good.

Like a dark cloud hanging over him, he spotted the unwanted figure of Adam Fallon sitting on the steps leading to his house. He wore baggy shorts and a backwards baseball cap. Whatever Adam had been doing lately must have been lucrative for him. He wore several gold chains and an expensive looking watch. Jake's smile disappeared. He took a deep breath and continued walking to his house.

Adam stood. "Jake, thank God you're here. Man, I've been waiting for hours. Your mom wouldn't let me in the house but said I could sit by the steps."

This was the first time he had seen Adam since his incarceration. Adam had never showed up for his trial, probably thinking Jake would dime him out. Jake never did, a decision he regretted from his first day in jail.

"I'm in big trouble, man." Adam walked toward him. Blood flowed from an open wound his right hand. "Some things didn't go down the way they were supposed to. You see there was this shipment..."

Jake raised his hand. "I don't want to know. Whatever it is, leave me out."

"You don't understand. I need your help. If I don't get—"

"I don't want to get involved in your problems. I've had enough of that for one lifetime."

"Jake, I don't have anyone else to turn to. Come on, man, you've always been there for me. Doesn't our friendship mean anything to you?"

Jake's eyes narrowed. "You got some nerve. I did six months of hard time for something *you* did. I took the fall for you. You could have come forward and admitted that you robbed the liquor store, and I didn't have any idea what was going on, but you never said boo. Now you're trying to lay a guilt trip on me. I'm getting my life back together. If our friendship meant anything to you, then you wouldn't jeopardize that."

Adam put his arm on Jake's shoulder. "Come on, man. I have no one else to turn to. I'd be there for you if you needed me."

Jake pulled away from him. "No, you wouldn't. It's always been one-sided between us. You've always made a mess of things, and I've always bailed you out. Let me ask you this. What you're asking me to do, does it involve anything illegal?"

Adam didn't answer.

"Just what I thought. You got yourself into a jam and you're going to have to get yourself out of it."

"But, Jake, they're going to hurt me bad."

Jake shook his head. "Look, if you need a place to stay for a few days, or a meal or something, I'll help you, but anything else, back the hell off."

Adam had the look of a dejected child. "So that's the way it's going to be?"

Jake nodded.

"Some friend you turned out to be. I need your help, and you turn your back on me."

Jake stood firm.

Adam glared at him and walked away, muttering under his breath.

Jake felt a twinge of guilt. What if he really was in danger? Could he just leave him high and dry? After thinking of Kenna's sweet, smiling face, he had no other option.

He went inside the house.

He found his mother sitting on the sofa in the living room. Her eyes were red as if she had been crying. She looked up at Jake and smiled. "How did it go tonight?"

Jake sat on the checkered sofa next to her. "Good. You okay?"

His mom blew her nose. "Seeing Adam tonight dredged up bad memories. Things have been tough the last couple years, but I'm done feeling sorry for myself. Sometimes life deals you a bad hand, but you have to pick up the pieces and move on. First your dad dying, and then you in jail. I couldn't cope. I'm sick and tired of feeling miserable. I have a beautiful little girl and a young man trying to restart his path through life who need my help. I've been so self-absorbed that I haven't been there for you two."

Jake slipped his arm around her shoulder. What a night. All he wanted was a pleasant evening out with June. He wasn't prepared for this emotional turmoil. "We've been through some rough patches, and there'll be hard times ahead. That's why we have to lean on each other. We'll be stronger for it."

She kissed his forehead and straightened his shirt. "You have blood on your collar."

Jake frowned as he looked at his shirt, trying to think how he got it. During their fight, Chad had not been bleeding. Then he remembered Adam had a cut on his hand from doing God knows what. "It's nothing."

"Listen, Jake, don't let that boy drag you down again."

Jake nodded. "There's no way I'll ever do anything to let you or Kenna down again. That's a promise."

Chapter XI

Cordy pulled Kenna aside before they entered school. School was about to start, and the other kids were all walking inside. "We have to talk to Mia about Mark."

Kenna looked around to make sure no one else was listening. "I know. I wanted to last time, but Mia's been acting weird lately."

"Still, we have to get back to Mark Saleski soon. Otherwise, he's gonna write us off as a bunch of wackos."

They had spoken to Mia three times since emailing Mark Saleski. Each time, she intended to tell Mia that they had spoken to him and get inside information to prove to Mark that they really talked to her. The last few times, Mia had been erratic with long lapses in between answers to their questions. On several occasions, Kenna had thought she had bowed out of the conversation before she resumed communicating with them. When Mia spoke, it came in ragged bursts, not with the normal smooth flow of the planchette that Kenna had become used to feeling. Her responses often didn't make sense, as if she was distracted. Kenna had a good idea what was bothering her. The one time she had brought up Cotter, Mia ended the conversation abruptly.

Kenna rubbed her eyes. "We'll talk about Mark this time. We'll get right into it. No messing around. I promise."

"Good," Cordy said. "I was starting to think you were wimping out."

Kenna scowled at her. "I'm not wimping out. Ben's the one who's always afraid."

Cordy smiled. "Don't worry about Ben. I got him wrapped around my little finger. Boys are so easy to control."

Ahead of them, Ben was waddling up the steps leading to the front entrance. His backpack was so stuffed he was having trouble walking. Every few feet, he had to hike it up so it wouldn't fall.

"Hey, Ben," Cordy called out. "Four o'clock at Kenna's house. We're going to tell Mia about Mark. Be there."

"Um, okay."

Cordy had a beaming smile. "What did I tell you?"

"You could be a little nicer."

Cordy frowned. "Why should I be?"

"You're like a diva."

"What's that?"

"I'm not sure," Kenna replied.

"Whatever. So, we'll meet at your house, and we're not leaving until we get that information from Mia."

***

Kenna felt like a celebrity at school. Everyone was asking about her brother's fight, even the older kids who never bothered with her. She soaked in the spotlight, not because she wanted the attention, but because she was so proud of Jake. She wanted to stand on top of a mountain and let everyone know how awesome he was. When she described the fight, she gave them a blow-by-blow detail, skipping over the part where she had closed her eyes when Jake was down, and his opponent was throwing elbows at him.

She tried to think about Jake's fight and not about Mia. When Cordy insisted they talk to her about Mark Saleski, she had inwardly groaned. Normally, she looked forward to speaking with her spirit friend, but lately she had been getting bad vibes during their conversations.

Just before school ended, she tried to talk Cordy out of it, but her best friend was adamant. When Cordy called her a chicken, there was no way she was backing down.

***

Right after school, they went to Kenna's house.

"Did you bring the question?" Kenna asked.

Carlos sighed. "I already told you I have the copy of the email in my backpack."

Kenna nodded. "All right. I guess we're ready."

Kenna didn't need the email. She had memorized the secret question they were supposed to ask Mia. The question only Mia could know, which would convince Mark that they truly spoke to her beyond the grave. Grown-ups were so hard to convince, especially lawyers. Jake had told her lawyers were no damn good. That was probably because his lawyer had lost the case that sent him to prison.

They had pestered Mark with emails until he finally relented and provided them with the secret question. He obviously still felt something for Mia, or he wouldn't have bothered.

Once inside their house, Kenna called out, but as expected, nobody answered. Mom was stuck at work for another hour, and Jake was at the dojo. She figured he would have taken time off after his fight, but he was back training the next day.

"All right. Let's do it," Cordy said.

Kenna hesitated.

"What's the matter?" Ben asked.

Kenna replied, "I'm scared."

Ben's eyes widened. "You're scared?"

Kenna turned away. "Crazy things have been happening lately."

Ben nodded. "We should drop this whole thing."

Kenna frowned. "No. Mia's our friend."

"She'll understand," Ben said.

Cordy put her hand on Kenna's shoulder. "We should do anything we can for her."

"Enough with this," Carlos said. "Just get the board. Gary let me borrow the new Halo game, and I need to get back and play it when we're done."

"Is that all you think about?" Cordy rolled her eyes.

As they went to the basement, Kenna experienced an odd sense of déjà vu. Would Cotter show up again? Probably not.

After all, they had communicated with Mia over a dozen times, and he had only appeared twice.

They got the board and took their familiar positions. Kenna sat with her legs crossed and stared at Ben. His face no longer had that look of apprehension as if he had just stepped into a yard full of barking German Shepherds. Maybe it was her admission of being scared that helped him.

They circled the Ouija board with the planchette. It was dark inside the basement. Kenna told Carlos to go put on the second set of lights. She preferred the atmosphere to be cheery when they spoke with Mia.

"Mia, are you there?" Kenna asked. Lately, Mia had been responding quickly, but they hadn't spoken to her in a few days. Hopefully, they had not lost their connection.

Ben looked up at Kenna, his face full of concentration. "Mia, it's Ben. We want to talk to you."

Kenna continued to circle with the planchette. "Mia, please speak to us."

"Maybe she's taking a nap," Carlos said. "Or maybe she's on a hot date."

Cordy flicked Carlos on the head.

"What's that for?" Carlos asked.

"Like she's really going out on a date."

"How do you know what she does up there?"

Kenna let go of the planchette. "Cut it out. I need to concentrate."

"Yeah, quit your yapping," Ben said.

Before Kenna called out again, the planchette spelled out MISSED YOU

"We've missed you too," Kenna said. "We've been, um, busy with stuff. You know, like school and everything. So, how's everything in the spirit world?"

TRYING TO GET BY

"I hear you," Ben said. "I feel that way all the time."

After some small talk, Kenna said, "Mia, there's something we haven't told you. We've been talking to your old boyfriend, Mark Saleski."

The planchette tugged violently. YOU HAVE

Kenna glanced at her friends. "We thought it would be a good idea to send him a message from you. The thing is, he kinda doesn't believe that we talk to you."

"Yeah, most people don't believe in ghosts—I mean spirits," Ben added.

Before Ben finished speaking, the planchette started moving across the board. WHY YOU TALK TO HIM

"Well, we didn't actually talk to him," Ben said. "We emailed him. Email's done through computers and stuff. They didn't have it back when you were alive. I'd explain it better, but I doubt you'd understand."

Ben was starting to ramble, so Kenna cut him off. "We thought you would like to let Mark know that we talk to you, and you still care about him."

There was a long pause before the planchette spelled out WHAT YOU SAID TO HIM

Kenna wiped the sweat off her brow before re-gripping the planchette. "Well, we told him you're doing fine, and you still think about him, but he didn't believe us."

HOW IS HE

Ben tilted his head. "Okay, I guess. He's a partner at a law firm."

ALWAYS KNEW HE WOULD BE LAWYER

"Like we said, we didn't actually talk to him on the phone or in person or anything like that. The way we communicated with him is sort of like how we're doing with you." Kenna paused to give Mia time to comment, but there was no resistance on the planchette. "We have to get him to believe we actually speak to you. To make sure we really speak to you, he wanted us to ask you something that only you would know."

There was an unexpected pull on the planchette. WHAT

Kenna took a deep breath. "Okay, he wanted to ask where you guys went after your senior prom and what he gave you?"

The response was rapid. CLIMB STEPS ART MUSEUM GAVE ME BRACELET SAID 4EVER.

Cordy said, "Aw, that's so sweet. I told you she was the love of his life. To be broken apart at such a young age. That's so sad."

Kenna felt the air lighten around her. Mia's presence continued to grow stronger. It was as if she was standing next to them.

"Thank you for telling us," Kenna said. "He'll have to believe us now. Is there anything you want us to tell him?"

There was a long pause before the planchette moved to No. Then it moved to Good Bye.

For a while, nobody spoke. Carlos broke the silence. "That went better than I thought it would."

Kenna nodded. "Did it feel like, I don't know, like Mia was happier?"

Ben smiled. "Yeah, it was like a nice summer breeze."

Cordy pressed her index finger against her cheek. "It was more like the smell of lilac on a spring day."

"No, no," Carlos said. "It was like when you get to the final level in Mortal Kombat and you kill off the last bad guy."

Kenna shrugged. "Maybe it's different for each of us. But did you guys feel something? It wasn't just me?"

"I definitely felt something," Carlos said.

Ben and Cordy nodded.

After her friends left, Kenna couldn't get the feeling out of her head. Mia's physical manifestation was significant. She just couldn't figure out why.

Chapter XII

Carlos ran across the school yard with a piece of paper in hand. Ben ran behind him, having a hard time keeping up. Ben had short legs and a wide frame, so running fast was not something he did. Carlos had a look of wild-eyed excitement. "Hey, guys, check this out!"

Cordy and Kenna had been jumping rope. They broke away from the other girls.

"What is it?" Kenna asked.

Cordy frowned. "Yeah, you're gonna wake up the dead."

Carlos stopped to catch his breath. "I got an email from Mark Saleski." Last night, they had emailed Mark, detailing what Mia had revealed the last time they talked to her, private information only Mia would know. Kenna had no idea how Mark would react to it. She had crossed her fingers when they sent the email and had been mentally crossing them ever since.

Nearby, a group of kids were playing four square. They were too close to the other kids for her liking. This was their own private business. Nobody else needed to know about it.

"Let's go to the gazebo," Kenna said. Kids hardly ever congregated there. When they reached it, she asked in a high-pitched voice, "What did he say?"

Carlos waved the sheet of paper in front of them. "I have it right here."

Cordy snatched it from him, and Kenna looked over her shoulder.

The email read: *How the hell can you possibly know that? I was devastated when Mia died. Part of me died with her. But that was so long ago, a lifetime really. Now you're stirring old memories that should be left alone. I have to find out how you learned this and if the impossible is true. Can you really communicate with Mia? I won't be able to sleep at night without knowing. I'd like to meet you. From your letters, I assume I'm dealing with more than one person. Let me know where and when, and I'll be there.*

Kenna took the paper away from Cordy and read it again, focusing on each word. She could hardly believe Mark Saleski wanted to meet them. Then reality bit her. What would he think when he saw they were just kids?

Cordy snatched the paper from Kenna. "This is awesome. It's just what we wanted."

Kenna folded her hands, deep in thought. "Okay, how about we meet him after school? Somewhere nearby so we can walk there."

After some haggling, they settled on a diner between school and their homes.

***

During the week leading up to their encounter with Mark Saleski, Kenna kept wondering whether or not this was a good idea. She hoped this would help Mia feel better about being dead. Maybe they could pass along a message from Mark.

She was certain Mia would welcome it. She had asked about Mark the last time they communicated with her. Kenna had been purposely vague with her answers, not wanting to get Mia's hopes up.

Hopefully, they could convince Mark they were telling the truth. Of course, he might just tell them they were nuts and walk out.

Kenna felt so jittery. The only one who seemed relaxed was Cordy. She couldn't stop talking about it in between classes, at recess, after school, or on the phone. She fashioned herself as this matchmaker who was going to get Mia and Mark back together again. The only problem was that Mia was dead. Anything short of bringing her back to this world would make that impossible.

After their final class, they gathered together by the flagpole in front of school. Carlos wore shades and a backwards hat. Ben's face was pale. At least she could count on him being more afraid than her. Cordy was chatting up a storm. She had planned out exactly what they were going to say to Mark.

They arrived at the diner five minutes before the scheduled meeting time. They ordered two Cokes and a root beer. Kenna didn't want anything because she felt queasy.

"This is so cool." Carlos sipped his soda. "You know, it's like we're undercover agents in some secret meeting."

Cordy smacked Carlos' shoulder, causing his drink to spill. "This isn't a comic book. This is real life. Be serious."

Carlos smirked. "Well, I think it's cool. It beats soccer practice."

Kenna glanced at her watch every few moments. Five minutes after their scheduled meeting time, she started to get worried. "Maybe he's not going to show and we're wasting our time. What were we thinking?"

Ben slid across the booth. "Maybe we should just leave."

Cordy yanked him back to his seat. "You're not going anywhere. Just chill."

Kenna's eyes lit up when a man wearing black dress shoes, pleated pants, a Tommy Hilfiger button down shirt and a striped tie entered the diner. His thick hair was beginning to get gray. He had a neatly trimmed mustache and beard, also growing grey. In his hand, he held a briefcase.

Kenna nudged Carlos. "That must be him."

"Yeah, I think so," Carlos said.

Cordy and Ben turned and stared at the man.

Kenna put her hands on the table and leaned in, speaking in a low tone. "All right, let's play this cool. Let's make sure it's him. Don't all stare at once."

Carlos disregarded her advice and ogled the guy.

The man scanned the diner, a heavy frown forming on his face.

A hostess walked up to him. "Will there be anyone else joining you today?"

He continued to look around. "I'm meeting people."

The hostess smiled. "If you like, you can wait here, or I can get you a table."

The man ignored her and continued looking.

"This has to be him." Kenna rose from the table amid anxious looks from her friends and walked over to him. "Excuse me. Are you Mr. Saleski?"

His face tightened. "Yes, that's me."

She extended her hand. "I'm Kenna."

Mark Saleski frowned. "Is this some kind of joke?"

Kenna shook her head. "No, it's not."

"You're just a kid."

"I realize that."

"And I suppose those are your friends at that table?"

Kenna nodded.

Mr. Saleski sighed and ran his hand through his hair. "I can't believe I've been talking to a bunch of kids. This is nuts. Why didn't you tell me you guys were like eight years old?"

"I just turned ten. We figured you wouldn't show if you knew we were kids, so we didn't mention that."

"All right. I'm leaving."

"Please, Mr. Saleski, don't leave. We may not have told you how old we are, but we never lied about it. You just never asked. And we haven't lied about Mia. We really do talk to her. That's why you're here. If you didn't think there was at least a chance, no matter how small, that it might be true, you'd have blown us off a long time ago."

Mark pursed his lips.

"I swear to you we're telling the truth. Hear us out. You're already here, so you don't have anything to lose."

Mark grinned. "Except my dignity. Well, you've made a persuasive argument, young lady. You just might have a future as a lawyer." He shook her extended hand. "I'll listen to what you have to say."

"Awesome."

Kenna led him to their table. "Mr. Saleski, this is Ben, Carlos, and Cordy."

He shook each of their hands, pulled up a chair, and sat at their table. He folded his hands. "So, how do you communicate with Mia?"

Cordy smile brightly. "We use an Ouija board."

Mr. Saleski's brows rose. "An Ouija board? But those are phony."

Ben shook his head, his face grave. "It isn't, sir. I thought so, too, but it's real, very real."

"Well, how did it happen? Did you try to talk to Mia?"

Cordy shook her head. "No, it was like a total accident. I mean, we were just goofing with it, and then the planchette started moving, and it was Mia talking to us."

Mr. Saleski's eyes narrowed. "So, what do you talk about with Mia?"

Ben shrugged. "Different things. We've asked her about all sorts of stuff that happened in her past."

Kenna nodded. "Yeah, that's how we found out about you."

"How did that come about? Did she randomly start talking about me?"

Kenna shook her head. "We asked if she had any old boyfriends before she died, and she spelled out your name with the planchette."

Mr. Saleski folded his hands. "Tell me about the physical act of communicating with her. How does that work?"

Ben replied, "Me and Kenna hold the planchette, and we just kind of move it around. Then when she starts speaking, it moves on its own, and you just go with it. It spells out words and stuff. We ask her questions, and she responds. We've never been able to communicate with any other spirits other than Mia. Believe me, I didn't think any of this stuff was real until we actually started doing it."

Kenna was surprised that Ben was so talkative. He was usually timid around grown-ups.

"So, what did Mia say about me?"

Cordy's face lit up. "She still loves you. You can tell that. Not just by her words, but there's this whole vibe you can feel. It's hard to explain, but it's like the atmosphere in the room totally changes."

"Yeah," Carlos added. "It's like she's there with you."

"She told us about her accident," Kenna said

Mr. Saleski's face sagged as he lowered his eyes to the table. "That was really tough. I've beaten myself up so often over the years about that. I wasn't with her that day."

Kenna didn't want to pry, but she felt compelled. She took a deep breath. "She mentioned you had gotten into an argument."

Mr. Saleski's eyes went wide. He leaned in close to them. It was like he finally believed they spoke to Mia. "We did. It was a stupid argument in retrospect, although at the time it seemed important. We hadn't spoken to each other for a few days. I thought I would make her feel bad, and she would cave in. You see, my uncle worked at a law firm in Connecticut and he had offered me a summer internship. Mia wanted me to go. She said it would be a good opportunity. I…well I didn't want to go. I thought if I spent the entire summer away from her, we would drift apart, and she would find someone else. I didn't want to lose her, and then…" Tears formed in Mr. Saleski's eyes. "I lost her anyway."

"You really loved her, didn't you?" Kenna asked.

Mr. Saleski wiped away tears. "I sure did."

Kenna stared into his eyes. "But she's not gone. She's dead, but her spirit is with us."

Mr. Saleski sighed. "I don't know if that's comforting or not."

"She seems happy most of the time," Cordy said. "But she does have issues."

Kenna glared at her.

"What do you mean?" Mr. Saleski asked.

Ben looked around the table, and when nobody volunteered to answer, he said, "There's this bad spirit named Cotter, who's causing Mia problems. We're not sure what the deal is since she doesn't like to talk about him, but it can't be good."

Mr. Saleski's face tightened. "Is she in danger?"

Kenna felt a sudden urge to change the direction of the conversation. "We're not sure. I'm really glad you decided to come today, because Mia still cares about you."

Mr. Saleski took a deep breath. "I must be crazy for talking about this with a bunch of kids. Hell, the whole situation is crazy, but I've never forgotten about her. My marriage is a disaster. Right now, I'm in the middle of an ugly divorce. Hopefully, your parents will stay together. Divorce is bad business. I have a son just entering high school and a daughter a few years older than you. They're not taking it well. My son was just recently arrested for drug possession, and based on the crowd my daughter runs with, she probably isn't far behind." He closed his eyes. "God, I miss Mia. I think my problem is that I've measured everyone else against her, and nobody can meet her standards. Maybe it was because I was young and didn't know any better. Everything that happens when you're young seems so much better and more important as you get older. It was devastating to lose her."

Kenna sniffled as tears welled in her eyes.

Cordy clutched Mr. Saleski's arm. "That's so sad."

"Hey, it ain't all bad," Carlos said. "Mia's still out there, even if she ain't with us."

Kenna nodded. "That's right. If you'd like, we could pass on a message to her, or maybe you want to talk to her yourself."

Mr. Saleski paused for a moment. "I'm not ready to talk to her, but what the hell, maybe there is something you can tell her. Tell Mia the cup is still full."

Kenna's brow furrowed. "What does that mean?"

"It was just a saying we had. We were silly kids. If you truly communicate with Mia, she'll tell you."

Kenna smiled. "We'll tell her that the next time we speak to her."

Chapter XIII

Jake knelt on the mat, calling out instructions. "All right, Robin, buck out of there. Thrust your hips and roll right. Good job. Now get to your feet."

Robin and June were grappling on the mat. June was on top of her, and Robin was trying to get out from underneath. She was making a valiant attempt, but Robin lacked physical strength. Meanwhile, June was doing an excellent job of maintaining top position.

A few of the other students stood watching them grapple. Lawrence shouted encouragement, and Robin finally got to a standing position.

Jake patted Robin's back. "Not bad. Take a break and switch positions."

Lawrence grabbed his arm. He had the excited look of a kid who had just tied his shoes for the first time. "Hey, Jake, I finally figured out how to put on a triangle choke. I was practicing with Pete. Let me show you."

"Sure thing." Jake smiled. He had thought of teaching mixed martial arts as a way to make money and keep himself sharp while training for his next opponent. Little did he know that he would actually enjoy it.

The tenor and attitude of his class had changed after his students had gone to see his fight in Atlantic City. At the beginning of the next class, he had brought a digital copy of the fight provided by the event promotor and analyzed it with them, showing step by step what he had done and why he had done it.

Watching his fight and attending the after-party had been a bonding experience for the class. Ever since then he had noticed a change in their attitudes. His students were more receptive to what he was telling them, and the intensity increased in class. Many students sported noticeable bumps and bruises at the end of the sessions. They also exhibited a greater sense of cooperation. Even Lawrence, who used to dominate his time, waited patiently while he worked with others.

Jake did his best not to show June preferential treatment at the dojo. So far, she did not seem to mind.

He went across the room where Lawrence hit the mats with another student. They grappled for a minute before Lawrence applied a triangle choke to his sparring partner.

Lawrence pumped his fist. "That was so awesome."

"That's the result of you working hard at improving your craft. Keep at it. You have to keep practicing, or you'll lose it."

Lawrence put his hands on his hips. "I love this stuff. It's the only thing I look forward to when I'm at work. I was at a meeting today, and my CFO was pissing me off. I wanted to go across the table and choke the son of a bitch out. Either that or fire him."

Jake chuckled. "Take your aggression out at the dojo, where it belongs."

"Well yeah, I'm not going to actually do it. I just had this urge. You know what I'm saying? I still might fire him, except he is good at his job."

Jake thought back to his encounter with Chad Garrett at the Starbucks, wishing it had never happened. Maybe he could have tried harder to talk himself out of the situation.

The rest of the session flew by. He finished by showing the entire class the proper technique to use when trying to get out from underneath a bigger and stronger opponent.

He said good-bye to his students as they filed out. June lingered. After everyone left, he clutched her arm. "Hey, you're getting good. Your ground game is coming along. Now we need to work on your striking."

June folded her arms. "So, the other night, were you trying to blow me off?"

Jake felt his face blushing. "No." That was the last thing he wanted her to think. "I really had to go to work early. In fact, I'd like to get together with you. Soon."

"Yeah? I'm not doing anything tomorrow night. However, I can be persuaded into going out if someone were to ask," June said.

"In that case, I'd like to take you somewhere."

Before he could think of where he might take June, Joe Renken walked up from behind and slapped his back. "Hi, June. Jake, good news."

Jake turned around. "Oh yeah?"

"I just lined up a fight for you at the end of the month."

"So soon?"

Joe shrugged. "Why not? You didn't sustain any damage in your last fight, and I want to get you out again. You need the experience. Plus, you opened some eyes in that last fight. That guy you went up against is a high-level wrestler. He had been looked at as a serious prospect until you decimated him. Now, you're the prospect. A couple representatives for major organizations want to check you out in person. It's good to strike while the iron's hot."

June grabbed his hand. "That's awesome."

"So, who am I fighting next?"

"The kid's name is Paulo Santos. He's a hotshot out of Brazil's Chute Boxe Academy. I don't know much about him, but he's highly regarded and also looked at as a prospect. Those Chute Boxe guys have wicked Muay Thai, and he's Brazilian, so you know he's going to have strong jiu-jitsu. I'll get some tape on him, so we can come up with a game plan."

"All right," Jake said. "Let's do it."

"And I'm also working on a sponsorship deal for you with a local Ford dealership."

Jake grinned. "Awesome. Some extra cash wouldn't hurt."

"Just keep training your ass off, and you'll go places. Mark my word." Joe peered over at June. "I trust you're not going to weaken my boy here. I need him strong for his next fight."

Jake's face went red. They hadn't taken their relationship to that level. The most physical they had gotten had been on the mats at the dojo.

June pulled him close. "Don't worry. I'll make sure he's in good shape."

Jake wasn't sure how to take that comment. After a few moments, Joe and June began laughing, so he joined them, not sure what was so funny.

Joe patted him on the shoulder. "I'm proud of you, kid."

After Joe left, June smiled. "I'm proud of you, too." She gave him a light kiss on the lips. "Call me."

Jake stared at her as she sauntered out of the dojo. Things were going great. He wasn't accustomed to things working out this well. That was probably why he had a sneaking suspicion things were about to get a whole lot worse.

Chapter XIV

Kenna opened her eyes and stared at the ceiling. She always fell asleep with no problem, but tonight she couldn't stop thinking about Mia, Mark Saleski, and dying. Her conversations with Mia proved there was life after death, but it also proved this existence wasn't always happy.

She had thought speaking with Mr. Saleski would fix everything. He had been receptive to what they had told him, passing on a message to Mia. So far, that hadn't solved anything. When they had tried to contact Mia the last time, she had not responded. Kenna had gotten used to her picking up on them as soon as they attempted to communicate. Since then, terrible thoughts had been running through her head.

She glanced at her alarm clock. It was well past midnight. She was going to be a wreck at school tomorrow if she didn't sleep.

She closed her eyes and turned on her side. A slamming sound came from downstairs. She snapped her eyes open and sat up. For a few moments, she stared in silence at her darkened bedroom. Her first instinct was to get Jake. He would protect her. Then she remembered Jake had gone out with June. Maybe he had come home. They must have had a late night, which she assumed was a good thing.

Kenna hoped things would work out between them. It had been a stroke of genius when she and Cordy had reintroduced them. June was perfect for her brother. She was super cool, smart, confident, and always in control. Kenna wanted to be just like her when she got older.

Kenna got out of bed, checked Jake's bedroom, and found that he was not there. As she approached the stairs, she noticed the kitchen lights were on. A burglar wouldn't turn on the lights. She walked downstairs and spotted Jake in the kitchen.

He put down his glass of water. His face seemed brighter than normal. For a while, after he had come home from prison, he had been brooding. Major improvement. Definitely a good date with June.

"Why are you still up?"

Kenna shrugged. "Couldn't sleep. So, you had a hot date with June?"

"It went well."

Kenna smiled. "That's awesome. She's really nice."

Jake nodded. "Yeah, I like her a lot. So, what's keeping you up? I'm sure you didn't stay up late just so you can ask me about my date."

Kenna yawned. "What do you think happens to us after we die?"

"Jeez, that's morbid. Why would you ask that?"

Kenna shrugged. "So, what do you think happens?"

"Well, if you lead a good life, you go to heaven. At least that's what we've always been taught, and I don't have any reason not to believe that."

"Do you think bad things can happen to you there?" Kenna asked.

"I certainly hope not. Where's all this coming from? Are you thinking about Dad?"

Kenna looked down. She hardly thought about him anymore. That was terrible of her not keeping his memory alive. "You know that thing with the Ouija board?"

Jake nodded.

"Well, we've been speaking to the spirit of this girl who died."

Jake's face tightened. "What? Is this some kind of joke?"

Kenna folded her arms. "No. I wouldn't joke about that."

"You're talking to a *spirit*?"

Kenna nodded. "I think she might be in trouble. I'm worried about her. You see, Cotter, this bad spirit, harms her. The last time we tried to speak to Mia, she didn't answer."

Jake folded his hands under his chin. "I don't know what to tell you. I don't know anything about spirits or what happens after you die. All I can tell you is that there are certain things you shouldn't mess with. Look, I wouldn't tell you what to do unless you were in danger, but I would leave this Ouija board thing alone."

Kenna sighed. She shouldn't have expected Jake to know how to deal with the situation. It's not like he ever communicated with dead people. This was something she and her friends would have to figure out on their own.

"Somethings are just better if you let them be," Jake said. "And I think communicating with a spirit is one of them. I seriously doubt any good could ever come from it. You with me?"

Kenna nodded.

Jake patted her shoulder. "It's late. You need to get to bed."

Kenna smiled. "Okay. Can you give me a piggy back ride to my room?"

"Of course." Jake knelt on the floor. "Climb aboard."

Kenna climbed on his back and wrapped her arms around his neck. He carried her up the stairs and dropped her off in her room.

Jake hugged her. "Good night. Sleep tight."

"You too."

Kenna crawled into her bed. She was going to ignore Jake's advice. They would have to try contacting Mia again. Hopefully this time, she would respond.

***

Ben stood by the bank of the creek, throwing rocks. Kenna stared blankly at the water as the sun set in the background. The chill in the air made her shiver. She should have brought a jacket. They would have to leave soon. The dark skies in the distance suggested a storm was coming.

"What are we going to do?"

Ben put his hands in his pockets. "How am I supposed to know?"

They had tried twice more to reach Mia with no luck.

"Do you think we like lost our connection with her?" Kenna asked.

Ben sat next to her. "I don't know. Maybe it's for the best. You ever think we might be in over our heads?"

Kenna frowned. "You sound like Jake"

"Then he's probably right."

Kenna waved her hand. "No way. We need to tell Mia about Mark. This can be the most important thing that has happened to her since she died. She needs to know he still cares about her."

"Well, maybe it isn't a coincidence that ever since we told her that we emailed him, we haven't been able to reach her."

Kenna's face tightened. "Hmm. You think she doesn't want to talk to us anymore because of that?"

Ben shrugged. "Maybe she has something to hide."

"Like what? She's dead."

"I don't know. I just don't think it's an accident that we haven't been able to talk to her. I mean, for a while, it was instantaneous. You know what I'm saying?"

Kenna nodded. She grabbed Ben's hand. "We can't give up. I won't give up on her."

"Why is this so important to you? We all talk to Mia and stuff, but you're obsessed with it."

Kenna looked down at the rocks. "I don't know. This is our chance to do something important. Most of the time, it feels like nothing we say or do matters, but this is different. This is…" Kenna struggled for the word. "This is significant.

"Ben, I need you with me on this. Maybe because we're the ones who first spoke to Mia, or maybe because you're more reliable than the others, but I need you to stick with me, no matter what. Don't give up."

"I won't. Are you sure we're doing the right thing?"

"Yeah, I think so."

Ben smiled. "Then the only thing to do is to keep trying to reach Mia. Maybe next time we'll get lucky."

Chapter XV

"You have to face it, Mia's gone," Carlos said in his all too cool voice.

Kenna felt like smacking the back of his head. "No, she isn't. How can you say that?"

Carlos raised his hands. "Hey, don't get all mad at me. I'm just keeping it real. We tried reaching Mia four times, and she ain't responding."

Kenna put her hands in her pocket. They had tried different combinations of people holding the planchette on the Ouija board, but nothing worked. Still, she wasn't ready to give up. Not yet. Not after speaking to Mark Saleski.

She turned to Cordy, the wind on this blustery late fall afternoon had left her friend's long blonde hair tangled as they walked through the park, sticking to the path that ran alongside the creek. Cordy tried to keep it down, but she was fighting a losing battle. "What do you think?"

Cordy shrugged. "I don't know. I mean, I want to talk to Mia, but she's not responding any more. Maybe Carlos is right. Maybe she's gone."

Kenna shook her head. She couldn't accept that. Her pleading eyes turned to Ben.

Because Ben spoke less, his words always meant more. "I think Mia's still out there. I don't know why, but I do."

Kenna pumped her fist. "Then we have to keep trying. We're not going to give up. As soon as we get to my house, we'll try reaching her again."

"Whatever you say," Carlos said. "I got soccer practice, so let's make this quick. It's not like it's going to work, anyway. We're just wasting our time."

Ben turned to Carlos. "Sure, it will. You have to have faith."

Kenna wore a big smile as they continued walking along the path. She patted Ben on the back. She knew she could count on him. When the chips were down, there were few people she could rely on. Jake was at the top of the list, but Ben was there as well. He was a rock.

Cordy grabbed Kenna's hands. "Hey, you have to come over my house later. My parents are going out, so June's babysitting. We can ask her all about her date with Jake."

Carlos made a gagging sound. "I'd rather get poked in the eye than hear about that."

Cordy's face tensed. "You know, I can arrange that for you."

"No need to get all violent," Carlos said.

Kenna couldn't help feeling trepidation as they walked to her house. They had to reach Mia this time or their little group might fracture. It was getting harder to keep everybody on board. Not to mention she was concerned about Mia. She couldn't stop thinking about her spirit friend. It was eating away at her. She was having trouble sleeping at night and concentrating at school.

Her mom was not home when they arrived. She was surprised to find Jake home, carrying a basket of laundry. He spent most of his time training at the dojo or teaching. She wished that she could spend more time with him, but she knew how important training was for him.

"Hey, Jake," Kenna called out. "We're going to be hanging out in the basement." She wasn't about to tell him they were going to use the Ouija board. He would not approve, and what he did not know would not hurt him.

"Mom's working a double shift tonight, so I'm supposed to make you dinner and make sure you don't damage the house. Do you have any dining preferences?" Jake grinned. "Keep in mind, my culinary skills aren’t the best."

Kenna smiled. "Well, since you’re not training for a fight now, we can eat junk food."

"Sorry, no such luck. I'm fighting in two weeks, so my diet's going to be real strict."

Kenna's brows rose. "Get out. You already have another fight? But you just had one."

"Joe wants me to get in right away. This show he booked me for is a big deal. If I beat my next opponent, it could be a huge boost for my career."

Kenna might be his kid sister, but she still felt protective of him. "That's not enough time. Are you going to be ready?"

Jake shrugged. “I'm in shape. I didn’t take any damage in the last fight. We're just going to have to do some crash game planning for my next opponent."

"Who are you fighting?" Kenna asked.

"Some Brazilian dude, Paulo Santos. He's supposed to be good, even better than my last opponent."

"That's okay," Cordy said. "You're better."

"Yeah, you'll kick his ass," Carlos said.

Jake frowned. "Hey, watch the language. Anyway, I'll be all right. Joe knows what he's doing. I trust him."

Kenna put the name of Jake’s opponent in her memory bank. Later tonight, she would look up his fights on You Tube. Then she would try to find everything she could possibly find about him on the Net. Jake wasn’t the only one who had to prepare for his fight.

She folded her arms. "All right, so we have to eat healthy. Do you know how to make stir fry?"

Jake shrugged. "I could probably wing it if we have the ingredients."

Cordy's face lit up. "I have an idea. How about you invite June to come over and help you cook? She has to babysit me and my sister tonight, anyway. She can walk to my house from here."

Jake's eyes narrowed. "I don't like it when you two are scheming."

Cordy batted her eyelashes, looking much older than she was. "Well, if it wasn't for us, you two would never have gotten together."

"Good point," Jake said.

Cordy handed Jake his cell phone, which had been sitting on the table. "Well, what are you waiting for? Call her."

"Is she always this pushy?" Jake asked.

"Definitely," Ben replied.

Kenna began to usher her friends downstairs. "All right, we'll be in the basement." She turned on the lights and went straight for the Ouija board. She kept telling herself, *it's going to work this time*.

"You want me to work the board with you?" Ben asked.

Kenna nodded.

Cordy sat on the floor with her legs folded, while Carlos draped himself on the sofa. Ben knelt on the floor.

Kenna's heart thumped. "You guys ready?"

Ben nodded, while Cordy and Carlos gave her their assurances.

Kenna set the Ouija board in front of them. She lightly touched one end of the planchette, and Ben did likewise. She tried to control her trembling hands as they rotated around the board.

Kenna tried to speak, but words would not come out, so she cleared her throat. "Mia, it's your friends. We need to talk to you.

If you're out there, please respond. It's really important. We spoke to Mark Saleski. He has a message for you."

Kenna clenched the planchette tighter. It was all she could do to keep her hands from shaking. She glanced at Ben, who was staring laser beams at the board. If they couldn't reach Mia, it was not because of a lack of effort.

"I don't think it's gonna happen," Carlos said.

Kenna shot him a cold stare. The last thing she needed was his negativity.

They kept circling with the planchette. Kenna was considering giving up until she felt a tug. A jolt of electricity ran up her arms, making the top of her hair stand. She had never felt anything like that before.

"Mia, is that you?" Kenna asked in a high-pitched voice. "Are you there?"

The planchette meandered to Yes.

Kenna breathed easier. Thank God. She thought she was going to have a heart attack. "Mia, we've been trying to reach you. Where have you been?"

The planchette spelled AWAY. Kenna frowned, but before she could follow up with a question, it spelled BACK NOW.

Ben said, "Mia, we recently met Mark Saleski. We told him all about you."

OK.

Kenna momentarily removed her hands from the planchette and glanced at Cordy. That was hardly the reaction she expected. Last time, the vibe she got when they spoke about Mark was a mixture of wariness and excitement. This time, Mia seemed indifferent.

Carlos got up from the couch and knelt behind Kenna. "Aren't you gonna tell her about what went down?"

"Anyway, we spoke to Mark," Kenna said. "At first, he was, like, really reluctant. He didn't want to talk to a bunch of kids or anything, but we convinced him to listen to us."

No response from Mia.

"Yeah," Ben said. "He told us that he still cares about you."

Kenna was about to continue the narrative about their meeting with Mark, when she felt a violent tug on the planchette. She blinked rapidly. A cold shiver ran through her body.

She watched wide-eyed as the planchette spelled TIME SHORT NEED HELP.

Kenna's heart began to race. She was beginning to feel icy fear deep within her. "What is it, Mia? What can we do to help?"

TROUBLE NEED HELP.

"Of course, we'll help you," Kenna said. "Just let us know what's going on and what you want us to do."

"Yeah, just let us know," Ben added.

The planchette went from letter to letter in jerky movements, nothing like the fluid strokes she had gotten used to. It spelled out HELP ME PLEASE.

Mia's words had a desperate pleading quality to them. Kenna felt helpless. Mia was dead. What could they do to help her? "How?"

SAY THESE WORDS

It took several passes with the planchette before they got exactly what Mia wanted them to say. Cordy ran to get a pen and paper to write it down.

Kenna released the planchette. She was feeling dizzy and her head ached. She was getting a crazy vibe from Mia, unlike anything she had ever felt before. It was disorienting just holding the planchette. "Did you get it?"

Cordy nodded.

"All right," Kenna said. "Let's say it."

Ben removed his hands from the planchette. "Are you sure this is a good idea? We don't even know what saying these words will do. There's something really weird going on with Mia today."

"Yeah, she seems freaky," Carlos said. "I don't like it."

Cordy glared at him. "Don't you trust Mia?"

"I never said I didn't," Ben replied. "It's just that maybe we should wait and try to figure things out, you know."

Kenna stared at the back of the room where she had previously seen Cotter's silhouette and those creepy red eyes. She hesitated for a moment. She remembered Jake telling her that some things were better left alone. Maybe he was right and dealing with the spirit world could only bring trouble. On the other hand, this had to be about Cotter terrorizing Mia. They had to help her. "Let's do it, Ben."

She and Cordy both stared at him. Meanwhile, Carlos chewed on his fingernails.

Ben raised his hands. "Okay."

Cordy sat to their side, practically hovering over the board. Her face was tight, her eyes focused on the planchette. Carlos knelt directly behind Kenna, his hands folded underneath his chin, almost as if he was in prayer. Kenna and Ben grabbed the planchette and circled it around the board, repeating, "By the power of wind and fire, I give you passage. *Eachlais*."

She wasn't sure if they were pronouncing that last word right since she had never heard it before. It probably wasn't even English.

It felt like the calm before a big storm. Something was about to happen, something big. For the first time, she felt some of Ben's skepticism, but she trusted Mia. She was their friend.

A strong wind blew across the basement. Cordy's long hair flopped in the wind.

"What's going on?" Carlos asked.

Holding onto the planchette, Kenna and Ben continued to repeat, "By the power of wind and fire, I give you passage. *Eachlais*." She glanced into Ben's troubled eyes. His face seemed worn. He looked older, like a miniature version of what he would look like forty years from now.

A strong wind continued to gust through the basement. Kenna sniffed the air. It smelled like something was burning. The air shimmered around them. It was as if the individual air molecules had become big and were moving around, colliding with each other.

Ben began to wheeze. His asthma acted up in times of stress. She wanted to stop, but it was too late. She felt a compulsion to see this thing through to the end. They continued repeating the words.

"What's going on?" Carlos shouted in the thick air. His voice sounded warbled. "Something's on fire."

Cordy tugged at Kenna's arm. "What's happening?"

Kenna did not reply. Instead, she kept repeating the words Mia had told them, like she was in a trance. She couldn't stop even if she wanted to.

A massive spike of electricity surged through her, knocking her backward. For a moment, her head felt as if it was going to explode. Intense, searing pain ripped through her body, followed by pressure, as if someone was trying to pull apart her head. Carlos cushioned her fall as she landed on him.

Ben let go of the planchette and leaped across the Ouija board. He grabbed Kenna's hand. His eyes looked frantic. "Are you okay?"

Kenna blinked rapidly. Whatever she had felt earlier had passed. She no longer felt that heavy pressure in her head. She still felt woozy, but it was passing by the moment. "I think so."

Just then, she felt a shove from behind.

“Hey, get the fuck off me,” Carlos said.

Kenna turned her head, not believing what she had just heard. Carlos had never spoken to her like that before.

Ben’s face tightened. “Hey, what’s the matter with you?”

Carlos shoved Kenna aside and got to his feet. “Nothing. Just get off my case, asshole.”

Kenna stared at Carlos in disbelief.

“Why did you push her?” Ben asked.

Cordy grabbed Kenna’s hand. “Are you okay? It was like someone zapped you or something.”

Kenna shook her head. “I don’t know. I’ve never felt anything like it.”

Carlos snickered. “Ya think, girlie? I can give you something you never felt before.”

Ben’s face turned red. He grabbed Carlos by the shirt. “Why did you say that to her? That’s not cool. You have to say you're sorry right now.”

“Get off my grill,” Carlos said. “I ain’t sayin’ shit to the little bitch.”

Kenna put her hands on her hips. “Why are you acting like this?”

Carlos glared at her. "Because I can. Now step aside, you whiny little bitch."

Ben's hands shook as he stood in front of Carlos. "You better say you're sorry, right now."

Instead of apologizing, Carlos sucker-punched Ben in the face, knocking him to the ground. Ben clutched his jaw.

Kenna's mouth opened wide. "Why did you do that?" She stammered. "Get out of my house, right now."

"I was already leavin'. You kids are cramping my style. Later. Much later." Without turning back, Carlos went up the stairs, leaving Kenna dumbfounded.

Chapter XVI

Jake had a jump in his step after getting off the phone with June. She had readily agreed to come over, even offering to stop by the grocery store to pick up ingredients for their meal.

He was glad Cordy had suggested calling her. The girl might only be nine, but she had a good head on her shoulders, at least when it came to relationships.

He whistled as he folded his laundry. He did not know what he did to deserve June, but he wasn't going to do anything to jeopardize their relationship. For the first time, he had found someone special. She had looks, charm, kindness, and self-confidence. After his stint in jail, he figured no one worth a damn would want to have anything to do with him.

After he was done with his laundry, he tidied up the house. He wanted everything to be just right. She had told him she would be right over, so he had little time to waste.

The doorbell rang. He frowned and looked at the clock. It was too soon for June to have gone to the store and arrive at his house. When he opened the front door, he felt sick to his stomach.

Without an invitation, Adam Fallon stepped inside the house. "Jake, it's so good to see you."

Jake took a step back. "What do you want?"

Adam smiled. "You're my best friend. I wanted to see how things were going."

“What do you want?”

Adam looked around. “All right. Here’s the deal. I was doing some running for this guy. I was supposed to deliver his stash, but my buyer stiffed me. He expects the smack to be gone, so I can’t exactly have it on me. I have another guy who can take it off my hands, but not for a few days. So, I just need you to hold onto…”

Jake gripped his wrist. “You gotta be kidding me. You brought heroin into my house.”

Adam grimaced. "Just chill, bro. I need you to hold it for a few days. Nobody's going to find it here."

Jake took deep breaths to control his rage. "I don't know what made you think I would help you, but there's no way in hell I'm going to hold heroin for you. Get this shit of my house now."

Adam looked down. “Jake, you don't know the kind of heat I'm facing. I need your help. Come on. Hook me up just this one time. I promise I won't ask for any more favors. I can't keep it right now and I don't trust anyone else with it.”

Carlos approached them. Jake wouldn't have noticed him because of his heated conversation with Adam, except that he was walking with this weird strut. Carlos didn’t have a strut when he walked. The only noticeable thing about his normal walk was that his shoulders dropped. Now he had this overconfident, overbearing manner that suggested the world owed him something. He bumped into Adam, almost knocking him over, before walking out the front door without saying a word.

Jake followed him to the front door. The kid had a blank expression and looked as if he was lost. The strut was gone.

At the same time that Carlos was leaving, June was walking out of her car. He had forgotten all about her. He wished he had gotten rid of Adam before she arrived.

June had a wide smile as she carried a bag of groceries. "Hi, Jake." She kissed him on the cheek and looked over his shoulder. "Oh, I didn't know you had company. Hey, Adam." She put down the bag.

"Actually, Adam was just leaving."

Adam's demeanor changed. Earlier on, he had been jumpy. Now he looked like he did not have a care in the world. He put his arm around Jake's shoulder. "What's the rush? I just got here."

Jake frowned. What the hell had gotten into Adam?

Adam approached June with a hungry look in his eyes. "It must be my good fortune that you just got here. You're looking mighty fine today." He felt his jacket pocket and looked down as if noticing the heroin for the first time. "If you wanna party, I got some good stuff. Real good stuff. Whadaya say, baby?"

June took a step back, glaring at him. "I don't think so."

Jake spun him around. "What's come over you? Back off."

Adam raised his hands. "Chill, bro. I didn't realize this was your bitch. That's cool. I don't mind sloppy seconds. Or we can both do her at the same time."

Blood rushed to Jake's face. He felt like grabbing the son of a bitch by his throat and choking him out. It took all his restraint not to do just that. "You're leaving right now."

Adam smirked. "Like brother, like sister." He took a long look at Jake, as if sizing him up. Adam knew how good of a fighter he was. Was he crazy? After a few moments, he backed down. "I can see where I'm not wanted." He walked toward the door with a stupid grin on his face.

Jake followed him. This was not the Adam he knew. The guy was a weasel but never this brazen.

Adam walked down the steps. He turned and sneered. "I didn't want that filthy whore anyway. Fuck you both."

Jake clenched his fists, trembling with rage. "You asshole." He rushed after Adam, about to throttle the bastard, but June held him back.

"He's not worth it," June whispered. "Just let him go."

Jake shook his head. "I can't let him go after he said that about you."

"You can and you will."

Adam gave him a middle finger salute. "That's what I thought, you pussy. You think you're some tough guy. You ain't shit, Jakey. Let him come after me. I'll put you in your fucking grave, boy. Go ahead, fuck with me. Before this is all said and done, I'm going to make you feel a world of hurt. It ain't over between us."

Jake frowned, watching Adam walk away. What the hell had just happened? He turned and stared at June, who had her lips pursed.

"I hardly knew Adam in high school, but I had no idea he was such a jerk. Why were you ever friends with him?"

Jake folded his arms and turned to look at Adam, but he was already gone. "Look, I'm not going to defend him after what he did to me with the robbery, but this…this isn't the Adam I know. He's not brave enough to say that kind of crap, at least not to someone's face. He's the kind of guy who always backed down from a fight and avoided confrontation. I don't get it."

"So, what did he come here for?" June asked.

Jake looked down. "He wanted me to hold some heroin for him."

"He sounds like an asshole to me. I hope you told him to go to hell."

"I did. But what just went down, I still can't figure it out."

June waved her hands. "What's there to figure out? He's a jerk who duped you into taking a fall for him. Now, he's trying to take advantage of you again."

"I suppose." Jake took a deep breath. Something about his confrontation with Adam left him disturbed. He had known Adam his whole life and had never seen him act like that. It was as if his entire personality had just undergone a Civil War and the unrepentant bastard part won out.

June rubbed his shoulders. "Relax. You're all tense."

He turned, and June kissed him. She put her arms around his waist. "Forget about him. So, I take it you're culinary challenged and need help."

Jake smiled. "You can say that."

"Can you at least chop vegetables?"

Jake nodded. "No problem there."

"Good. Let's get to work."

Chapter XVII

Cotter walked down the street and smelled the fresh air, never having felt more alive. He had always taken life for granted. Now, he appreciated every moment on this God-forsaken world.

He was glad to be away from those brats and that punk kid, Jake. Kid fashioned himself sort of tough guy. He didn't know what tough was. Jake had never been knifed in the back or jumped by a rival gang. He would never survive the streets. He was just a wet behind the ears poser.

The girlfriend, on the other hand, was a fine piece of ass. Obviously, she had to be misguided being with that loser, but he could show her a good time. Good girls like that always enjoyed walking on the wild side.

He wasn't done with Jake. Not by a long shot. The kid would get his, but until then, he had to take care of some business. There were debts to be paid and good times to be had. The best thing was that he could do whatever the hell he wanted and not face any consequences. This was the deal of the century, thank you very much. It was as if someone had written him a blank check.

Of course, he had limitations. For instance, he couldn't go wherever he felt like. He would kill to get away from this dump and head to Vegas or NYC, maybe South Beach. His limitation was that he had to be near his lifeline, little Kenna, at all times.

Since she was likely to stay in the area, he was also stuck here. No matter, he would make the most of it.

He rubbed his hands together. Where should he start? He was going to paint the town, get hammered, shack up with a sleazy woman, and get some much-needed revenge. People had wronged him in the past, and he was going to pay them back.

To get started he needed some green in his jeans and a nice ride. He checked his pockets and smiled at the bill fold. He peeled back twenties. Just under four hundred bucks. Not a bad start. Judging by the smack in the bag in his inside jacket pocket, the kid was dealing.

Now to get some wheels. He had the key of some unknown car, but rather than try to find it, he was going to help himself to someone else's ride. For someone of his many talents, this would be no problem. He had lifted more cars than he could remember back in the day. Rather than mess with a new car with unfamiliar technology, he looked for something tried and true. He found a Mustang, circa 2007. That would work just fine.

The sap who owned the car had conveniently left the door unlocked, so he lifted it in less than a minute. He put the car in gear and flew down the street, hollering like a madman. This was like Christmas Eve. Who was he kidding? Christmas Eve had always sucked. The old man would get a load on, turning into a stupid drunk, digging in on his mom before turning to him and his sister. His old man was probably still alive, rotting in a nursing home. Too bad he was far away. He'd like to play the bastard a visit and jab a knife into his ribs.

He turned on the radio and cranked it up when he found a rock station playing Guns-N-Roses.

He stopped at a *Wawa* to pick up junk food and a massive soda. He needed fuel to get started. His next stop was a hunting and fishing supply store where he bought a buck knife. He didn't have the time to buy a piece just yet. This would suffice for now.

He drove down Ridge Pike. Payback was a bitch; that's what they always said. Well, they were right. He was getting payback tonight. Snitches deserved to get their balls cut off. He didn't know if he would get that exotic, but he would do his best.

He parked his car outside of Brother John's. The bar was bustling. That would work in his favor. He walked to the front door, pulled out the kid's wallet and looked at the driver's license. It said he was twenty-five. Looking at the picture, he doubted it, but the driver's license looked authentic enough. This place wasn't too picky about its clientele. The bar staged illegal poker games and sports betting. An underage drinker with questionable identification would be no big thing.

He flashed his driver's license to the goon at the entrance. The goon nodded and let him through. He knew the man from Graterford where they had done time together, although the goon wouldn't recognize him now.

He worked his way to the bar and ordered a beer and a shot of tequila. He chugged the beer and downed the shot. Now he was ready for action.

He worked his way back, pretending to go to the bathroom before taking a left and walking through an unmarked door. He entered a room that was staging a poker game. A disinterested broad who'd had a boob job sat at the desk.

"When's the next card game starting?" he asked.

She barely looked up at him. "About a half hour."

"Good deal. I think I'll get a drink before then."

The broad went back to doing her nails. "Suit yourself."

He made sure she wasn't looking when he slipped through the opposite door of the one that led to the bar. He slunk through a corridor until he ran into some no-neck bastard, who looked as if he ate glass for breakfast.

"No one allowed back here," No-Neck said.

"Oh, sorry about that." He made as if to turn around, but instead charged No-Neck, knocking him off his feet. He head-butted No-Neck on the bridge of the nose, causing blood to flow freely from it. He then punched his bigger foe in the face, dropping him to one knee. He used the back of his head like a ping pong ball, smashing it against the floor until he lost consciousness.

Wearing a wide grin, he got up and dusted himself off. He dragged No-Neck to a nearby broom closet and shoved him inside.

Next stop was Harry Black's back office. The little worm had done him wrong in a past life. Black had been tripped up by the cops on a wiretap and immediately squealed. They didn't even have to squeeze him to get him to talk. Because of that spineless bastard, he had done five hard years in the joint. While in the joint, he found out Harry had sold him out. He had vowed at the time that he would get the son of a bitch back one day. Well, today was that day.

He stepped inside without knocking on the door. Harry Black was reading over today's odds. He looked up, his lips curled into a snarl. "Who the fuck are you?"

He smiled. "An old friend."

"I don't know you," Harry said.

"Don't you remember? We did the Greiss job together. Not to mention I supplied hookers for those bachelor parties you used to run. In fact, we got along just great until you sold me out to the cops about my gambling ring in South Jersey."

Black's eyes narrowed. He leaned forward. "Cotter? That's impossible. He's fucking dead. Not to mention, you look nothing like him. You're just some punk kid trying to stir things up. Get the fuck out of here."

Cotter smiled. "I ain't goin' nowhere. Not until we have ourselves a nice conversation. We've got some catching up to do."

Harry Black reached for the gun he kept in his top drawer, a move Cotter was anticipating. He lunged at Black and knocked him off his chair. Cotter grabbed a staple gun from the desk and smashed his face with it, relishing the terror in Black's eyes. This was too much fun. He shot staples into Black's forehead and reveled as the fat bastard wailed. It was like the sound of a beaten dog. Cotter pulled out the buck knife from his jacket pocket, jammed the butt of the knife onto Black's nose, then flipped the blade open.

He held the knife up high. "You dimed out the wrong guy. Nobody fucks with Cotter." He plunged the knife into Black's fat gut. He stabbed Black in the abdomen, chest, and neck. It was a bloody mess. So much for keeping it neat, but damn, it felt good.

He had to get out of here, but before he did, he needed some loot. Fortunately, he knew where Black kept it. He didn't have enough time to crack the safe but found cash in the bottom drawer of his filing cabinet. He counted twenties and hundreds. Now he had cash and a gun. All he needed was a woman of loose moral fiber and he'd be set. He took a deep breath. It was good to be alive again.

Chapter XVIII

After clipping Harry Black, Cotter washed up in the bathroom. His clothes were a mess. He would get new threads that were more his style.

He slipped out back without anyone noticing him. Even if they had, he didn't care. He was not going to be on the hook for Black's murder. This kid Adam Fallon would take the fall. Tough shit for him.

After driving to a store and picking up a pair of slacks, a silk shirt, and a fedora to complement the look—all stolen of course—he drove to a club in Conshohocken. The music in the club had changed, and he wasn't digging the new tunes. He recognized a bartender, an old associate from back in the day. The bartender had done a stint in the joint for dealing. Cotter was able to unload the smack Adam had been carrying to the bartender for a reasonable price. Now his wallet was fat with cash.

He hustled some losers at a pool table, beating a pair of wet behind the ear yuppies five times before they figured out they were not in his league. Just to add insult to injury, he lifted one of their wallets as they left. He took the cash and dumped the wallet.

Later, he picked a fight with a college boy who had too much to drink and was getting loud at the bar. Cotter suggested he and college boy take it outside. College boy took him up on the offer, but before they made their way out of the club, Cotter sucker punched him in the back of the head.

College Boy had it coming since he was dumb enough to turn his back on him. Who said books made a person smart? He proceeded to give him an ass kicking before leaving the club.

He left the smoke-filled club with the music blaring in the background. The night air felt cool, crisp, and alive when it touched his face. He had built up a good sweat from his fight with College Boy.

He lit a cigarette. A red-head wearing too much makeup came up to him to make conversation. She had been digging his work inside the club, first hustling the yuppies and then beating up College Boy. She was a hot dish, all the more appetizing when he found out she worked as a dancer at a local strip joint. Her name was Stella—not that it mattered. After tonight, she would not be able to recognize him again.

They got into his borrowed Mustang.

"So where do you want to party tonight?" Stella asked. "My place or yours?"

Cotter had no idea where Adam Fallon lived. "Definitely yours. Too much heat on me. I want to lay low."

Stella nuzzled against him as he started the car. "This isn't your car?"

Cotter shrugged. "It's mine tonight."

"You know, you look awfully young, but you sure know how to handle yourself."

"I've been around." Cotter had stolen his first car when she was still in diapers. "And I definitely know how to handle myself. More importantly, I know how to show you a good time."

Stella squealed. "Now you're talking. I have some blow back at my place."

"Sounds good to me." Whatever got her off. He wasn't into the hard stuff. Sure, he had dabbled in it from time to time, but he had never developed a taste for it, always too ambitious to let that stuff deteriorate his mind.

"I haven't seen you before. You from around here?"

"This ain't my normal stomping grounds." Cotter stopped himself from laughing. His normal stomping grounds were a world away. If he got her high enough, she might even believe him.

A wannabe tough guy in a Corvette pulled up beside them. He had seen the type before. Like driving a sports car made you a big deal. Mr. Corvette stared at Stella.

"Now that's a nice ride," Stella said.

Cotter said, "Oh yeah? Wanna trade up for it?"

"What do you have in mind?"

"Watch this." Cotter lowered his window. "Hey, Cuz, you wanna race?"

The guy in the 'Vette rolled his eyes. "Spare me. I'll smoke you."

Cotter raised his brows. "Is that right?" He peeled a bunch of twenties from his front pocket. "I got five hundred bucks here that says you can't."

Mr. Corvette narrowed his eyes. "You're on."

"We'll race to Trooper. You got the money to put up?"

"Sure do."

Cotter raised his windows. "This asshole doesn't have the money. No matter. That ain't what I'm after anyway."

When the light turned green, the Corvette shot off. It was late at night, and traffic was virtually absent on the street. Almost immediately, Cotter turned onto a side street, then made a right onto a street that ran parallel with their original street.

"What are you doing?" Stella asked.

"Just watch. This ain't my first rodeo."

Mr. Corvette had probably slowed to look in his rear-view to see where Cotter had gone, abandoning the race. Cotter accelerated down the parallel street until he was four blocks from their starting point. He made another right, going back to the street on which they had started. Just as he suspected, the Corvette was slowly approaching. Cotter turned onto the street, floored the accelerator, and drove straight at the Corvette.

"Holy shit," Stella said. "What are you doing?"

"Relax, baby."

Mr. Corvette went wide-eyed as he approached. He slammed his brakes and swerved to avoid Cotter's car.

Cotter hit the brakes, threw his head back, and laughed. The color slowly returned to Stella's face. After a few moments, she began to laugh.

Cotter looked at the other car. "Looks like our friend ain't happy. Too damned bad for him."

As the driver of the Corvette approached him with a deep scowl, Cotter got out of the car.

Spit flew from Mr. Corvette's mouth. "What kind of shit are you trying to pull?"

Cotter smirked. "You know, I was going to let you walk away, but since you're pissing me off, I'll have to take your wheels." He pulled out the gun he had stolen from Harry Black's office and pointed it at the driver.

Blood rushed from the other man's face. He raised his hands. "Hey, just chill out. You don't need to do this."

Cotter tilted his head. "Oh, but I do have to do this. Now you got two options. Either leave your car and walk away or eat some lead. By the way, I don't give a shit which option you pick."

A wet spot emerged near the man's groin, which told Cotter exactly what his decision was going to be. The man's voice faltered. "Look, I don't want any trouble. I have a wife and two kids at home."

"Like I give a shit." Cotter motioned with his gun. "Now start walking."

Cotter thought he was going to cry. What a pussy. "Okay, I'm leaving."

"You're damn right you're leaving."

Stella emerged by his side with a big smile and flushed cheeks. He could tell she was getting off on the adrenaline rush. He always had a way with the ladies. She called out, "And we don't want you comin' back either."

After the guy was out of sight, Ronnie Cotter turned to Stella. "You ready to have some real fun tonight?"

Chapter XIX

Jake had been in his bedroom watching his next opponent's fight on YouTube—it was grainy footage of a fight that literally took place in the jungles of Brazil—when the doorbell rang. He had watched this fight three times, each time noticing new tendencies from his Brazilian foe. Joe Renken was working on getting additional footage of his other fights. Santos was good, no doubt, Jake's toughest opponent yet. He was going to have his hands full in this fight.

Kenna was at school, and his mom was at work, so he went downstairs to answer the front door. After opening the door, he clenched his fists at the sight of Adam Fallon.

"What the hell do you want?" Jake was ready to thrash him, but his former best friend looked so utterly pathetic, he couldn't summon the rage he felt yesterday.

Tears streamed down his face. "Jake, something bad happened. I'm sorry for everything I did to you but I need your help. I have no one else to turn to."

Jake took a deep breath. He had to be the biggest idiot in the world for not slamming the door on Adam's face, but his former friend looked as if he had been through seven kinds of hell. He remembered how yesterday Adam had suddenly turned into an unbearable jerk as if a switch had been flipped. He looked like a totally different person today. Something seriously wrong was going on here. "Come in."

Adam clutched his arm. "Thanks, man. I appreciate it."

"What's going on?"

Adam sat on the sofa and sobbed. "That's the whole thing. I have no idea. I…The last thing I remember was being in your house last night, and I, um, was trying to get you to hold my heroin."

Jake ground his teeth. "Yeah, you son of a bitch. I can't believe you pulled that crap, especially after I took a fall for you."

Adam looked down. "I'm sorry, man. I shouldn't have done that. I'm an asshole."

For a while neither said anything. Adam looked like a beaten dog.

"All right, then what?"

"I don't remember anything after that. It's all a big blank."

Jake folded his arms. "You don't remember when you said those filthy, vile things to June?"

Adam's brow furrowed. "Who's June?"

This was getting weird. "June Madsen. She's my, um, friend. We've been seeing each other. We went to high school with her."

Adam raised his brows. "Oh yeah, I remember her. You're going out with her?"

"You don't remember June being in my house yesterday?"

Adam shook his head. "I would remember that. She was hot."

"Well, you said some nasty things to her."

Adam frowned. "I did?"

"Yeah. I was about to kill you. She held me back."

"I don't know what to tell you, bro. I don't remember any of that. I wouldn't say anything bad about your girl."

Jake took a deep breath. What Adam had done was so contrary to anything he had ever seen him do, and Jake had known him his entire life. "So, you don't remember June, or flipping me off?"

Adam shook his head. "Flipping you off? What do you think, I have a death wish? Why would I pick a fight with you? You could snap me like a twig."

Jake couldn't argue the point. "What happened after that?"

Adam released a muffled sob. "Nothing. It's all blank. The next thing I remember I'm wandering aimlessly on a street in Norristown. I…had a knife and this gun." He pulled out a pistol.

Jake's eyes went wide. "Where the hell did you get that?"

"Wish I knew. I've never owned a piece before. I don't even know how to shoot one."

In the robbery that had landed Jake in jail, Adam had been using a prop gun. He was too chicken-shit to use a real one.

"There was blood on the knife, my clothes, my car. I don't know how it got there." Adam clutched his arm. "Jake, what's going on? Am I going crazy? Something bad went down. I could feel it."

Jake took a deep breath and looked into Adam's eyes. Yesterday, when he had been a complete bastard, there had been this evil glint in his eyes that Jake had never seen before. That look was gone. He was the same old Adam Fallon. "I thought something was off with you yesterday. One minute, you were trying to peddle drugs to me like a weasel, then you turned into this complete unbearable creep. Not that you weren't an asshole before, because you were. You were just a different kind of asshole."

"I have no idea what happened to the drugs. If I don't get them back, I'm going to be in deep shit."

Jake glared at him. "Remind me to throw you a pity party."

Adam wiped away his tears. "I don't care about the drugs now. I just want to know what went down and why I can't remember anything. This is freaking me out, man."

Jake walked to the window, wondering if he should believe Adam. The story seemed outlandish, but he appeared to be genuinely spooked. He didn't believe in multiple personality disorder, figuring it was just psychological mumbo jumbo, but if it existed, then maybe it was manifesting in Adam.

"Even though you screwed me over, I'd help you out if I could, but I don't know what I could do. Maybe you should see a shrink."

Adam motioned toward the gun. "What if I did something, you know, really bad last night?"

Jake stared out the window, not knowing what to say.

"What if this happens again? What if I black out and can't remember anything?"

Jake nearly jumped at the sound of rapping on the door. He frowned at Adam, who shook his head, his face turning white.

When Jake opened the front door, two police officers stood in front of him. One was a tall, black man with wide shoulders and a stubby nose. He contrasted with his partner, a short, slightly overweight, Italian looking guy with a pointed nose.

"You Adam Fallon?" the Italian cop asked.

Jake shook his head and pointed his thumb. "He's Adam."

"Is that your vehicle parked outside?" the black cop asked.

Adam looked hesitantly at Jake. "Um, yeah."

"You're under arrest," the Italian cop said.

"What did I do?" Adam began to hyperventilate.

As his partner cuffed Adam, the Italian cop said, "Well, let me see. We've got you on two counts of murder, robbery, kidnapping, criminal endangerment, and a litany of other charges. You been a busy boy, and you ain't very smart about covering your tracks." He read Adam his Miranda rights, something that brought back horrible memories.

Adam looked as if he needed a lifeline, but Jake could do nothing for him. His face was pure contorted anguish.

"And what's your relationship to the suspect?" the black officer asked.

Jake hesitated. After his experience with incarceration, he was not going to say anything that was not the absolute truth to these police officers, even if it meant hanging Adam out to dry. "We used to be friends. No longer."

"Did you see him last night?"

Jake nodded. "He was at my house until about 5:30. He left and showed up again fifteen minutes ago."

"Are you aware of his whereabouts the previous evening?"

Jake shook his head.

"Did he tell you what he was up to last night?"

"He says he doesn't know," Jake said.

The officer frowned. "He said he doesn't know what he did?"

Jake nodded. "That's what he told me."

The officer handed Jake a card. "We'll be in contact with you later."

"I'll answer whatever questions you have."

As they took Adam away, Jake could not decide if he should feel remorse or satisfaction at the poetic justice of Adam being arrested. Mostly, he felt confused.

Chapter XX

When Kenna answered the door, the last person she expected to see was Carlos. She didn't think he was still her friend after yesterday. At school, Kenna and her friends had purposely stayed away from him.

Three sets of cold eyes stared at him as he entered her house.

Carlos took a step back. "Hey, what's going on? You guys have been ignoring me all day."

Cordy folded her arms. "Hmph. If you don't know what's wrong, then there's no point in telling you."

"What did I do?" Carlos asked.

Ben got in his face. "What did you do? *What did you do?* Are you kidding me?"

Carlos shrunk backward.

Kenna shook her head. "Come on. Just own it."

Tears streamed down Carlos's face, the first time Kenna had ever seen him cry. "I really don't know. Just tell me. The last thing I remember we were in the basement talking to Mia, and then…I was walking outside, just, I don't know, wandering. I was lost. I was walking around for about fifteen minutes before I figured out where I was at. I was scared."

Kenna held back tears. Whatever happened yesterday with Carlos, it was obvious he felt bad about it. Maybe that was why he was acting like it didn't happen.

Cordy softened her stance, but still kept her distance. "You were so mean. You even punched Ben in the face."

Carlos had the appearance of a wounded dog as he stared at Ben. "I punched you? I would never do that. We're friends."

Ben's face tightened. "You did, and it hurt, but what hurt more was what you said to Kenna."

Carlos shook his head. "I don't know what I said to Kenna, but whatever I said, I didn't mean it. You have to believe me. The three of you are my best friends in the whole world." His eyes pleaded with them.

***

Jake was brushing his teeth after eating a plate of celery sticks, when he heard commotion from downstairs. Eating clean and healthy was getting old. He would kill for a pizza with every possible topping on it. After that he wanted to wash it down with a big bowl of ice cream, but that would have to wait until after his fight, assuming Joe didn't try to sign him up for another fight right away.

The day had been hectic. The police had called him in for questioning. After finding out about his criminal record, they had become more interested in him. To his surprise, he felt calm during the interrogation, even though it took place in the same precinct where he had been questioned following his arrest. He had nothing to hide. He answered all of their questions honestly and to the best of his knowledge.

From what he could gather, as crazy as it sounded, Adam had gone on a criminal rampage after leaving his house. Jake had airtight alibis for the time frame in question. June, Kenna, his mom, and Cordy could all vouch he had been home during that time. He had also spoken with Joe.

He was still in disbelief that Adam had been arrested on two counts of murder. *Murder? Adam?* It hardly seemed possible. Then again Adam had a gun—presumably the murder weapon. All the same, why would Adam kill someone? If he had committed those crimes, was it possible he could truly not remember what he had done?

Jake didn't want to be involved in this mess. He had dealt with law enforcement enough for one lifetime. When he had called his mom at work to tell her, she had gone hysterical, insisting he never have contact with Adam again.

He walked down the steps and looked in on Kenna and her friends. They seemed to be laying into Carlos pretty good. What was that all about? They usually got along so well. He nearly dropped his toothbrush when he recalled the dazed and confused look Carlos had when leaving the house yesterday. It had been around the time Adam had transformed into a rude jerk.

Jake ran back to the bathroom, rinsed, put away his toothbrush, and went downstairs toward the basement. When he saw Carlos crying, Jake felt an odd sense of déjà vu.

"I really don't know. Just tell me. The last thing I remember we were in the basement talking to Mia, and then…I was walking outside, just, I don't know, wandering. I was lost. I was walking around for about fifteen minutes before I figured out where I was at. I was scared."

Jake slowly descended the stairs. He was not sure who Mia was, but the story sounded eerily similar to Adam's. Although Carlos may not have gone on a criminal rampage, he had done something to upset his friends. Jake's heart went out to the kid. He looked terrified and confused.

"I punched you?" Carlos asked. "I would never do that. We're friends."

Normally, he would let Kenna and her friends resolve their own issues. They were responsible kids, more than he was at their age, but he had to intervene. Some weird shit was going on here.

"Hey, guys, I couldn't help notice you're laying into Carlos pretty hard."

Cordy folded her arms. "Well, he deserves it after what he did."

Jake put his hand on Carlos' shoulder. "We all do things we regret. If anyone should know, it's me. But I know Carlos is a standup guy and deserves a second chance. I'm sure if you guys did something you weren't proud of, you would want a second chance. And hey, if your friends aren't going to cut you a break, then who will?"

His speech wasn't particularly eloquent, but it seemed to deflate the tension in the room. Cordy's mean scowl turned into a frown. Ben had looked ready to slug Carlos, but now was staring at his sneakers.

Kenna gave Carlos a hug. "It's okay. I know you didn't mean what you said."

Ben put his hand on Carlos' shoulder. "And I know you weren't yourself when you hit me."

"You can hit me back," Carlos said.

Ben smiled. "You'll owe me one."

"What about you, Cordy?" Jake asked. "You were willing to give me a second chance."

Cordy played up the drama with her overly exaggerated facial expressions but eventually relented. "Oh, okay. I forgive you. Maybe you had some brain tumor or something that made you act crazy. You better not do that again, or else."

Jake nodded. "Good. You're all friends again. Let's stay that way. We need friends. How else are we going to make it through this crazy world?"

Crazy was the right word. He couldn't make heads or tails of what was happening. He was a simple guy, and he liked his problems simple, so why did they have to be so damned complicated?

***

"Bye, Mom." Jake waved as he and June left the house.

"Don't stay out late," his mom said. "And if Adam tries to contact you, tell him to stay away."

"Adam can't contact me. He's in jail, and I don't think they're letting him out any time soon."

His mom narrowed her eyes. "Well, they shouldn't. He's no good. He's just trying to drag you down. You take care of my boy, June."

June smiled. "I will."

Earlier that day, his mom had gone on about how proud she was that he was dating June, and that was exactly what he needed in his life. He couldn't agree more.

Jake had hoped that going out with June tonight would take his mind off what had happened with Adam, but it stuck with him like a sore tooth. On their way to the movie theater, he said, "Something really weird is going down with Adam."

June raised her brows. "Let me see. A seemingly ordinary boy, albeit a drug dealing jerk, goes on a crime spree, including allegedly murdering two people. Yeah, I would classify that as weird."

Jake shook his head. "No, I don't mean that. I mean the whole part where he said he didn't remember anything."

June shrugged. "Maybe he's in denial and wants to forget what he did. Or maybe he's just getting in defense mode and planning on going the insanity route."

"I don't know. He seemed legitimately spooked. There's something else. Later that day, Kenna and her friends were scolding their friend, Carlos. I found out from her later that he sucker-punched Ben and said some really nasty things to Kenna, so bad she wouldn't even repeat them to me. Carlos was in tears because he didn't remember any of it. The kid wasn't acting."

June stared at him, a startled expression on her face. "Really? That is kind of weird."

"Tell me about it. So, let's say both Adam and Carlos are telling the truth—and it's not like they could know about each other's stories—then what's going on here? Could they be related somehow?"

June stared out the window. "There is such a thing as transient global amnesia."

Jake frowned. "Huh?"

"It's like a stroke in the sense that the person has complete temporary short-term memory loss, but unlike a stroke, they have no other cognitive disruption. It comes on all of a sudden and lasts a few hours. The person knows something isn't right but can't figure out what's wrong with them."

"Yeah, but they're young."

"It doesn't just happen to old people."

"Even so, what's the chance this would happen to two people at the same time and same place? I'm guessing this global amnesia thing isn't common."

June nodded. "The odds would be astronomical."

"So then how do you explain this?"

June shrugged. "I can't, but I don't believe Adam. He's not exactly a credible witness."

"I don't think Carlos is a liar. Even if he was, I can't imagine he'd concoct such a crazy story."

"Then what's your explanation?"

Jake took a deep breath. "Wish I had one. I was hoping you would."

"It could be an odd coincidence."

"It doesn't feel like one. Something bad's going on here. I can feel it."

"So, what should we do about it?"

"I don't know."

She leaned over and kissed his cheek. "Forget about it. At least for tonight. Enjoy the moment."

He glanced at June. She looked amazing, making him wonder how in the world he got so lucky to have her in his beat-up old Hyundai next to him as his date. He would forget about all that craziness, at least for tonight.

Chapter XXI

Kenna watched with clenched fists as Jake sparred with his opponent. Normally, he trained when she was in school, denying her the opportunity to see him in action, but it was a Saturday, and she and Cordy had asked if he could take them to the dojo. He seemed reluctant at first, but she had talked him into it. She could usually convince Jake to do what she wanted. Plus, he owed her and Cordy for their matchmaking gem.

Cordy chewed her fingernails. "Is he all right? He's getting hit a lot."

In the background, the sounds of someone working a heavy bag and people shouting encouragement pervaded the dojo, but Kenna tuned it out to focus on Jake. In the main room, a Brazilian Jiu-Jitsu class was in progress. They were in a back room, where there was a boxing ring. Kenna and Cordy stood on training mats. There were a handful of other observers, including Joe Renken, who had a stoic face as he watched the action. Joe had arranged for some visiting Muay Thai fighter from Thailand to spar with Jake. Jake kept pressing the action, even though he was taking a beating.

"He's fine. He needs to do this to get better." Kenna reassured Cordy, but she wasn't so sure herself. His opponent had kicked Jake's legs at least a dozen times, causing them to turn red and puffy from welts.

Jake's head rocked back when his opponent landed an uppercut to his jaw.

"He doesn't look fine." Cordy stood and yelled, "Come on, Jake, give it to him."

Kenna grabbed her friend's arm. "Stand back. You're blocking my view."

Jake wobbled after taking a hook kick from the Thai fighter.

Kenna dug her knuckles into her chin. "Come on, Jake."

Kenna breathed easier when they took a break from sparring. She turned to Cordy. "I'm still weirded out from the last time we talked to Mia."

Cordy nodded. "Me too. Everything went crazy. Not to mention that whole thing with Carlos."

"With everything that happened, I almost forgot about our conversation with Mia. When we mentioned we had spoken with Mark Saleski, it seemed like she didn't even care. And then she wanted us to say those words."

Cordy frowned. "Yeah, it was like asking the wind and fire to give passage or something. I don't even know what she was talking about."

"It was so odd. The basement got, like, really windy. And it felt like someone had pushed me, even though there was nobody close enough to do it. That's when I fell into Carlos, and he started acting like a jerk."

"Do you think that had something to do with the way Carlos was acting?"

"Maybe we should contact Mia again and ask her."

"I'm not sure that's such a great idea." Cordy looked down. "She was acting all weird. It gave me the creeps."

Kenna grabbed her arm. "We can't give up now. Mia needs us more than ever. Something happened the last time we talked to her. It felt like my head was getting ripped apart." "Maybe something worse'll happen next time."

"That's why we have to contact her again. We need to find out what happened and how we can help. Don't you see? We're the only ones who can help Mia. We have to be there for her."

"Okay. I'll do it. I'm not sure Carlos will."

"I'll talk to Carlos." Kenna's eyes went wide. "Ooh, Jake's about to start fighting again. Hopefully he'll do better this time." Unfortunately, the sparring session only got worse for her brother.

***

Cotter pulled into a parking space near the school. Two elementary schools were in this area, and he was not sure which one the girl attended. If this one did not pan out, he would try the other elementary school, and then the Catholic school.

He was driving a 5 series BMW. Apparently, the fella whose body he had taken over was some sort of businessman. Poking around the guy's desk at his house, Cotter found all sorts of memos and hand-written notes that didn't mean shit to him. What mattered was that the guy had a sweet ride and an even sweeter wife. He had nailed the wife three times in the past twenty-four hours. She probably hadn't had sex like that in years.

The guy, his name was Ryan something, had a big house with a nice back yard and a pool. It would be nice to inhabit his body for a while, but eventually things would fall apart. For instance, he had no intention of going to Ryan's work. That would become a problem. So far, he had fooled the guy's wife, but sooner or later she would realize there was something seriously different about her husband, even if she was enjoying the sex.

He would eventually move on to another body. This lack of stability could present a problem for someone else, but not to Cotter. Compared to where he had been and what he had done since his death, this was nothing. Living in the shitty existence of his afterlife had been unbearable. Being back here confirmed something he already knew—life had it all over death.

He would screw the guy's wife a few more times. Before things got hairy, he would make his jump. In the meantime, he had to keep tabs on little Kenna.

Normally, he didn't give a shit about brat kids. Never had any during his life—that he knew of anyway. Kenna was a special kid; special to him anyway. Because of the circumstances surrounding his rebirth into the world, she now had a guardian angel. He was going to make sure she stayed nice and safe. Not that he expected her to encounter any problems, but if she did, he would protect her. He could certainly do a better job of it than her asshole brother.

The worst part of this whole deal was being tied to this little girl, but he could live with that. She was only ten or eleven, so it wasn't like she could get into big trouble. Barring a family vacation, he didn't see her moving around. If she did, he had no choice but to follow her or kidnap her, and he sure as shit didn't want to have to lug around a little girl.

A whole mess of students walked out of the school building. Had to be recess. He recognized that blonde girl who had been with Kenna on the day of his reentry into the world. A minute later, Kenna walked out of the school building.

Cotter managed a big smile. "Bingo." Now he knew where she lived and what school she attended.

Not wanting to arouse suspicion, he exited the parking lot. Even after parting ways with Ryan, or whatever his name was, he might keep the car. He could get new plates and tags. It didn't matter if he got caught with a stolen vehicle. He had the ultimate get out of jail free card.

Last night on the news, they showed that Adam Fallon had been arrested for two murders, including Harry Black. He had a nice long laugh over a shot of bourbon. Who knew framing someone would be so easy?

He whistled as he drove. There was more payback to be had, wrongs to be righted, and people who would find an untimely demise for crossing him. Then there was Kenna's brother. They hadn't run into each other since that first time, but they would soon. Cotter's encounter with that punk stuck in his craw. He was going to make good ole Jake's life miserable.

Chapter XXII

"What if it's like last time? What if I blank out again? I was like five blocks from your house before I finally knew what was going on." Carlos put his hands in his pockets.

Cordy walked in from the kitchen, carrying a pitcher of iced tea.

"If it happens again, we'll be there for you," Kenna said. "We're not going to let you wander around the neighborhood aimlessly. You need to trust us."

Carlos sighed and filled his cup with iced tea.

"Don't be a baby," Cordy said. "It's not like you went out and killed somebody. You were just mean to us."

"He punched me in the face," Ben said.

Cordy touched his face. "You can't even notice the bruise anymore. I swear, boys are such wimps."

Kenna said, "I know it's scary, but we need to do this for Mia."

"What makes you so sure?" Carlos asked.

Kenna shrugged. "I can't explain. It's like part of Mia is inside me. I have this deep connection with her."

Carlos finally relented. "All right. Let's do it. Maybe we'll find out what happened."

Kenna retrieved the board from its hiding spot in the utility closet. She was certain her mom and Jake never went in there. Even if they did, she doubted they would find it.

Kenna put the Ouija board on the floor. Looking at Carlos's trembling hands, she wondered if they were doing the right thing. Her gut told her they were. Jake said after his last fight that no matter how much he prepared, and no matter how much he studied his opponent, when he was inside the cage, he followed his instincts. He tried to stick to his game plan while fighting, but his next two or three moves were always dictated by what he saw in front of him. That was what she was doing now.

Kenna sat on the floor with her legs crossed. Ben sat opposite her. They locked eyes. Ben was a rock. Cordy was her best friend, but when things got tough, Ben was the friend she could count on the most.

The each grabbed the planchette and moved it around the board. Kenna did not feel any psychic connection yet.

"Mia, it's Kenna. We need to speak to you."

Ben wore an expression of intense concentration as they rotated the planchette. He spoke in a monotone. "Mia, if you're there, let us know."

After a few minutes, Kenna frowned. She wanted to stay upbeat but could not help feeling discouraged. It used to be easy so easy to reach Mia.

A vibrant odor, similar to the scent of the ocean, filled the air. Kenna felt a surge of electricity in her fingers. Goose flesh sprang on her arms. She looked up, her eyes wide.

"Is she there?" Ben asked.

Kenna nodded.

"Mia, it's Kenna. I'm here with my friends. Are you there?"

Kenna smiled as the planchette slowly moved to yes.

Cordy pumped her fist in the air. "I knew she would answer."

Kenna began speaking rapidly. "I'm so glad that you're here. After all that weird stuff, I wasn't sure what to think. I know things got rushed the last time we spoke to you, but we had a chance to speak with Mark Saleski."

The planchette began to move with a strong jerk.

SPOKE TO MARK

Kenna nodded. "Yeah, we did. That's what we were trying to tell you last time."

HOW IS HE

"He's doing good," Ben said. "He misses you. His family life isn't so great."

Kenna nodded. "Yeah. He still thinks about you a lot. That's what he told us. He's, like, in the process of getting a divorce. I think it's because, you know, he doesn't love his wife like he loved you."

Carlos frowned. "Do you have to go and make this all sappy?"

Cordy punched his arm. "Of course she does. Girls love this stuff."

The planchette spelled MISS HIM

Kenna's entire body tingled. It was as if Mia's feelings from the spirit world were flowing into her. Kenna pulled away from the planchette and took a deep breath. She blinked rapidly, trying to get her bearings. Mia's emotions were overwhelming her.

Ben looked up at her. "You okay?"

She nodded. "Uh-huh." During their last conversation with Mia, their normal spiritual connection had not been there.

"He said to let you know that his cup is still full," Kenna said.

OUR SAYING

An overwhelming feeling of joy surged through Kenna's body. She closed her eyes and swayed backward. She felt as if she had just soared into the sky and had landed on soft clouds, which were keeping her afloat. When she opened her eyes, she was surprised to find tears trickling down her cheeks. Without having to ask, she knew Mia was happier than she had been in a long time.

Those same nagging doubts that Kenna had been feeling earlier flooded into her.

"You didn't seem excited the last time we told you about what Mark had said." Kenna tensed. It was like all the joy she had been feeling burst out of her like a balloon popping.

The planchette jerked violently. NEVER TOLD ME

Ben frowned. "What are you talking about? We told you. You weren't interested. Instead, you wanted us to chant that saying with that strange word at the end."

WHAT CHANT

Carlos crossed his arms. "How doesn't she know about that? She's the one that kept telling us to say it."

A growing despair filled Kenna. When she spoke, her voice was shrill. "Don't you remember those words you wanted us to say?"

The movements on the planchette began to take on a desperate quality as the device moved across the board. Normally, Kenna could feel where it wanted to go and help guide it, but now it was moving on its own.

WHAT WORDS

"I don't like this," Ben said.

Kenna frowned. "I don't like it either. In fact, I'm getting a really bad feeling about this."

"I still have the words written down." Cordy reached into her pocket and fished out a crumpled sheet of paper. "Here it is." She handed it to Kenna.

Kenna straightened out the sheet of paper. "You told us to say 'By the power of wind and fire, I give you passage. *Eachlais*'. You told us to say it over and over. Then something weird happened."

For a while there was no response from Mia.

"Mia, are you there?" Kenna asked.

"What's going on?" Cordy asked.

Kenna shrugged. "Wish I knew."

"I don't know why she can't remember. I definitely remember it." Carlos sighed. "I don't think I'll ever forget it."

"Mia, are you okay?" Kenna asked.

The planchette slid across the board to No.

Kenna's heart raced. "What's wrong?"

VERY BAD.

"What's bad?" Ben asked.

The planchette kept going back to No. It was as if Mia was freaking out in her own way, causing Kenna's panic to grow.

"What's going on, Mia?" Kenna felt cold dread as the planchette spelled COTTER. "What does Cotter have to do with this?"

The planchette moved quickly. BOASTED COULD ENTER UR WORLD

Ben frowned. "What do you mean, enter our world?"

MUST HAVE FOUND WAY

Kenna wanted no part of Cotter. It was bad enough knowing he hurt Mia, but him being here was much worse.

"How could he do something like that?" Kenna asked.

LEARNED

"Learned what?" Kenna asked.

HOW 2 RETURN

Ben shook his head, his face incredulous. "He could do that?"

The planchette spelled BIG TROUBLE.

Kenna's anxiety was becoming a three-alarm-fire. "What can we do?"

STOP HIM

"But how?" Kenna asked. "We're just kids."

The planchette repeated STOP HIM.

Kenna was near tears. "How can we possibly stop him?"

GET HELP

Kenna looked at her friends in despair. The situation had gone from very bad to hopeless. She had no idea what to do, and based on the looks on their faces, neither did her friends.

Chapter XXIII

Kenna felt numb as she put away the Ouija board. How had it all gone wrong? Contacting Mia had been fun and exciting, even after seeing the silhouette and those red eyes. They had made a friend in Mia, and Kenna had been so eager to help her. Somehow, Cotter had entered their world, and it was all her fault.

Ben looked to be on the verge of tears. "What are we going to do?"

Cordy folded her arms. "I don't know."

"We need to get help," Kenna said.

"But who can we talk to?" Cordy asked. "Who's gonna believe us?"

"Jake," Kenna said without hesitation. "I trust him more than anyone else in the world. He'll help us." He would be mad at her for continuing to use Ouija board when he told her to stop, but if she was in danger, he would move mountains to save her.

Cordy nodded slowly.

"Okay, let's talk to him," Carlos said. "I trust Jake, too. He'll help us out."

***

Jake's body ached after another day of hard sparring. As he drove home, he could barely move his neck, and his abdomen felt like it had been pounded repeatedly and relentlessly by a sledgehammer.

He went all out during training today, as he had for the past week. His upcoming fight was the biggest of his life. An impressive victory could propel his blossoming career. Sponsors had been showing interest in him recently, and he even signed a deal with a local car dealership yesterday. Furthermore, this would validate himself in his own mind as a fighter. Paulo Santos was the toughest opponent he had ever faced. Jake had seen footage of one of his fights, where he chopped down his opponent with nasty looking leg kicks and then finished the fight with a knee to the head from the clench that sent his opponent to La La Land. If Jake could win this fight, then he could make a career being a mixed martial artist. A loss would mean he would have to start over and work his way up from the bottom. He kept telling himself that if he lost, he could still use this as a learning experience, but in his heart, he knew how devastating it would be. As much as he tried to be mentally tough, he knew his psyche was fragile. Doing time in prison had done that to him.

He wasn't going to lose. He was preparing himself for this fight as if it was life and death. That's why he went all out in practice, working himself to exertion, having heavy sparring sessions that would make a lesser person quit.

Finding himself dozing at the wheel, Jake opened the driver side window and turned up the radio. He felt physically drained, yet tomorrow would bring more of the same. He would bust his ass at the dojo again, leaving the gym aching and depleted.

Jake dialed June's cell phone but got her voice mail. He left an awkward message on her phone, asking about her day was and if she was interested in getting together Friday night. He wished he was a smooth talker. He would see her at the mixed martial arts class he taught tomorrow but hearing the sound of her voice always uplifted him.

He arrived at his street and parked his car. His mom wasn't back from work. He had planned on viewing footage on his Brazilian opponent, but all he wanted to do now was lie on his bed and close his eyes.

He picked up the mail and walked toward the house. When he first entered, he thought the house was deserted until he heard rustling from the basement, probably Kenna and her friends. He was glad to see they were getting along again after their blow up with Carlos the other day.

He drank two full glasses of water since there was no Gatorade in the refrigerator. He closed his eyes, feeling dizzy. Maybe it would be best to lie down. Nine days away from his fight with Paulo Santos, he couldn't let the pressure get to him. That would be his enemy on fight night.

Jake plopped himself on the sofa and rested his feet on the coffee table. He was starting to doze when the shuffling of feet coming from the basement awoke him. As he rubbed his eyes, Kenna and her friends emerged. "Hey, what's going on, guys?"

"Jake, we need help."

The urgency in Kenna's voice startled him. She sounded horribly frightened.

He sat upright, the last vestiges of slumber being swept away. "What is it?"

Kenna's eyes filled with tears. "Something really bad happened."

"What? What happened?" None of the four kids appeared to be injured. Maybe they broke something in the basement, but there was nothing valuable down there.

"You know your old Ouija board that we've been using," Kenna started.

Jake narrowed his eyes. "Yeah? The one I told you stop using, you mean?"

"We did something wrong," Kenna said. "And now things are getting out of control, and we don't know what to do."

Cordy nodded. "It's really bad, Jake." She had this sad look on her face, like her favorite pet had died.

Jake frowned. Kenna had mentioned using his old Ouija board, and that she had seen something strange, but he had not put much credence into it. It was just a silly toy. Combined with their overactive imaginations, it was little surprise they had conjured up crazy things they thought they saw.

Jake raised his hands. "All right, guys, calm down. Whatever's going on, we'll figure it out." He tried to keep his voice steady, not wanting to talk down to them. "Who wants to start?"

For the next ten minutes, Jake let them speak. Kenna started, but Carlos and Cordy frequently interrupted her. Ben sat silent as they told their tale. It was one of the craziest stories he had ever heard.

Jake folded his hands and tried to process this insanity. The damndest thing was that they seemed so sincere. He wasn't sure about the other kids, but Kenna never lied to him. At least he had never caught her in a lie. She was sometimes brutally honest, even when he wished she would have more tact. He didn't see her making up a wild story, but what was the alternative? That they were telling the truth?

"Let me get this straight. You guys were messing with my Ouija board and you've been in contact with this ghost named Mia."

Cordy shook her head. "She's a spirit, and we've spoken to her like dozens of times."

"Okay, so you're communicating with this spirit and you emailed some dude who was her boyfriend back when she was alive. Then you met up with this guy. Do you realize how terrible of an idea that was? I can't believe you would do something like that. You don't know anything about him. He could have been a child molester or a murderer."

Kenna gave him a severe frown. "He was Mia's boyfriend. Plus, he's a partner at a law firm."

"All the same, I would have felt better if you asked me to take you to meet this guy. You never know who you're going to run into. Some people seem alright on the surface but turn out to be creeps. Anyway, so there's this bad spirit…"

"Cotter," Kenna said.

"Who terrorizes Mia," Jake said. "So, I don't get this last part. What did this Cotter fellow do?"

Kenna looked down, a guilty look on her face. "Mia thinks he found a way to enter our world."

"And this was because you guys repeated a phrase he told you to say while you were communicating with him on the Ouija board?"

Kenna nodded. "And he told us to say this foreign word we had never heard before."

"Look, I'm not saying I don't believe you, but you have to realize how nutty this sounds."

In a very soft voice, Kenna said, "We're not making this up. It's all true."

Jake put his hand on her shoulder. "I never said you were making this up. I'm just saying it's hard to sign off on. I mean, talking to spirits with an Ouija board is one thing, but one of them actually coming alive, that's tough to swallow."

"We wouldn't be telling you this if we didn't think something really bad was happening," Kenna said. "We need your help, Jake."

"I promise you I'll help you in any way I can." Jake closed his eyes and took a deep breath. What could he do? His sister needed him, and as impossible as her story seemed, she seemed genuine. "Let's get the Ouija board out. I want to talk to Mia."

Chapter XXIV

Cotter glanced at his growing stack of chips. Just eyeballing it, he had to be up ten large. He was fleecing these boys in this high-stakes poker game. They thought they were dealing with some clueless yuppie. This Ryan guy, whose body Cotter had taken possession of, certainly looked like one. Instead, they were dealing with a card shark of the highest magnitude.

Cotter was a formidable player, but he never played by the rules. He could crush these hammerheads with his card skills alone, but what was the fun in that?

One of the players, a twenty-something guy wearing a goatee and sporting thick arms covered with tattoos, was staring him down, as if that would intimidate Cotter. He had gone toe to toe, knife to knife with much bigger fish. Mr. Tattoo, who fashioned himself as a tough guy, probably had a hunch Cotter was cheating but wasn't smart enough to figure out how. "I'll call your hundred."

Cotter smiled. This guy was going down hard on this hand. There had to be a few grand in the pot already.

When they laid their cards down, Mr. Tattoo was all confident with his two pairs— jacks and tens. His smile faded quickly when Cotter showed three kings.

"Sorry, big guy," Cotter said. "I guess it's not your night."

Mr. Tattoo slammed his fist on the table. "You're cheating."

Cotter narrowed his eyes. "That's a hell of an allegation, one I don't take lightly."

Mr. Tattoo stood with his fists clenched. "I know you're cheating."

Cotter raised his hands. "I've played an honest game. If you think I've been cheating, I suggest you show proof."

Mr. Tattoo gave him a cold stare but said nothing.

Charlie Watts, an old associate of Cotter's from his previous life who had organized this card game, said, "I don't want any trouble. I haven't seen any cheating, and I'm an old hand at this sort of thing. If you have anything to back your claims, then bring it to the table. Otherwise, you're going to have to leave."

Cotter held back his smile. Charlie Watts was a big ole' country boy who was as tough as shoe leather, not the kind of guy a sane person would want to mess with. Having run poker games for the better part of two decades, he was known for keeping order. Considering he was almost six and a half feet tall and north of three hundred pounds, people were usually intimidated by his size alone. If they had seen him in action, they would be downright scared. Granted, it had been nearly a decade since Cotter had last seen him fight, but age only appeared to season this tough bastard.

Mr. Tattoo's face tightened into a scowl. He cashed his chips—what was left of them—and left.

As he was leaving, Cotter called out, "Have a good night, darling."

"I'll be seeing you later," Mr. Tattoo said.

Cotter went back to the card game. "Some guys are just sore losers. Now, where were we? You know, I usually don't do so well at poker. Just last week, I dropped two grand at the casino. I guess tonight's my night."

Cotter won at a more moderate pace after that. The other players seemed to be wary of him. At least he got satisfaction from wiping out Mr. Tattoo. Cotter had been roping marks like him for years.

Just yesterday, Cotter had opened a safety deposit box to store his cash. He had pilfered Ryan's bank account. Good ole Ryan was going to be in for a big surprise after Cotter vacated his body, which would be any day now. He should have exited already, but Cotter wasn't done with the guy's wife just yet. She had a bit of a wild streak under her good girl demeanor. She had made a couple of promises that enticed Cotter to stay longer. Not more than a day or two, however. Ryan's employers had already called several times, inquiring why he hadn't been to work.

Ryan's employers would probably can the poor bastard. Cotter felt a strong urge to return and see what kind of damage he had wrought in this sucker's life. The dude would be devastated. Cotter felt like a kid on Christmas Eve. The world was his for the taking. He could do all sorts of shit he always wanted to do and not face any consequences for his actions. What a beautiful world he was living in.

After Cotter cashed his chips, he left the smoke-filled house. The house was on the middle of the block in a run-down North Jersey neighborhood. There was nothing special to distinguish it, and Charlie ran a tight ship, so the cops would have no reason to hassle them.

He walked out of the house humming a new tune he had heard on the radio. So much had changed since he was alive. People now had these smart phones. That Ryan guy owned three iPhones. Cotter was perplexed trying to figure out how they worked. He asked the guy's wife how to use it to make a phone call, and she looked at him like he was crazy. Hey, he didn't need a friggin' computer, just a damn phone.

At Ryan's house they had two laptop computers, an iPad, modems, and wireless internet. He didn't understand what half this shit meant, let alone how to use it. Why did people need all these computers? If he was going to stick around in this new world, then he would have to catch up to this technology.

As he walked to Ryan's BMW, Cotter pondered if he should hit another spot or go home and bang Ryan's wife. Decisions, decisions. He had to stash away tonight's winnings, but that could wait until tomorrow. He removed the keys to the car, which weren't keys at all, just some remote control thing. He didn't even have to put a key in the ignition. The scientists and engineers had been busy since Cotter had died.

Just as Cotter was about to get in the BMW, Mr. Tattoo stepped in front of him. Cotter couldn't help but smile. This jack-off was a glutton for punishment. Like it wasn't bad enough he just got cleaned out playing poker.

"I know you were cheating." Mr. Tattoo was trying to put all kinds of menace in his voice. *Ooh, scary.*

"What do you know?" Cotter taunted. "You don't know nothing. You're just a punk. I've taken shits more intimidating than you."

Mr. Tattoo raised his hands in a fighting stance. "You're going down."

Guys like Mr. Tattoo were useless. He had big biceps, big shoulders, and a bulky physique. Big muscles might look good on the beach, but they didn't do jack shit for a person in a fight. Those big muscles only served to slow a person down and tired them out quicker. In life, Cotter had been tall and wiry. He had always used those long limbs to his advantage, taking out bigger guys. Plus, he didn't fight fair.

Mr. Tattoo swung a looping overhand right. Cotter went in toward him, ducking under the punch. He put his left arm around Mr. Tattoo's waist and hugged him tight so that he couldn't break free. With his right hand, Cotter reached into his jacket pocket and brought out a knife. He flicked the knife open as Mr. Tattoo struggled.

Cotter stared into Mr. Tattoo's eyes and found fear. He was certain at that precise moment, Mr. Tattoo figured out he had just messed with the wrong motherfucker. He was the one going down, and he was going down for good. "Go to sleep, darling." Cotter plunged the knife into the man's back.

Mr. Tattoo's eyes went impossibly wide. He gasped, letting out a choked breath.

Cotter removed the knife, and Mr. Tattoo fell to his knees. For good measure, Cotter slashed the man's neck, cutting his carotid artery. Mr. Tattoo fell face first into the asphalt.

"You just couldn't leave well enough alone. Guess that was the worst mistake you ever made."

Cotter wiped the blood off the knife. Just as he was about to put the knife away, a smile lit his face. He put the knife on the ground next to Mr. Tattoo's body. Good ole' Ryan's fingerprints were all over it. Tough shit for him. Cotter laughed out loud and entered the BMW.

Chapter XXV

Jake followed Kenna and her friends to the basement with trepidation. Ouija boards were just toys to goof around with or devices that charlatans used to con people. They couldn't actually be used to communicate with the dead. Then why was his heart racing? Why did he have goosebumps on his arms? Why did his stomach feel queasy?

Nobody spoke as they stood in front of the Ouija board.

Jake put his hands on his hips. "Okay, what do we do now?"

Kenna sat on the floor at one end of the board. Ben took a seat opposite her.

Kenna looked up at Jake. "Ben and I usually hold the planchette. We call Mia, and she responds."

Jake took a deep breath. "Okay."

Ben looked up at Kenna with soulful brown eyes. "I don't know if I can do this anymore. Nothing good's come out of this."

Kenna reached out and touched his hand. "Maybe you've been right all along, that we should never have done this, that we caused a whole lot of bad things to happen. But it's too late to stop now. We let Cotter into our world, and we have to do something to stop him. We gotta make this right. I know you're scared, Ben. I'm scared too, but we have to finish what we started."

Ben nodded.

As Jake watched the exchange, he couldn't help but feel touched at witnessing his sister's maturity and compassion.

Jake stared intently as they put their hands on the planchette. As they circled the piece around the board, they seemed to be in deep concentration.

"Mia, it's Kenna. We need to speak with you."

Kenna's eyes lit up. Jake felt a certain electricity in the air. It was hard to describe, but something changed, and it wasn't just in his head.

"Are you there?" Ben asked.

The planchette moved to yes.

Jake watched their hands closely, trying to figure out if they were moving the piece or if it was going on its own, but it was impossible to tell.

"Is it definitely her?" Cordy asked.

Kenna nodded.

Jake turned to Cordy. "What do you mean?"

Cordy bit her lower lip. "It's hard to explain. Kenna has this deep connection with Mia. The one time we spoke to Cotter, she felt something different."

Jake wanted to ask more questions but, instead, focused on the Ouija board.

"Mia, my brother Jake's with us. He's going to help us with Cotter."

The planchette moved from one letter to another and spelled GOOD.

"Mia, do you know how Cotter was able to leave the spirit world and enter our world?" Kenna asked.

The planchette went to No.

Jake asked, "Are you sure you guys aren't moving this thing to spell what you want?"

Kenna's face tightened. "The planchette's moving because Mia's speaking to us." She sighed in exasperation, then her face lit up. "Mia, if me and Ben let go of the planchette, can you move it on your own?"

The planchette moved to Yes.

Kenna stared into Ben's eyes. "Okay. Let go of it."

Simultaneously, Ben and Kenna both removed their hands from the planchette. The tension in the air was palpable as all eyes in the room locked onto the Ouija board. Jake could hear his own breathing.

Jake went wide-eyed as the planchette shot across the Ouija board and landed in the carpet by Carlos' feet. Jake gasped.

Carlos pointed at the planchette. "Did you see that?"

Jake slowly nodded. He had wanted to believe his sister, but it was hard for his mind to accept the supernatural, where things went bump into the night. Even his practical mind could not deny what he saw. Whatever happened from here on out, he was all in. As her big brother, it was his job to protect her, and he would do whatever he needed to make sure no harm came to her.

Kenna looked up at him. "Do you believe us now?"

"I never disbelieved you," Jake said. "I just had a hard time wrapping my mind around this. Ask Mia what she can tell us about this Cotter."

Kenna relayed the question.

The planchette spelled out MEAN THUG CONMAN.

Jake nodded. "Okay, I get the idea. So, this Cotter fellow's a bad dude."

The planchette continued HURT ME.

"What else can you tell us?" Kenna asked.

CRIMINAL

"Cotter was a criminal?" Ben asked.

The planchette moved to Yes.

"Did he die in jail?" Ben asked.

Once more the planchette settled on Yes.

"Does she know why Cotter decided to enter our world?" Jake asked.

Kenna asked the question.

The planchette moved to No.

"Hmm." Jake began to pace around the room. So, Cotter was a criminal who had used this Ouija board, not to mention Kenna, to come back to this world. Just like when preparing for a fight, Jake needed to learn more about his adversary. "What did Cotter do to land himself in prison?"

Jake watched with a wary eye as the planchette spelled out MURDER, then THEFT, and finally DRUGS.

"Sounds like a real sweetheart," Jake said.

Great, so he had a murdering, thieving, drug dealer on his hands. He had met enough of the type in prison. Jake sighed, remembering his own days in the pen. He had led a solitary existence, not making friends or even talking to anyone unless it was absolutely necessary. During his stint, he had two different cell mates. Other than their names, he knew hardly anything about them.

Learning that he was a professional fighter, several gangs inside the joint had tried to recruit him, but he respectfully told them he was not interested. He had tried hard to avoid fighting while in jail, but it was inevitable it would happen. Twice he had been jumped by inmates. In both cases, he had soundly and convincingly thrashed his attackers. Nobody tried a third time, although he had heard rumors from other inmates and even correctional officers that he should watch his back, something he did religiously while in jail.

The only good thing about his prison experience was that if he had to face this Cotter, at least he had dealt with his type before.

"What can Mia tell us about how he entered our world?" Jake asked.

After Kenna repeated the question, the planchette spelled NEED LEARN MORE.

Jake had additional questions, but Mia could not give any substantial answers. She assured them she would find out about what had happened, and what could be done about it. By the end of the session, Jake's head was spinning.

After Kenna put the board away, she looked up at Jake expectantly. “Well, what should we do?”

“Right now, nothing. We don’t know where he’s at, what he looks like, how he can operate in our world. We don’t even know the rules of the game. Mia didn’t give us a whole lot work with. Until we learn more, there’s nothing we can do. Let’s give Mia time to figure this out, then we can come up with a plan.”

Kenna shuddered. “But what if Cotter comes after us? He’s dangerous.”

“Look at this way,” Jake said. “This happened over a week ago, and he hasn’t shown up yet. That means he probably won’t come after you. If he does, I’ll be here to protect you. I won’t let anyone hurt you. That’s a promise.”

Ben looked at him with his soulful eyes. “It’s not just that. If Cotter’s out there doing bad things, then it’s our fault. If it wasn’t for us, none of this would have happened.

Jake put his hand on Ben’s shoulder. “Listen, buddy, you had no way of knowing any of this would happen. This isn’t on you. What’s done is done. Now we have to fix the problem, and I’m going to help you.”

As Jake led the kids upstairs, he wondered if he believed that he was capable of doing what he claimed. He knew strange things were afoot and was wise enough to realize it may be beyond his capabilities to stop Cotter, but one thing was certain, he would not let this spirit harm Kenna or her friends.

Chapter XXVI

After what Jake had witnessed in the basement with the Ouija board, his grandiose plans of getting rest and studying footage on his next opponent were out the window. Restless, he paced the living room and then took a walk around the block.

He still could hardly believe it. The incident with the Ouija board and their contact with Mia shook his whole belief system. The problems he had been facing seemed simple in comparison to the ones he now faced.

Jake's mom picked up on his unease when she arrived home from work. She regarded him with a curious look but didn't say anything at first. As she cooked a meal of chicken breasts, brown rice, and green beans at Jake's request, she said, "Sit down. You're making me nervous."

Jake sat at the kitchen table but couldn't stop fidgeting.

"What's bothering you? You don't normally get this antsy about fighting."

Jake looked up at his mom, who had a severe frown. Their relationship had been strained by his going to prison, and he was certain it would never be the way it used to be since a certain amount of innocence had been lost. All the same, he was trying to regain her trust. Lying to her wouldn't help matters, but the truth wasn't an option. Believing in Kenna's story had taken a giant leap of faith on his part. There was no way in hell his mom would believe a word of it.

"I guess the whole thing with Adam's been bugging me," Jake said. This wasn't a lie since the incident certainly disturbed him.

Still cooking, his mom looked him in the eye. "Listen, Jake, I know you and Adam had been best friends since you were little tykes, but you have to face it, the boy's just no damn good. You let him bring you down before, but he's behind bars now, and he can't harm you. You need to forget him. He's going to be put away for a long time."

Jake found her sudden shift amusing. The last time they had spoken about Adam, he had assured her that Adam could no longer do him any harm. "I wish it were that easy. You weren't there when the police arrested him."

"If I was, I would have thrown him out on his ass."

Jake sighed. Under normal circumstances he would agree with her, but after seeing Adam's haunted eyes and shaky demeanor, he wasn't so sure.

Jake changed the subject. "Are you going to let Kenna come to the fight?"

"I suppose her going last time didn't produce any long-term psychological effects. She certainly has been pestering me about it. I suppose if June will take her, then she can go."

"You could always join them," Jake suggested.

His mom gave him a look that suggested he had lost his mind. "I'm a nervous wreck when you're fighting. All I do is pace around the house until you call me to tell me everything's all right. You have no idea what it's like. If I were actually there watching someone punch you in the face, I would have a heart attack."

"Well, if you change your mind, let me know. I still have a few tickets for the show."

"That's quite all right. I'm sure Kenna will give me a blow by blow breakdown of everything that happened."

Jake frowned, thinking about how frightened his sister had been earlier. He didn't like to see her like that. He wanted her to be her happy, care-free self again.

***

June laid both palms flat against the table and stared at him open-mouthed. "Are you serious?"

Jake nodded. "Deadly serious."

They sat at a booth in the Starbucks. Jake had wanted to take June out to a nice restaurant now that he could afford to do so, but he could not take any chances with his diet this close to the fight. He promised her he would treat her to a nice dinner after this fight.

June, for her part, did not seem to care. She seemed just as content going to a Chipotle as she would to Ruth's Chris Steakhouse. Still, Jake wanted to show her that she was special to him. For tonight's date, they settled on a movie at the IMAX theater and then coffee at Starbucks. When he asked for his plain and black, the barista looked at him like he had three heads. He had offered to get June a snack or a desert, but she refused since he wouldn't be able to indulge in the treat as well because he was cutting weight. She was too good to be true.

"That's crazy."

"I know it sounds crazy, but it's true. I saw it with my own eyes."

"But anybody can fake using a Ouija board."

Jake folded his hands and kept his voice even. "I'm well aware of that, but two things convinced me. First, Kenna is ultra-honest. But what really swayed me was that Mia, the spirit they talk to, was able to move the disc on her own without either Ben or Kenna touching it. Now, I know that sort of thing can be faked by a clever street magician, but there's no way these kids could manage that."

"What do you mean, it moved on its own?"

"It's just like I said. They asked Mia to move the planchette on her own. They took their hands off it, and it flew across the room."

"You're not putting me on? This is all real?" June asked.

"This is as real as real can get."

June sighed. "If you so strongly believe this, then I'll take your word for it."

"You do?" This was hardly the response Jake was expecting. He expected her response to be complete skepticism. He hardly thought she would accept the story with that little of a struggle.

"Most people don't believe in ghosts. Not me. I had one in my old house."

Jake narrowed his eyes. "Yeah?"

"The ghost lived in the house I grew up in. I used to feel this presence in my room at night. The room would get frigid. Sometimes, I swear this ghostly presence was right next to me. I would try to talk to it when I got really scared. I thought if I could speak to it, become friendly with it, then it would make me less scared."

"Did it respond?" Jake asked.

June shook her head. "I wish it did. At least that way I would know for sure. Instead, I had this haunting feeling all the time."

"So, what happened?"

"We moved. I don't know if it's still there. I wonder about it often. Do you believe my story about my ghost?"

Jake nodded.

"Well, I'm with you on this Ouija board business. I trust you, Jake. I know you wouldn't deceive me. And if this is legit, then you're going to need my help."

Jake smiled, a warm feeling settling in chest. Even though he was an ex-con, she seemed to have unwavering faith in him. If their relationship was going to last, and he sure as hell hoped it would, then he needed her trust. He also needed her help. June was intelligent, and she could piece things together he couldn't.

"So, go over everything one more time," June said.

Jake relayed what he knew, both what he had witnessed, and what Kenna had told him.

June sat in contemplative silence while Jake sipped his bitter coffee.

June lifted her finger in the air. "I have a theory."

"Shoot."

"This might explain another mystery. You know how Carlos had that experience where he blacked out, and Adam claims he has no memory of his killing spree. What if…What if they can't remember anything because this evil spirit was in them, controlling them somehow?"

"Huh?"

"Think about the timeline. The day they think this Cotter guy crossed over was the same day Adam killed those people and Carlos blanked out. Right?"

Jake tilted back his head. "Yeah. So, what are you getting at?"

"Well, maybe Cotter needs to occupy a body. If a spirit in our world didn't have substance, then what would it be?"

"I don't know," Jake answered.

"If a spirit didn't have a body to house them in, then it would just be air. I doubt they could spontaneously generate a body. Therefore, they would have to occupy someone's body."

Jake nodded slowly. "Kind of like possession."

"In a manner of speaking. Not in the demonic sense, but possession nonetheless. So, Cotter comes through the Ouija board, and then what happens? He finds a body close by."

"Carlos."

June put up her index finger. "Ask Kenna and Ben if either one of them blacked out at all. Is there any point where they can't remember what happened? They were holding the planchette, so it makes sense that Cotter entered through one of them first. But maybe that lasted only a moment before Cotter makes his way to Carlos, which explains why Carlos acted out the way he did. It would also explain why he couldn't remember anything."

Jake took a sip of coffee, letting his mind run through the possibilities. "If your theory's right, then what happens to the person while Cotter is occupying their body?"

"What did Carlos say about that time period?"

"He doesn't remember any of it. He said it was like everything went blank."

June shrugged. "I don't know. Maybe they go into some void. Maybe they go to the spirit world."

"But if that was the case, then wouldn't Carlos have some recollection of this?"

"Based on the information we have, that part's a little sketchy. Still, I like my theory."

Jake nodded. "Yeah, I think you're onto something. It makes sense to me, anyway."

"That brings us to Adam."

Jake closed his eyes. He didn't know what to think about Adam. His emotions ranged from sorrow to anger to ambivalence. "If Adam's telling the truth, then basically what happened to him mirrors what happened to Carlos, except in a more extreme way. He did something horrible, out of character even for him, and he has no memory of it."

June rested her chin on her folded hands. "I think you may have been right all along about that. You knew Adam wasn't himself. It's distinctly possible that if the spirit took over Carlos, then he could have done the same to Adam."

"What a mess. So now Adam is sitting in jail awaiting trial for crimes he didn't commit. Double murder, no less. That's messed up."

June nodded. "Tell me about it. He may have done you wrong, but he doesn't deserve that."

"So, let's play it out. After being in Carlos's body, he jumps to Adam, goes on this crime spree, dumps him later."

June shook her head. "The time frame doesn't fit. By the time I reached your house, Carlos was gone, but Adam was still there. If your theory is right, Cotter was in possession of Adam at that time, right?"

Jake nodded.

"But you told me Carlos was wandering for a bit, that he wound up a half mile or so from your house before he came back to his senses."

Jake nodded. "He was disoriented and wasn't sure where he was at. Eventually, he figured it out and went home, but there was a gap between when he left and when he came back to his senses. It doesn't work out. Cotter would have to occupy them at the same time." Jake sighed. "Just thinking about this makes my head hurt."

"We're missing part of the puzzle. We're on to something, but we need more information."

"I feel bad for Adam. We should do something to help him."

"Like what?" June asked. "Petition the authorities to let him go because a malevolent spirit was in control of him at the time he committed those crimes. Oh yeah, they'll believe that."

Jake said nothing.

"We need to concentrate our efforts on stopping Cotter, or at least finding him. If he killed before, he's going to kill again."

Jake took a deep breath. "Yeah. That's a safe bet."

"I want to be there the next time Kenna contacts Mia. I have questions for her. Then maybe we can put together a plan."

Chapter XXVII

Jake helped June put on her jacket as they exited the Starbucks. He was glad to be with her tonight. She brought sanity to this unreal situation. Her presence made him feel that things were going to be all right. He wished he could express his feelings to her, but that was not his strong suit, and he would wind up saying something that sounded stupid.

"Kenna and her friends are really beating themselves up over this," Jake said.

"They're just kids," June said.

Jake waved his hand. "Oh, I know. I'm not blaming them. They couldn't have known all this craziness would happen. They got in over their heads."

"What did you tell them you were going to do?"

"Nothing. There's not much I can do. How can I possibly find this Cotter guy? It's not like we know what he looks like, especially if he can possess people."

June folded her arms as they walked to Jake's car. "There has to be a way."

Jake put his arm around her shoulders. The night was chilly, but mostly he wanted to be close to her. "Notifying the police would be useless. They would laugh at us."

June stopped walking. "What about that guy Kenna contacted? Mia's old boyfriend."

Jake paused. "I guess he bought their story. He gave them a message to pass onto Mia."

"Maybe that's someone we can talk to."

"Not sure what good it would do. He is a lawyer. He might bill us for it."

June chuckled. "I'll make sure he's off the clock."

They continued walking to the car. Jake let June inside of the passenger's side, then entered the driver's side.

After Jake starting driving, June said, "If I'm right about Cotter being able to jump into a person and possess them, seeing what happened when he was inside Adam, I'm betting he's still committing all sorts of crime. Maybe we can track him that way."

Jake nodded slowly. "Good thinking. You know, you're really smart. And I just thought you were a pretty face."

June punched him in the arm.

Jake smiled. "Well, I'm glad you're here. I'd be lost without you."

"I'm glad to be here."

Jake was driving on a back road to June's house when he noticed the same black SUV that had been driving behind him since they left Starbucks. It was hard not to notice because there was no other traffic on the road. The SUV kept its distance, about a block behind him.

He continued to drive until he reached a red light. Looking up at the rear-view mirror, his eyes went wide. The SUV wasn't slowing down. In fact, it was speeding up, driving straight at them.

"Oh, shit." Jake hit the accelerator, but it was too late. The SUV crashed into the back of his car, jolting his car forward. Jake's Hyundai spun around, only stopping when it hit a curb.

While the car spun, Jake held the steering wheel to brace himself. An older model, his car was not equipped with air bags. Other than having been shaken from the crash, he felt fine.

He turned to June, whose face was white. "You okay?"

June nodded. "I think so."

"You sure? Do you think you need to go to the hospital?"

"No. I'm okay. What the hell just happened?"

Jake looked out the window for the black SUV. After catching sight of it, like the flick of a switch, he was seething with rage. Through gritted teeth he said, "This asshole in the SUV came straight for us, and instead of stopping, he accelerated. I saw him the whole time. The son of a bitch did it on purpose."

"You sure?"

"Yeah, I'm sure. I'm going to have a talkin' to with this asshole."

"Jake, be careful."

He got out of the car and slammed his door shut. In the background came the sound of June's door closing.

He marched to the black SUV. The driver was wearing a baseball cap and was laughing uproariously. Jake saw red.

Forget about talking, he was going to beat the snot out of this jackass.

"What the hell's wrong with you?" Jake shouted. "You could have killed us."

The driver remained in his car, laughing and having a good old time. He gave Jake a middle finger salute.

Spit flew from Jake's mouth. "You think that's funny? I don't think that's very fucking funny."

The guy in the car continued to laugh and point, bringing Jake's rage to unhealthy levels. Without thinking, Jake delivered a front kick with enough force to smash the driver side window. Glass flew at the driver, who was no longer laughing.

Jake flung open the driver's side door.

June shouted, "Be careful!"

Ignoring her, Jake grabbed the man by the shirt and dragged him out of the car. "What's wrong with you? Why did you smash your car into us?"

The man chuckled. "Look at that. I got ole Jakey mad."

Jake froze. He had never seen this man before. "Do I know you?"

"You may not know me, but I sure know you, Jakey."

Jake did not take his eyes off the man, but could feel June's presence behind him. He narrowed his eyes, getting a sick feeling in his stomach. "How do you know me?"

"You managed to get under my craw, Jakey-boy. You and me, we got unfinished business."

A sudden thought came into Jake's head. "Cotter."

The man narrowed his eyes. After a few moments, he grinned. "Well. Well. Very impressive. You're not as dumb as you look, and God knows you couldn't be. Yeah, I'm Cotter and I'm gonna make your life hell. Then I'm going to kill you."

"Just like you killed those people when you were inside Adam's body?"

Cotter narrowed his eyes. "Catchin' on quick, I see. Well, those were the ones the police know about. Let' just say I've been a busy boy. Some people got in my way. People like you."

"Why are you here?"

Cotter shrugged. "Why not? You see, life dealt me a shitty hand. Nothing ever went the way I wanted it. But now, I can do whatever the hell I want, and there's not a damn person who can stop me. Hell, I can commit the worst, most heinous crimes you can think of, and I'll never get imprisoned for it. I'm living the dream, brother."

June stepped forward. "You don't belong here, Cotter. What you've done is an abomination. You need to go back to where you came from."

"Look who it is, the nice piece of ass from the other day. You know, you'd be much better off with me than this piece of shit. Trust me, I'd show you a real good time. I'll have you coming back for more. They always do."

Jake grabbed his arm. "Don't talk to her like that."

"And what are you gonna do, Jakey? You think you're all bad. You're nothing. I'll mess you up."

"I'm going to stop you. Right here and now." Jake glanced at June. "Stay back."

Just as she was moving away, Cotter threw a sucker punch that clipped the side of Jake's head. The blow staggered him, but he had been hit harder than that before. Operating on instinct, he shot in for a double leg takedown and drove Cotter's back into the asphalt, giving him time to clear his head.

Based on how he reacted, Cotter had no clue on how to fight off his back. Jake quickly transitioned to the mount position, pinning Cotter down and pelting him with punches and elbows.

In between the blows, Cotter reached up and poked him in the eyes. It clouded Jake's vision. His eyes watering, he could do little to stop Cotter from slipping out of his grasp.

Jake got to his feet, blinking hard. He was about to shoot in for another takedown, when Cotter pulled out a knife.

Cotter flicked out the blade, but Jake was at a safe distance.

"So, what are you gonna do now, Jakey? I've been lookin' into you. I know all about how you're this professional fighter, like that's supposed to impress me. You see, I play dirty. Let me tell you, those rules don't apply here."

Jake stepped back. He was going to have to change his tactics. Cotter's knife changed the dynamics of this fight. What Cotter wasn't taking into account was that he knew more than just mixed martial arts. Joe had schooled him on self-defense since he was nine.

Jake feinted left, and Cotter swiped at him with his knife. Jake countered with a stiff kick to his leg, causing Cotter to step back. When he came forward again, he had a noticeable limp.

Cotter snarled. "So that's how you want to do it?"

Jake nodded. "Yeah, that's how I want to do it."

Jake kept himself at a distance. Cotter tried to stab at him twice, and each time Jake was out of range of the knife. On the third attempt, Jake punched him on the side of the head just above the ear, wobbling Cotter.

Seizing the advantage, Jake followed up with short punches to his ribs and then a roundhouse kick to the head, which sent Cotter to the ground.

He went to seize his knife hand to disarm him, but Cotter slashed his shoulder. Jake grunted in pain and scrambled out of the way. He had to get the knife out of play, but Cotter was savvy and had anticipated his move.

Cotter was now laughing. "You liked that one. I betcha you don't see that trick in the cage. Come on, darling. Let's dance."

Jake nodded slowly. Blood oozed from his shoulder. He couldn't tell how badly he was wounded, but it hurt like a bastard.

This time, Jake moved in quickly, feinting with his right hand. When Cotter made a move to block it, Jake seized the wrist of Cotter's knife hand. Holding the knife away, he landed a series of kicks to Cotter's ribs which dropped him to his knees. Jake landed five consecutive punches with his right hand while holding the knife away with his left. Blood gushed out of Cotter's nose.

Jake applied a kimura to Cotter's right arm. As he twisted Cotter's arm back, applying pressure to his elbow joint, Cotter dropped the knife. Jake rolled him over, continuing to apply pressure to his elbow joint until Cotter howled in pain.

Jake couldn't resist. "I guess you're not used to this on the streets."

Jake let go of Cotter and grabbed the knife, harmlessly tossing it near June, making sure it was out of Cotter's reach.

Cotter stumbled backward, holding his right arm, which dangled loosely. Jake would have liked to have done major damage to his limb, making it unusable for the foreseeable future, but he had been preoccupied with the knife.

Cotter kept backing away, but Jake was not about to let him escape. He would finish this tonight.

In the background, a dog barked. Jake glanced up and found an unleashed Rottweiler trotting down the side of the road. Cotter moved toward the Rottweiler. It growled as it approached. Jake narrowed his eyes and followed Cotter, not about to let the bastard get away.

"Come here, doggy." Cotter motioned with his fingertips and made a smooching type sound.

The dog kept its ground, all the while growling at Cotter.

"Nice and easy. I got a treat for you. Just come on over here, and I'll take care of you good."

"What are you doing, Cotter?" Jake asked.

"Don't you worry about that," Cotter said.

Jake was worried. He had no idea what Cotter was up to, but one thing was certain, he was up to no damned good.

"Come here, big guy," Cotter said.

The Rottweiler slowly approached. Cotter put out his hand, and the dog licked it.

Cotter went slack. The dog growled, then charged at Jake.

From behind June screamed, "Jake, watch out!"

He couldn't react in time. The dog knocked him to the ground and began trying to bite his neck.

June wrapped her arms around the Rottweiler and tried to pull it away from Jake. He took the opportunity and kicked at the dog, but not before it bit his hand.

The Rottweiler turned on June and growled at her. It jumped on her, knocking her off her feet.

Jake ground his teeth. "Son of a bitch." He scrambled to his feet and dove, laying a shoulder tackle on the dog, causing it to tumble out of the way.

Keeping one eye on the Rottweiler, Jake extended his hand and lifted June to her feet. "You okay?"

June grabbed her elbow. "I think it bit me. What the hell is wrong with this dog?"

"I think Cotter's taken control of that dog."

The dog circled around them. For all of Jake's fighting experience, he had no concept of what to do against a dog. He got into a fighting stance, ready to defend himself and June if it attacked again.

The dog barked a few times, then made as if it was going to attack, only to back away at the last second, as if it was playing with them. It raised its head and howled. The Rottweiler urinated before trotting away.

"What the hell," June said.

They slowly approached the man as if he was a rabid animal. Jake's head started to spin with the craziness of tonight's events. It all had happened so fast, and little of it made sense. The only thing he was certain of was that what Kenna had been telling him was true. Cotter was alive and he was dangerous.

The man was on his knees, a blank stare on his face.

Jake stopped a few feet from him. "Hey, bud."

No reaction.

June nodded toward the man. "He's out of it. Look at his eyes."

The man looked horribly frightened, confused, unsure of what was going on, and altogether incoherent.

Chapter XXVIII

"What are we going to do?" Jake asked. "Before long, a car's gonna drive past here and see the wreck. They'll call the police for sure."

June stared into his eyes, a fierce look of determination on her face. "We have to leave."

"But there was an accident here. Not to mention I beat this guy up pretty good. We can't flee the scene."

"Sure, we can, Jake. This is a no-win situation. What can we possibly tell the police? If we bring up Cotter, they'll think we're crazy and throw us in jail. This guy looks out of it. He won't remember any of it. He won't even know he's been in an accident. We'll go to my place, get my car, I'll follow you in your car, and we'll abandon it somewhere. I'll drive you home, and tomorrow you'll report it stolen. Got it?"

Jake stood in place and pressed his closed fist against his forehead, trying to think this thing through.

"Listen, Jake, I'm not in favor of breaking the law. In fact, I've never done it before, but we have to act quickly, and this is our only way out."

Jake rubbed his face. He hated doing what he was about to do, but June was right. The situation would be impossible to explain. The man by the car would have a sore arm and some bruises but was otherwise uninjured. Jake's car was damaged but still drivable. It wasn't worth more than a few hundred dollars anyway.

Jake nodded. "Okay. Let's go."

Without saying another word, they rushed into the car and started driving. Jake took back roads on the way to June's house, praying they wouldn't find any police on the road.

"I can't believe we're doing this," Jake said.

"It's awful, but it's beats the alternative. Are you okay with dumping your car?"

Jake waved his hand. "That's the least of my concerns. Now that I have some cash, I was going to get rid of this clunker. It's broken down on me a half-dozen times, anyway." Jake turned toward her. "Do you know how much trouble we'll be in if we get caught?"

"We're not going to get caught."

Jake pulled up to June's house.

"All right. I'll get my car and meet you at the bottom of the street. Where are we going to ditch your car?"

Jake said, "I know a place. Follow me."

He waited for June to pull up with her car. As they drove slowly down the road, Jake's heart raced. There was a lot next to an abandoned building in Norristown that had most of its windows broken. It was not the kind of place he would normally visit, but these were hardly normal circumstances.

He pulled the car into the parking lot. There was nobody around except a vagrant on the opposite side of the street. The man appeared to be speaking to himself. A car drove down the street but paid no mind to Jake.

Jake drove alongside a building and parked the car. After killing the engine, he debated whether or not to leave the keys behind. After a moment's hesitation, he decided to take them.

June left the passenger door open for him. He got inside, and she immediately drove away.

Jake said, "This is nuts."

"What we're doing now, or the fact that earlier tonight you got into a life and death fight with an evil spirit?"

"The entire situation."

For a while, neither of them said spoke. When they were near Jake's house, June put her hand on top of his. "It's going to be okay."

Jake stared out the window at the dark houses that they were passing. "Is it? Let's be honest. This may be out of our league. From what we know about Cotter, he can switch in and out of people with no problem. Hell, he can even take possession of a dog. We'll never know who he is and what he looks like until it's too late. And it's not like I can ignore him. Apparently, he has it in for me."

"We'll figure this out, Jake."

June pulled her car in front of his house. She leaned in and kissed him. "It's going to be okay. Call me tomorrow."

Jake nodded. "I will."

***

Jake was a wreck the following day. He filed a police report for his missing car, claiming it had been on his street the night before. He felt horrible about the lie as he filed the report but kept telling himself it beat the alternative—the truth. That option was a dead-end.

He was listless in training, just going through the motions with no intensity to any of his actions, something Joe picked up on right away. As Jake's sparring partner tagged him with repeated strikes, Joe yelled from the corner of the cage, "Get your hands up. You're dropping your guard too low."

Jake's sparring partner nailed him with two jabs, followed by a low kick to his leg.

From the corner, Renken barked out instructions. "What's wrong with you? Get your head into the game, Jake. You come out like this against Santos, and he'll eat you for breakfast."

Jake tried to do as his coach instructed, but he was a step too slow. As he swung a wide right hook, his sparring partner dropped him with a short counter. More stunned than hurt from the punch, Jake struggled to his feet.

Joe entered the cage and waved his hands. "Enough. Enough already. You're getting your ass handed to you. Your head ain't in the game." Renken got in his face. "If you don't start concentrating out there, I swear to you, I'm going to pull you out of this fight. Paulo Santos is a killer. What's wrong with you?"

Through cloudy eyes, Jake looked up at his coach. "I'm fine."

Renken shook his head. "No, you're not. Take off your gloves, hit the showers, and see me in my office."

Jake hung his head low and nodded. He was getting smacked around, even with his sparring partner going easy on him. Another sparring partner might not have been so forgiving.

Jake couldn't take his mind off the insanity of the previous evening. The fight against Cotter, the attack by the dog, the whole car fiasco, all weighed on his mind.

His body aching, he removed his sparring gear and made his way to the showers, but the hot water did little to clear his mind. Not exactly in the mood to chat, he walked to Renken's office, avoiding eye contact with others in the gym.

He waited in the office for five minutes before Renken arrived.

Jake looked up at him. "Look, I know I was fighting like shit out there."

Renken sat behind his desk. "That's all you have to say."

Jake shrugged. "I'm having an off day."

Renken stared into his eyes. "Don't bullshit me. I've known you since you were a kid. When you're out here, you're intense. You're a perfectionist. I don't even know what that garbage was out there today. It wasn't the Jake I know. That was somebody else in your body."

Jake blinked several times. He took a deep breath to regain his composure. He did not say anything. He just wanted to go home.

"What's wrong, Jake?" Joe leaned in toward him, his face softening

from his previous intense stare.

Jake waved his hand. "I'm fine."

"No, you're not. What's going on? Problems at home with your mom?"

Jake shook his head.

"Have a fight with your girlfriend? I know how that can mess with your head."

"No. Me and June, we're good. More than good. She's the best thing that's happened to me in a long time."

"You come in with a big bandage on your shoulder and your hand wrapped up, injuries you didn't have yesterday when you left. You get your car stolen." Renken walked around his office. "I don't like how Adam Fallon showed up at your house after he killed those people. You can't be hanging around people like that. They're bad news."

"I wasn't hanging around Adam. He showed up at my house. The police tracked him down there."

Renken's eyes blazed with intensity. "Listen, Jake, this isn't about your fight. Of course, I'm going to do everything I can to prepare you to beat Santos. I've been trying to get a regimen of quality sparring partners to work with you, mimic his style and what not, but that's whatever. I care about you."

"I know."

"You're like a son to me, Jake, and Goddamn it, I'm not going to lose you like I lost Chris."

Jake looked away. Joe almost never talked about his son, who died six years ago from a heroin overdose, about the same age as Jake was now. He remembered how despondent his trainer had been. He had been worried that Joe was going to commit suicide, but like a rock, he managed to pull through.

"Look, this isn't about fighting. Sure, I want you to fulfill your dreams and make it as a big-time fighter, and I'll be there to help you. Hell, someday you'll probably leave here to go to a bigger camp and get better training, and I won't stand in your way. You becoming a champion, that's not what I care about. I want you to become a good man, a solid citizen, someone your sister can be proud of. The rest of it don't matter. So, if you're hanging around the wrong crowd—"

"I'm not hanging around the wrong crowd. I wouldn't do that to my mom or June. I wouldn't do that to you, and I sure as hell wouldn't do that to Kenna. Trust me, I learned a lesson of a lifetime in prison."

"It ate me up every one of those days you spent inside. I kept asking myself what I could have done differently to have stopped you from going down the wrong path and prevent you from getting involved with all of that. It killed me."

"I didn't plan that robbery. I was just at the wrong place at the wrong time."

Renken nodded. "I know that now. I never really believed you were behind it. It didn't make sense, but you never denied the charges. Your defense was pathetic. And if something like that's happening again—"

"It's not like that."

"Then what is it? Something's not right with you."

Jake ran his fingers through his hair. "Trust me. If this was something you could help me with, I would turn to you. You've always been there for me, and I appreciate it. But you can't help me."

Renken folded his arms. "Why not?"

Jake was at a loss for words. He waved his hands. "You wouldn't believe me if I told you."

"Try me."

Jake sighed. Renken was such a straight shooter. There was no way he would believe this story about Cotter. He would think Jake was losing it and want to pull him out of his fight with Paulo Santos.

"Look, I know I looked like a pile of shit out there sparring today, but I'll be ready come fight night. I'm not going to piss away an opportunity like this."

"It's not about fight night. It's about you, Jake."

"I'm fine."

Joe threw his hands in the air. "Fine. I'm sorry you feel you can't talk to me about this, but that doesn't mean I'm going to turn my back on you. If you change your mind, I'm here. I won't judge you or anything. I just want what's best for you, and I'll do anything I possibly can to help you. You need to know that."

"I do." It was going to be on him to stop Cotter, and this was going to be the fight of his life.

Chapter XXIX

Kenna's face was solemn as Jake told her about his encounter with Cotter. He expected hysterics, but she sat stoically, not saying a word.

"It was really Cotter?" Kenna asked.

Jake nodded. "He admitted to it. Apparently, he has a grudge against me, so like it or not, I can't ignore him.

Kenna's lower lip quivered. "Is he going to kill you?"

There was no point sugar coating it. Kenna needed to be aware of the danger they faced. "I'm sure he'll try, but I'm going to make it hard for him."

Suddenly, Kenna clung to Jake for dear life. "No! I don't want you to die. I can't lose you."

Jake kissed the top of her head. "I'm going to beat Cotter, and I'm not going to let him hurt you. That's a promise."

Tears formed in Kenna's eyes. "I'm not worried about me. I'm worried about you. You don't know how horrible it was without you. I can't do it again."

Jake gently grabbed Kenna's arms and held her back. "Look, we can't change what happened. All we can do is stop Cotter. That means we have to talk to Mia again."

Kenna nodded.

"This time, I want to have June with us. She's super smart. She'll be able to help us figure out a plan."

"I like June," Kenna said. "I think you make a great couple."

Jake smiled. "I think we make a good couple, too. Bring your friends tomorrow after school. I'll bring June."

Kenna nodded. "I'm really sorry."

"Sorry about what?"

"All of this. It's all my fault."

"Kenna, it's not your fault. I know you wouldn't purposely do anything destructive like that."

After Kenna left the room, Jake went back to visualizing his last encounter with Cotter and what he would do differently the next time they met.

***

When Jake told June about contacting Mia, she told him she would skip her class to be there. Jake felt bad about it, but this was serious business. Cotter was playing for keeps.

Jake picked her up from class and brought her to his home. They arrived before Kenna and her friends.

Jake fixed June a glass of iced tea. These days, he was strictly drinking water or black coffee. A week and a half out from his fight, he was only seven pounds over his contracted weight and wasn't sweating shedding the remaining pounds.

"You ever use a Ouija board?"

June nodded. "Sure, but it was just silly kid's stuff. We didn't communicate with an actual entity. We were just pushing the disc around the board and making things up."

"Same here. You know, I've always been ambivalent about the whole life after death concept. I'm not overly religious. My dad used to take us to church before he died. But mom's not so much into it, and I suppose neither am I. Damn, if this isn't proof of life after death, then I don't know what is. Kind of eye opening."

"Well, I've never had a problem in believing in life after death," June said. "After all, I had that ghost in my house I was telling you about. A little religion might be good for your soul, no pun intended."

Jake shrugged. "Maybe you're right."

June peaked out the window. "Here they come. This is wild. I've never spoken to a dead person before, well except for Cotter the other night. What was it like communicating with Mia?"

Jake paused. "Strange. The air felt electric. I don't necessarily want to say I felt a presence, but I certainly felt something."

"Hmm. Well, I guess I'll see for myself. I have to say, I'm a bit nervous."

Jake arched his brows. "Why? It can't be worse than going face to face with Cotter."

Kenna opened the door, and she and her friends entered the house. The normally talkative group was unusually quiet.

"You okay?" Jake asked.

Kenna nodded. "I think so. I told them about your fight with Cotter."

Ben stepped up to him. "We're real sorry he tried to kill you. We didn't mean for this to happen."

Cordy hugged Jake. "It's all our fault."

Kenna joined in on the hug.

"It's okay, guys. I'm still standing. I'm not afraid of Cotter. He's nothing more than a thug and a bully. I've dealt with bullies before, and I've dealt with thugs in prison. We're gonna stop this guy. It's just a matter of figuring out how."

Jake tried to put on a brave face for the kids, but he wasn't feeling it. The truth was, Cotter scared the shit out of him, and he had no clue how to stop him.

After they broke the embrace, June put her hand on Kenna's shoulder. "I have an important question for you and Ben. On the day Cotter came through the Ouija board, did either of you have a black out, kind of like Carlos had."

Ben shook his head.

Kenna's brow furrowed. "Well, um, I don't know. I'm not sure what happened. It was like something smashed into me and knocked me over."

"You were on the floor," Cordy said. "You were, like, out of it for a little bit."

"Yeah, then when you got up, that's when Carlos started acting all mean," Ben said.

Carlos put his hands in his pockets. "I said I was sorry."

"I don't think that was you, but I'll get to that later. Go back for a minute. So, Kenna, this force hit you, then what happened?"

"She fell back into me," Carlos said. "I remember because, like, I wasn't expecting it. I think I tried to catch her, but she just knocked me backward."

June put her finger to her lip. She turned toward Jake. "That must have been what happened. Cotter went into Kenna. When she made contact with Carlos, he transferred into him. His possession of her sister was so brief that her fugue state lasted momentarily. He possessed Carlos for a longer period of time, which is why he was out of it walking around in a daze for longer. Adam was possessed for an even longer period of time."

Kenna looked up at June, and then Jake, with a lost look on her face. "Wh-what are you talking about?"

June bent down so she was at eye level with Kenna. She put her hands on Kenna's shoulders. "I think that once Cotter broke into our world, he's been able to take over people's bodies, and then transfer to other people."

"What do you mean?

"When Carlos was being mean to the rest of you, it wasn't Carlos. I believe what happened was that Cotter first transferred into you and briefly possessed you. My guess is that when you bumped into Carlos, Cotter transferred into Carlos and took possession of him. Then when Carlos went upstairs, he must have somehow transferred into Adam."

Carlos trembled. He looked like he was going to burst at the seams. "You mean he was inside of me." Carlos shook his head furiously. No. No. No."

Jake clutched his shoulder. "It's all right, man. It's over now."

This hardly seemed to console Carlos, who was hyperventilating, tears streaming down his face.

"That's why Adam's in jail right now," Kenna said in a measured voice. "He didn't actually do those things. It was Cotter who did them."

Jake nodded. "That's what we think."

"That sucks," Cordy said.

"That pretty much sums up this whole situation," Jake said. "It's time to talk to Mia."

"Right," Kenna said. "Let's go downstairs."

Everyone followed Kenna to the basement. Jake hoped Mia could provide insight on how to stop Cotter. They could use some help from beyond the grave.

***

Despite the utter despair she had felt earlier, once the Ouija board was in Kenna's hands, her anxiety left. Perhaps it was just in her head, but she could feel something of Mia just by touching the board. It was like wearing a comfortable pair of shoes. It felt right.

She remembered the first time they reached Mia. Kenna didn't think it would work. Sure, they were playing it up like they were going to talk to a ghost, and Cordy was acting all scared with her eyes wide and her overreactions, but even Cordy didn't think they could truly make contact with a spirit.

She reflected back to that first encounter. She vividly remembered seeing Cotter's scary red eyes. It had scared her silly, overshadowing the fact that they had spoken to a person who had lived and died long before any of them had been born. Mia had her own problems and concerns, not to mention memories of the life she had. All Kenna wanted to do was to give her some happiness.

So much had happened since then. It seemed like they first took out the board a lifetime ago.

Kenna set down the board and took a deep breath. After taking her normal place at one side of the board, she eyed Ben. "Are you ready?"

"Sure. What can go wrong?" Ben grinned.

Kenna couldn't help but smile. She wouldn't be able to cope with all of this without Ben.

Kenna glanced at June, who was clutching Jake's arm. If this was bringing them closer together, then at least something good would come from this.

She and Ben put their hands on the planchette simultaneously. During the first rotation, before either of them spoke, Kenna felt a tugging on the planchette. She looked up at Ben, who nodded.

"Mia, this is Kenna. Are you out there?"

Almost before she finished asking the question, the planchette moved to Yes.

"Wow, that was quick," Jake said.

Before they asked any further questions, the planchette began to spell out BEEN WAITING FOR YOU.

When there was no longer any resistance on the planchette, Kenna said, "A lot has happened since we last spoke. Cotter is in our world and he's doing really bad things. He's killed a couple of people and tried to hurt my brother. Jake is here, by the way, with his girlfriend, June."

Ben frowned. "We need to find out a way to fix all of this."

"They have some questions for you," Kenna said.

"Ask Mia if she knows how Cotter was able to get into our world," June said.

Kenna relayed the question.

The planchette moved to Yes and then spelled FOUND OUT.

"How?" Kenna asked.

The planchette moved smoothly from letter to letter spelling out POWERFUL MAGIC. There was a pause, and then it spelled DANGEROUS.

"Can he transfer himself from person to person and even person to animal?" June asked.

After Kenna proposed the question, Mia answered Yes.

Kenna relayed all of the questions her brother and June asked. Jake folded his arms and began pacing. "Is there something we can do to stop him? Can he be killed? Can we send him back to where he came from?"

Mia responded with, DONT KNOW STILL LEARNING.

Jake grunted. "Wonderful. In the meantime, Cotter's out there killing people and he's made a nice target of me."

Kenna released the disc and looked up at Jake. Her heart thumped. As much as her brother tried to sugarcoat what had happened and put on a brave face, she knew what kind of danger he was facing. He was scared, even if he wouldn't admit it. Jake never got scared. He was a fighter. He had to take on tough guys every day.

Kenna put her hands back on the planchette. "What can we do, Mia?"

FIND MARK

"Your old boyfriend?" Ben asked.

The disc went to Yes, then spelled WILL HELP.

June nodded. "Okay. We'll do that."

Without prompting, it spelled out TELL HIM ORCHARD POINT.

June frowned. "What's orchard point?"

Jake replied, "It's about twenty minutes from here. It's a scenic place overlooking a lake."

June shrugged. "Okay. When we see him, we'll mention Orchard Point."

Kenna continued asking questions, but Mia didn't know anything else useful. She told them she would learn more about how to defeat Cotter. Kenna was more than a little frustrated when she put the Ouija board away. Mia had to help them stop Cotter; she just had to help them.

Chapter XXX

Three days after contacting Mia, Jake drove his rental car to Mark Saleski's law office. After relaying Mia's request to Mark on the phone, Jake was surprised he actually agreed to meet them.

"So, what can you tell us about this guy?" Jake asked.

"Well, he didn't really believe us at first," Kenna replied. "But I could tell he wanted to. You see, he's divorcing his wife because he really misses Mia. She was his one true love." Jake raised his brows. "Did he actually tell you that?"

Kenna looked out the window. "Not exactly, but I know it's true."

"You might be jumping to conclusions," Jake said.

"Maybe not," June said. "Would he really agree to meet us if Mia was just a fling from long ago?"

Jake shrugged. "I'm not sure what the point of all this is. How is he going to help us anyway?"

"We won't know until we talk to him," June said. "At any rate, it can't hurt."

Kenna nodded. "He's a nice guy. You'll see."

"Nice lawyer," Jake said. "Sounds like an oxymoron."

Kenna frowned. "What are you talking about? He's not a moron."

"No, oxymoron. It's like putting two words together that are the opposite."

"Huh?" Kenna asked.

June waved her hand. "Your brother is just saying he doesn't trust lawyers."

Jake didn't actually harbor any ill will toward lawyers. He was just wary of getting anyone else involved in this tangled mess, but if Mia thought it was a good idea, he would defer to her. After all, she was communicating with them from beyond the grave so she had to know things that they didn't know.

Jake managed to find street parking a block from the law office. He took a deep breath on this chilly October afternoon as they walked to the office. "I hope we aren't wasting our time."

June said, "The worst he can do is laugh at us and call security to escort us out of the building."

Kenna folded her arms. "He won't do that. I told you, Mr. Saleski is a nice guy and he cares a whole lot about Mia."

"Yeah, I've heard your theory," Jake said.

When they entered the building, they stopped in front of an office directory. Mark Saleski's law firm was located on the third floor. After exiting the elevator, Jake followed June down the hallway and to the right. They opened the door to the law offices where a secretary with red hair and perky smile was there to greet them.

"Hi," June said and introduced the three of them. "We're here to meet Mark Saleski. He's expecting us."

The secretary looked down at a notebook. "Ah, yes, Mr. Saleski mentioned that. He's not with any clients right now, so you can go inside."

"Thank you," June said.

Jake and Kenna followed her to Mark's office.

"Mr. Saleski," June said.

Mark sat behind a mahogany desk, typing on a computer. He looked up and immediately went to greet them.

Mark had graying hair and a matching beard. He looked soft around the middle, perhaps thirty pounds overweight. He had on a shirt and tie, and wore glasses. He extended his hand to Kenna. "Hi, Kenna. Nice to meet you again. You must be Jake." He shook Jake's hand.

June extended her hand. "I'm June. Thanks for seeing us. I know you must be busy."

Mark waved his hand. "It's fine. I didn't have any client meetings this afternoon."

Jake, Kenna, and June took seats in front of his desk.

"I have to say I'm a little leery," Mark said, "but you mentioned this was urgent, and well, as hard as it is to believe, I can't deny the authenticity of some of the things Kenna spoke the first time we met. It's been on my mind ever since."

June cleared her throat. "Mia asked us to pass a message on to you. She said to tell you Orchard Point."

Mark appeared to be visibly shaken. He removed his glasses and wiped tears from his eyes. "Orchard Point. That was…our first time."

Kenna frowned. "First time for what?"

"Never mind," Jake said.

"I still have a hard time accepting that you can communicate with Mia. She's been dead for so long. But at the same time, I don't see how you can know the things you know without Mia having told you. She was the only person who would know that."

"I had a hard time buying into this as well," Jake said. "That is until I saw it for myself. But there's more to it than that."

"Which is the reason why we're here," June said.

Kenna blurted out, "All we wanted to do was to help Mia. We didn't mean to get in all of this trouble. It was all an accident."

Mark raised his hands. "Slow down. What's going on?"

"In the process of communicating to Mia, Kenna and her friends have resurrected a malevolent spirit named Cotter, one that Mia apparently knows and fears," Jake said.

Over the next twenty minutes, Kenna, Jake, and June relayed what had been going on, starting with Cotter's first appearances through their last communication with Mia.

Mark shuddered. "I think I'm going to need a stiff drink."

"The last thing Mia told us was to contact you, that you could help," June said.

"She did?"

Jake nodded. "I don't think I have to tell you that we have our hands full here. Cotter is a homicidal maniac who now has power he never did in life and seems to be out to get me."

Mark got up and began to walk around the room, rubbing his hands together. "Maybe we have something we can work with. Do you have any idea about the identity of the person who smashed your car?"

Jake shook his head. "We didn't get a license plate number or anything. We just wanted to get out of there as soon as possible."

"Sure, I understand," Mark said. "My thought was that if you had gotten the license plate number, and he still retained that body, then we could track him down. Of course, the more likely situation is that he moved on to possess another unfortunate person. The other thing I was thinking was that we could use his pattern of crimes from when he possessed this Adam fellow, not to mention when he was actually alive, to track him."

Kenna's eyes went wide. "Does this mean you'll help us?"

"Of course, I'll help you. It's the least I could do for Mia. God knows, I couldn't do enough for her when she was still among us. If I did, maybe she would be alive."

"But you weren't there when Mia drowned, right?" June asked.

Mark nodded with sadness in his eyes. "But if I was, she wouldn't have died. So, yes, I'll do what I can to help you. I have resources you don't. As I was saying, we can follow crime patterns not only since his rebirth, but also from the time that Cotter lived. You mentioned in your encounter with Cotter that he was getting back at people. Perhaps we could track down homicides involving people from his past. I have numerous contacts in the local police as well as the Philadelphia police force. Do you know his actual name?"

Kenna perked up. "Ooh. Cotter is his last name."

"And his first?" Mark asked.

Kenna closed her eyes and put her hand to her face. "Mia mentioned it once. It was, um, Robbie. No, that's not it. It was, um, Ronnie. Yeah, that was it. She mentioned it once when we spoke to her."

"You sure?" Mark asked.

Kenna nodded. "Yeah. And he died in prison. That should be able to help you."

"I'll see if we can get a criminal record, known associates, and the like." Mark rubbed his beard. "That's a start, but we still have to figure out how to track him down. If he can slip in and out of bodies like you say, then he'll be a tough nut to crack. Did Mia indicate any weaknesses he might have, anything we can exploit to stop this SOB?"

Kenna shook her head. "Mia didn't know, but she told us she was trying to learn more."

Mark took a deep breath. "Well, this won't be easy. First, we have to find him. He may come looking for you again, Jake."

Jake nodded. "I expect he will. When he pulled a knife on me, I wasn't ready for it. I'll be more prepared the next time we meet."

Mark said, "The next time, he might bring a gun to the fight."

Jake spoke softly. "I know, but I'm not going to run and hide. If he wants to come after me, then I'm going to be here for him. Look, the people in this room right now, that's all we got. If someone is going to do something about Cotter, it has to be us."

"Then we have to be careful," Mark said. "I have a gun at home I'm going to start carrying. I would advise you to take similar precautions."

"My weapons are my hands and feet," Jake said. "I'm a professional fighter. You might be right about Cotter coming after me with a gun, but if he does, I probably would be dead anyway. I don't own a gun and have never shot one. Given my criminal record, I seriously doubt that I could buy one—legally anyway."

"Be careful then," Mark said. "All three of you. Just because Cotter is targeting Jake right now, it doesn't mean he might not turn his attention on someone else. Just the fact that you are trying to bring him down will make you a target. Once I involve myself, I'm sure the same will hold true for me."

"So where do we go from here?" June asked.

"I'll find out about his criminal history, both as Ronnie Cotter and his current self. As for the three of you, be careful and lay low. And I would…I would like to talk to Mia. I don't know how I'll react, but I think it's important."

Kenna nodded. "Okay. We can do that."

Mark folded his hands. "In the meantime, I'll keep you posted on anything I find. I thought I said my final goodbyes to Mia all of those years ago, but I guess I was wrong."

Chapter XXXI

Jake left the dojo with a smile on his face. Just days away from his fight with Paulo Santos, he had his most productive day of training this whole camp, starting with a massive cardio workout in the morning. In the afternoon, he did light sparring before drilling wrestling techniques with two members of Penn State's wrestling team. He fared much better than he expected, stopping most of their takedown attempts and scoring some of his own.

Despite the setbacks during the previous week in training, he was now on point. Every aspect of his fighting was coming together nicely. Even Joe had commented on his progress, a far cry from his last critique.

Despite that, he was hardly overconfident. He had watched a DVD of a fight Paulo Santos had last year in Brazil. Santos had folded his opponent with a series of knees from the clinch. Jake wanted no part of that and would be careful not to get into that position during their bout.

For the past few days, Jake had been working with Joe to formulate a game plan for the fight. Although Jake had confidence in his striking skills, he thought it prudent not to stand in the pocket and trade punches and kicks with Santos. Despite his opponent's allegedly strong jiu-jitsu skills, Jake had seen no evidence of this on tape. He was clearly superior to Santos in wrestling, so his plan was to take Santos down, pound on him with punches and elbows, and look for a submission if it presented itself.

Jake would have liked for the bout to take place tomorrow. For the first time since this whole mess started, he had been able to get his mind off Cotter, even if for just a short while.

Jake spotted his car across the street, a new Toyota Corolla he purchased yesterday from the dealership that sponsored him for his upcoming fight. They had given him an irresistible deal on the vehicle. Although it was nothing fancy, it was a nice ride. Someday, he would drive a Lexus, but for now this suited him fine.

He slung his bag over his shoulder and began walking across the street. At the sound of tires screeching, he turned his head, catching sight of a thirty-something-year-old guy roaring down the road in a Corvette.

Jake's eyes went wide. The car was driving straight at him. Jake saw the malevolent glint in the man's eyes. Cotter. With quick reflexes born out of dodging punches, Jake jumped back to the sidewalk.

For a brief moment, Jake thought the Corvette had smashed into him, but it was only the impact of Jake slamming into another parked car.

Up ahead, the car came to a screeching halt. Jake glanced up and saw a big smile on the driver's face. No doubt about it. It was Cotter.

The car started driving in reverse, stopping just in front of Jake.

Cotter opened the passenger side window. "Better watch where you're going, Jakey. Things are getting dangerous around here."

Jake gritted his teeth. "You son of a bitch!"

Cotter revved his engine. He made as if he was going to come after Jake, but there was no way he could do that unless he was willing to jump the curb, something the Corvette was not designed to do.

Cotter used his thumb and index finger to make a gun and pointed it at Jake. He pretended to shoot with it, then laughed uproariously.

"Your time's limited, Jakey. One of these days, I'm gonna kill your sorry ass for real. Then your pretty girlfriend's gonna be all mine. She's gonna want some comfort, and I know how to give it."

Jake clenched his fists. He got to his feet and charged after the car, but it accelerated away. Without turning around to look back, Cotter extended a middle finger salute to him.

Jake stopped running. There was no point. He could never catch up to the Corvette. However, there was something he could do. Before it drove out of sight, Jake read the car's license plate. Repeating the number in his mind, he took out his smart phone and entered it.

***

The following day, Jake met with Mark Saleski for lunch at Panera Bread, Mark's treat. Jake would have appreciated it more if he wasn't three days away from the fight and still cutting weight. He only had five more pounds to shed, but he couldn't afford to take any chances with his diet at this stage. If he maintained his current weight, he could easily sweat off the remaining weight on weigh-in day, the day before the fight.

When Jake had spoken to Mark on the phone the previous evening, he briefly mentioned his encounter with Cotter but did not want to elaborate because his mom was nearby. He had told Kenna and June about it, nearly giving his sister a heart attack, while June had been in tears.

June wanted to meet Mark, but she was giving a presentation in one of her classes and couldn't afford to miss it. Jake promised to update her later that evening.

When Mark arrived at the restaurant, they took a booth.

"So, what happened to you?" Mark asked. "You were a bit vague on the phone. Are you okay?"

Jake told him about nearly getting hit by the car. "I got by unscathed. I have the feeling he wasn't actually trying to hit me, that he was just trying to get in my head."

Mark rubbed his beard. "Well, I tracked down Cotter's criminal record based on your sister's information. This guy's a real piece of work. His name was Ronald Cotter. He had been doing ten years in Rahway state prison and died three years into his sentence, shanked on his way to the prison yard. His rap sheet includes armed robbery, sexual assault, statutory rape, arson, extortion, and operating an illegal gambling ring. I spoke with a detective in Jersey, who told me those were only the things he got convicted on. They believe he was responsible for more, including murder. He was considered a small-time hood with big ambitions."

"What else do you have on him?"

Mark flipped the page of his spiral notebook. "He was thirty-nine when he died nine years ago. He dropped out of high school and was arrested four times by age twenty-one. He never married, but there were claims he fathered three children out of wedlock and never paid child support for any of them.

"Here is where things get interesting. Your friend Adam Fallon is currently awaiting trial for the murder of Harry Black and Ted Means, both known associates of Ronald Cotter. Furthermore, last week a man was arrested for two separate murders that occurred within days of each other. One of the people he is accused of murdering is Benny Walker, another former associate of Ronald Cotter."

Jake shook his head. "That son of a bitch. He's settling old grudges and having these poor saps take the fall for it."

Mark nodded. "That seems to be his game."

"So now what?"

"You have the license plate number of the car that tried to run you down?"

Jake nodded. "Uh-huh."

"Good. I have a private investigator who does work for our firm. I'm going to have him track this guy down. Hopefully, by his movement and activity, we'll be able to figure out whether or not he's Cotter. Then we'll decide where to go from there."

"You know, I was a little unsure about approaching you. I didn't think it was a wise idea to get someone else involved, but Mia suggested it, and my sister vouched for you. I'm glad I listened. You've been really helpful."

Mark drank his Diet Coke. "Thanks, but I haven't accomplished anything yet. Not while this psychopath is on the loose."

"All the same, I appreciate your efforts."

"You're fighting this Saturday night, right?"

"That's right."

"Be careful."

Jake frowned. "You think he'll use this as an opportunity to attack me?"

"If he tried to run you over with his car, then Cotter must be tracking you. In that case, he'll be aware of your fight. That seems like a logical move."

"Great," Jake said. "I'm already going to have my hands full with my opponent that night. The last thing I need is to worry about Cotter coming after me."

Mark raised his hands. "I don't want to put any undue pressure on you. Just be careful."

"I will. And the next time I get a hold of Cotter, I won't let him get away."

"Well, that may not be the best strategy. Keep in mind, he could always take possession of you."

Chapter XXXII

Cotter pulled his appropriated Corvette into the school parking lot and spotted the girl that was the link to this world. He made sure to keep tabs on little Kenna every day. Sometimes at school, other times near her house. He couldn't afford to lose track of her. If he wasn't in close proximity to Kenna, he would be banished to where he had come from. That wasn't going to happen. He was having way too much fun now, more than he ever had alive.

So far, he had managed to remain inconspicuous by playing it smart. He had switched bodies a half-dozen times already, so if she spotted him, he wouldn't always have the same look as his previous appearances. He was also switching the locations he used to spy on her.

Cotter waited as Kenna got on the bus with her two friends. That blonde girl and the boy with the sad face seemed to spend a lot of time with her.

Satisfied Kenna was fine, Cotter drove off. The red speedster was a sweet ride. A flashy and fast car tended to be a pre-requisite when he switched bodies. Who wanted to drive around some piece of shit?

The man whose body he occupied, Stewart something, was some sort of high-flying financier. Cotter didn't know what the man did, nor did he give a shit. The only things that mattered were the guy had a nice house, a nice ride, and a girlfriend who recently had a boob job. Probing further, Cotter discovered that old Stewey was twice divorced and had three children, none of whom lived in his house, which was a good thing since Cotter didn't have time for bratty kids. It was bad enough he had to keep track of Kenna.

The other interesting thing Cotter found out about Stewey was that he was quite the drug user. He had coke, crystal meth, and ecstasy pills in abundance in his house.

Cotter maintained his policy of staying away from the hard stuff but made sure he had a steady supply for Stewey's girlfriend.

After checking on Kenna, Cotter drove back to Stewey's house, a big place on a large lot in the burbs. Seeing as how Stewey owned his own business and wasn't married, Cotter could stay inside this guy's body for a while. He could ride this out a while, slowly emptying this fella's bank and investment accounts in the process. Life was beautiful.

Once he got back home, Cotter put his feet up on the expensive desk in Stewey's office, mentally trying to tally up the money he had swindled since his rebirth. He had safety deposit boxes at two different banks loaded with cash and valuables. In addition, he had a safe in the apartment he rented. By his estimate, he had at least two hundred grand in cash right now. He never had this kind of scratch when he was alive. The things he could do now were downright criminal.

Cotter poured himself some Scotch. He was still trying to get a handle on some of these high-tech devices, like this iPhone. What he needed was someone to give him a tutorial. He would ask Stewey's girlfriend, but then she would think he was some kind of dumbass. After all, he owned these things. It would make sense he would know how to use them.

At some point, he wanted to settle into someone's body in a permanent, or at least a long term basis. Before long, he would set up off offshore bank accounts in the Cayman Islands and create fake identities to go along with them. The biggest problem was that he had to be ready to move at a moment's notice. Wherever Kenna went, he had to follow. He had contemplated kidnapping her and bringing her with him where he went, but the last thing he wanted was to be saddled with some brat kid. To have her travel around with him, an unwilling companion, would be too complicated. That wouldn't work out for him at all, and he would only go that route as a last resort. He would have to figure out a way to accomplish his goals given his limitations.

Cotter poured himself another Scotch. Even with these complications in his new life, he would take it over the afterlife any day. People had all these grand conceptions about life after death, but they were all wrong. The afterlife sucked.

The afterlife was an amorphous thing, more of a concept than a place. The setting, landscape, and environment were in a constant state of flux. From one day to the next, things would change entirely, going from a rocky desert to a frosty winter land.

That wasn't the only thing that was inconsistent. Cotter could never keep track of time. Days blended into each other. Weeks and months melted away, yet moments tended to drag on for infinity. When he first died, he found the whole process disorienting. After thirteen years, he still couldn't get used to it.

What infuriated Cotter the most was there was no action to be found in the after-life. It was all quiet contemplation and serenity. Supposedly, this stage of his post life existence was meant for him to reflect on his life and come to peace with it. Whatever. It was all bullshit.

In life, Cotter had always been looking for an angle, trying to get one over on everyone else. He was always going for the big score, creating opportunities when nobody would give him one. No such thing existed in the afterlife.

From the moment he got there, Cotter wanted out. Yeah, he had been told about going to a higher level once he reached a certain point of enlightenment, but that higher level would probably be more of the same bullshit. The question was how to find a way out. He had made that his mission, and when he set his mind to something, he attacked it with bulldog persistence.

He had wandered through the seemingly endless world of the afterlife like a nomad, talking to as many people as he could. He kept hearing rumors of a really old bastard who had mystical qualities that awed the other lost souls. It took him a while, but he finally found the old bastard.

Cotter tried to befriend this mystic, a Spaniard named Francisco, but despite Cotter's best efforts, Francisco always turned him away.

Then he met up with Mia, the skinny bitch with the sad face. He tried to make his moves on her, but she wouldn't have it, which pissed him off. She thought she was hot shit, but she was nothing special, what with her hippy dippy attitude and Zen philosophies.

It took a while, but Cotter found a way to get to Francisco. The ancient Spaniard had a penchant for the newly dead. Cotter didn't know what he did with them, nor did he care. What limited the old bastard was that he hated getting out of his hovel and lived like a hermit. Cotter kept his eyes and ears open to find the newly dead, who arrived on a daily basis.

It took some serious negotiation, but Cotter finally made a deal with Francisco. Cotter would supply him with a slew of newbies, and Francisco would teach him how to get out of this shithole. Learning how to do that proved even more difficult than convincing Francisco to help him. Before he could attempt to exit the afterlife, he had to master elemental magic—no easy feat. He had literally been burned several times practicing it but, eventually, he got the magic down well enough to use it.

Once he felt comfortable with using the magic, he needed a conduit for his exit. That's where that hippy bitch Mia came into play. She so missed her old life, which was probably why she had yet to advance to the next stage, whatever the hell that was, that she was trying to communicate with people on the other side. Cotter formulated a plan. He would use Mia and her new friends to get back, something Francisco claimed had never been done before but was possible.

Cotter spent a good deal of time around Mia, observing how she interacted with those kids. She was old school, using a physical medium to communicate. He got the idea that he could mimic her actions and trick those brats to get him back into the world. They chanted the powerful words he gave them, and he worked his magic. Most wouldn't think it possible, but Cotter never underestimated his own abilities, especially when he was driven to accomplish his goals.

Cotter smiled as he knocked back some more Scotch. When he thought back to his old life, he realized how many people had underestimated him. His contemporaries from back in the day had always held disdain for him. His accomplishments never measured up to his aspirations or his boasts to others. But now…everything was different. He had gained the power of life over death. His ability to switch in and out of host bodies made him an unstoppable force of nature.

Opening the drawer to Stewey's desk, he pulled out a Glock. Fortunately, guns had not changed significantly since his last stint in this world. Stewey's girlfriend wanted him to take her out on the town tonight, but Cotter had other things in mind. For the past few days, he had been tracking down somebody who had tried to keep him down in his old life, an asshole who amused himself by belittling Cotter in front of important people, which was why he never got the respect he deserved.

Cotter packed the Glock in its holster. He set off to New Jersey in his Corvette. Over the last few days, he had been making inquiries, pretending to be a potential buyer of guns and ammo from a dealer named Lorenzo Ibarra.

Back in the day, Cotter had been trying to make a name for himself in the Jersey scene. Back then, Ibarra was still small time, dealing mostly in stolen merchandise he lifted off trucks and ships coming in from the port. One night, Cotter was playing pool with a couple guys when Ibarra and his crew rolled in.

Ibarra was a typical ball buster, always coming with the insults and sharp remarks. For whatever reason, Cotter was Ibarra's target. Every time Cotter attempted a shot, Ibarra yelled something to disrupt him. To make matters worse, Ibarra kept calling him Jew-boy even though Cotter wasn't Jewish. After the first few times, Cotter told him to cut the shit. He would have gone over to kick his ass, but he knew Ibarra was at a higher place than him and doing something like that could cause trouble.

Cotter kept hoping the greasy bastard would lay off him, but Ibarra wouldn't quit. Eventually, Cotter reached his limit and told Ibarra to step outside. Ibarra agreed, but before Cotter made it outside, three of Ibarra's men jumped him, one of them equipped with brass knuckles. The two pussies Cotter was playing pool with didn't even jump in to stop it. Ibarra's boys gave him a royal beatdown. He never got his shot at payback, since a week later Ibarra got pinched for armed robbery.

Cotter was a patient man. Death could do that to a person. Harry Black had been the first on the list. After Black, there had been a couple of others. Now, it was Lorenzo Ibarra's time. His pet project was Kenna's brother, Jake. He wanted to torment the kid for a while. Something about the punk's smug attitude irritated the hell out of Cotter. Maybe it was his self-righteous way, or how he came off as being better than everyone else.

He spent quite a bit of time thinking about how he could make Jake's life hell. He wanted to make the kid suffer and watch it up close and personal. He had contemplated dropping himself into Jake's body, killing some people, and leaving Jake to pick up the tab, but that wasn't his style. He wanted to watch Jake as his life unraveled and ultimately put a bullet into his head.

Cotter revved the Corvette out the driveway and drove north. He had it on good authority that Ibarra always ate at the same Cuban restaurant in New Brunswick on Thursday nights.

Cotter got a prime spot at the bar of the Cuban restaurant with a good view of the tables. He drank a Seven and Seven and waited patiently for Ibarra to arrive, who entered the restaurant just before seven that night with a hot blonde at his side.

As Ibarra was leaving the restaurant, Cotter followed him. He shoved aside the blonde and grabbed Ibarra's wrist.

"What the fuck's your problem?" Ibarra shook him off and stepped back.

"I been looking for you for a real long time and I've finally found you."

"Do I know you?" Ibarra asked. "I usually let my underlings deal with pieces of shit like you."

"You know, you talk a lotta smack," Cotter said. "I always thought your sharp tongue would get you in trouble. Well, tonight's that night."

A deep scowl formed on Ibarra's face. "Who the fuck are you?"

"What, you don't recognize me? You used to give me all kinds of shit back in the day, disrespecting me all the time."

Ibarra balled his hands into fists. "I don't know who you think you are, but—"

"I'm Cotter. That's who I am. Remember me?"

Ibarra frowned. "You're not Cotter. That little shit died in jail."

Cotter's eyes narrowed. "Still coming with the insults? Well that's the last one you make."

Just as Ibarra reached for something, Cotter pulled out the Glock and shot him in the chest. Ibarra rocked backward, blood pouring from a gaping wound, and fell to the ground. Ibarra choked on his own blood as he clutched his wound.

"Guess you should watch who you fuck with, asshole." Cotter put a bullet in Ibarra's head.

While this was going on, Ibarra's girlfriend was screaming her fool head off. To shut her up, he shot her twice.

As Cotter observed his handiwork, sirens pierced the air. He did not attempt to flee. He was in a whole new world now. The old rules no longer applied.

He looked up into the sky as it started to rain and belted out the chorus to "Singing in the Rain."

The police vehicle came to a screeching halt just in front of him. He continued to sing, ignoring their unwelcome approach.

"Drop your weapon," a Hispanic cop shouted.

"Glad to see you decided to join the party. We just got started. Sit down and stay a while," Cotter said.

"I said put your weapon down," the Hispanic cop shouted again.

Cotter turned to the white cop next to him. "Hey, bro, your partner needs to chill."

The white cop kept his gun trained on Cotter. "Drop your weapon now."

"Why don't you make me," Cotter said.

"Put down that weapon, or we will shoot," the Hispanic cop said.

"Fine," Cotter said. "You want me to put my gun down, I'll put it down." Cotter tossed the gun aside. "I guess you guys want to get this over with, so you can jerk each other off in the back of the squad car."

"Get on the floor, maggot," the white cop said. "Hands behind your head."

"Make me," Cotter said.

As the white cop approached him, Cotter spat in his face.

The white cop snarled and gave him a sharp punch in the ribs. Cotter gasped for breath. Two more body punches from the cop made Cotter double over. The last one didn't feel so good. Still, Cotter wasn't about to stop. A little pain and suffering never hurt anyone.

Cotter looked up. "Is that all you got? My grandma can punch harder than that."

That little jab didn't go over well with the cop, who balled his fist and went to slug him in the jaw. Cotter grabbed the cop's wrist just before impact.

He transferred himself into the cop's body instantaneously. The first couple of times that change in perspective was jarring, but now Cotter was capable of doing it without missing a beat. Instantly, Stewey slumped.

The Hispanic cop narrowed his eyes and leaned in toward Stewey. "What the hell was that all about?"

Now inside the white cop's body, Cotter turned toward his partner. "You know something. I always wanted to kill a cop. Never did it because it was too risky. Not anymore."

The Hispanic cop turned toward him, his brow creased. "What the hell are you talking about, Rick."

"It's like I said, killing a cop's always been on my bucket list." Cotter raised his gun and pointed it at his temporary partner.

The Hispanic cop's eyes grew wide. He looked at Cotter in horror. "What the hell are you doing?"

Cotter smiled and pulled the trigger. A bullet shattered the man's throat, blood and tissue bursting out. Blood splattered all over Cotter's face and police uniform. As the Hispanic cop's body hit the ground, Cotter felt a rush unlike anything he had ever experienced. Murdering a cop was all he thought it would be and more.

Cotter broke away from his reverie. After all, the job wasn't over yet. While all of this was going on, Stewey was lying on the floor with a dazed look. He bent over and touched Stewey's shoulder, and transferred himself back, another trick Francisco had taught him in his preparation to return to the land of the living.

Once in Stewey's body, Cotter got up from the asphalt. He tilted his head and cracked his neck. Police Officer Rick stood there looking like an idiot with his gun in hand. The man's eyes were wide and his face pale. He had a distant look in his face. That wouldn't last long, so it was best to get on his way. Cotter smiled widely. Oh, was this going to be a big mess. A cop killing another cop. Meanwhile, the bodies of Lorenzo Ibarra and his girlfriend were nearby.

Cotter walked away from the murder scene, once again belting out the chorus to "Singing in the Rain."

Chapter XXXIII

Jake held up his hands, covered by mitts, as Kenna punched them. She always enjoyed watching Jake hit mitts with his trainer and had convinced Jake to get her a pair of her own mixed martial arts gloves.

She had been hoping to accompany Jake for the weigh-in for his fight, but her mom did not let her go with him.

Her brother was in the process of rehydrating after cutting weight to get ready for his fight tomorrow. He had downed two bottles of Gatorade and cleaned off two plates of spaghetti and meatballs, his first real meal in weeks.

Jake yawned, pretending to be bored. "Is that all you got?"

Kenna scowled and began to punch his mitts harder.

"I hate to say this, but you punch like a girl."

Kenna scrunched her face and began to punch the mitts even faster with more intensity. "I don't punch like a girl."

Jake smiled. "That's more like it."

The butterflies in Kenna's stomach were fluttering rapidly. She always got like this before her brother's fights. She had scouted Jake's opponent just like she had his other opponents. So far, she had watched five different matches involving Paulo Santos on DVDs and YouTube. Her heart nearly stopped when she watched in slow motion as Santos knocked out his last opponent cold with a spinning back kick.

Kenna stopped punching. "You need to take the fight to the ground tomorrow night."

Jake raised his brows. "What, you don't think I have good striking skills?"

"No. It's just…this guy's really dangerous."

Jake removed his mitts. "Look, I know you're worried, but Joe and I have put together a sound game plan. I'm ready for Paulo Santos and I'm going to beat him."

"Yeah, but I don't want you to get hurt."

Jake shrugged. "I'm not going to lie to you. I might. It's part of fighting. But you can rest assure that I'm going to do all that I can to win without taking much damage. I'm just glad you're going to be there with me. It means a lot. You're my inspiration."

Kenna's heart began to swell. She had to turn away to prevent herself from crying. "I won't miss any of your fights. Ever. That's a promise."

Jake ran his fingers through her hair. "I'm gonna to hold you to that."

Jake's cell phone rang. He pulled it out of his pocket.

"Who is it?" Kenna asked.

"I'm not sure." Jake clicked on his phone. "Hello? Oh, hi, Mark."

Kenna's eyes went wide. "Is that Mark Saleski?"

Jake nodded.

Kenna shook his arm. "Put it him on speaker. I need to hear about what's going on."

Jake glanced at her. "Hold on, Mark. Kenna's here. I'm going to put you on speaker."

Kenna said, "Hi, Mr. Saleski. Did you call to wish Jake luck in his fight?"

"Not exactly," Mr. Saleski said. "I have some news to share."

"Go ahead," Jake said.

"I followed up on the license plate number you gave me. It belongs to Stewart Ruklick, a thirty-five-year-old financier from Exton. I've had my private investigator follow him over the past couple of days. He hasn't been going to work, and yesterday he was in a shady neighborhood buying what the investigator believes were illegal weapons. He also visited an apartment in Germantown. I'm trying to tap into Stewart's financial records, but that's going to be tricky."

"Sounds like this guy might be Cotter," Jake said.

"That's what I'm thinking," Mr. Saleski said.

Kenna frowned. "So, if we know it's Cotter, then what do we do about it?"

Jake stared at her. "You're not doing anything, Kenna. I'm not going to let you get in harm's way. Understand?"

Kenna folded her arms. "This is all happening because of me. If I can do something to help, then I'm going to."

"No, you're not," Jake said.

"Guys, guys," Mr. Saleski said. "I'm sure we can find a way Kenna can help us without exposing her to any unnecessary danger."

Jake's face tightened. "We'll see about that. I think the best thing to do is to contact Mia again, this time with you present. We'll see what she has to say. If she doesn't have any insight, then I'm going after the bastard. We have a score to settle, and he seems to hold a grudge against me. When I do go after Cotter, I don't want the rest of you involved. I want to do this alone."

"No," Kenna cried out.

"Jake, this guy is a spirit who is capable of transferring from person to person if your theory is correct. Just because you're a professional fighter, it doesn't mean you can defeat him."

Jake grunted but didn't say anything.

Kenna stared at her brother's intense gaze. "We shouldn't do anything until Jake's fight is over tomorrow night. He needs to stay focused."

"How about we reconvene on Sunday, if you guys aren't doing anything? Until then, I'll continue to have my private investigator follow Stewart, so we can be sure he really is Cotter."

"Okay," Jake said. "Sounds like a plan."

"Good luck tomorrow, Jake."

"Thanks." Jake clicked off his cell phone and gave Kenna a stern look. "You're not going anywhere near Cotter. You hear me?"

Kenna crossed her fingers behind her back. “I’m not planning on it. He’s scary.”

Chapter XXXIV

In his locker room, Jake paced like a caged animal. A half hour until his scheduled fight time, he was ready to go now.

"Take a seat, Jake,"

So focused, Jake wasn't aware of who spoke to him. "Huh?"

"Sit down," Joe said. "Time to wrap your hands."

"Oh yeah."

A member of the New Jersey state Athletic Commission was present to witness this.

As Joe applied the wrapping, he said, "Santos is going to come out swinging right away. You got to be alert from the jump. Don't brawl with him. That's his fight—not yours."

Jake nodded. He knew all these things. Joe was trying to drill it into his head, so he wouldn't have to think about it when he got inside the cage.

Joe stopped wrapping his hands for a moment to look Jake in the eyes. "Are you ready for this? I mean really ready?"

Jake's gaze didn't waver. "I am. All the other things that have been going on, I've shut them out."

Joe nodded. "Good. You're going to need intense focus tonight."

Neither one of them spoke for the next few minutes. The athletic commission representative stifled a yawn.

One of Jake's training partners opened the door to the locker room. "Hey, Jake, you got some company."

June and Kenna stepped inside of the locker room.

"Everything decent over here?" June called out.

"I'm good," Jake said.

Joe didn't take his eyes off what he was doing. "Give me another minute. I'm almost done."

June and Kenna remained in the background as Joe finished wrapping. The athletic commission guy made a final inspection, gave his approval, and left the locker room.

Jake gave Kenna a hug and June a kiss. "How did you guys get back here?"

"We know people," June said.

Kenna rolled her eyes. "These security guards are a sucker for a pretty face. I would hate to see them deal with real trouble."

June smiled. "At least we were able to catch you before your match. How are you feeling?"

Jake waved his hand. "I'm fine. I was a lot more nervous for my last fight. I'm ready to go." Jake paused to glance at Renken, who had walked to the other side of the room. "With everything else I've had to worry about, I haven't put much thought into the fact that this guy is going to try to take my head off."

"That's the attitude," Kenna said.

"Just worry about your opponent," June said.

Jake nodded. "I'll be all right."

June said, "We don't want to stay long. We just wanted to see you real quick."

"Good luck," Kenna said in a hopeful voice. "I'm going to be pulling for you real hard."

"I might be biased," June said, "since you're my trainer and all, but I can't imagine anyone being able to defeat you. You're an awesome fighter. You're going to do great out there."

Jake smiled. "Thanks. I appreciate the confidence."

They said their goodbyes and left.

Jake's training partner tapped his shoulder. "You ready?"

They were going to go through final preparations, which included light sparring and grappling. It was more of a mental exercise than a physical one. Jake wanted to feel some contact before his fight and work up a good sweat.

A few minutes into his preparations, Jake heard his ring tone coming from his carrying bag. He contemplated not answering his phone, but it might be something important. "Hold up."

Jake clumsily fumbled for his phone. "Hello?"

"Jake, I'm glad I got you." There was a sense of urgency in Mark Saleski's voice.

"Hey, Mark, what's going on?"

"I just got a call from the private investigator who's following Cotter." Mark sounded like he was out of breath.

Jake gave him a moment. "Yeah?"

"Unless he's switched bodies, Cotter is in the building you're fighting at."

Jake's eyes went wide. "He's here in Atlantic City? In Boardwalk Hall?"

"Yes. The PI lost him in the crowd, so all I know is that he went inside. I don't know where is right now."

Jake closed his eyes. "Oh, shit."

"I don't know what Cotter's planning, but you need to be careful. Did you fight yet?"

"No, I'm going on in fifteen minutes."

"Maybe you should pull out of your bout."

Jake's face tightened. "No way. It's too late now. I'm just about ready to go out there."

"Then watch your back, Jake."

"I will. Look, I have to go. I'll talk to you later."

"Okay. My PI is in the building. He's trying to find Cotter, but I imagine it won't be easy."

Jake disconnected the phone and took a deep breath. Like he didn't have enough to worry about.

***

Cotter worked his way through the crowd. After purchasing a ticket to the event, Cotter had been staking out the security guards, trying to find a certain type of guard, one who really didn't give a shit about his job and was just collecting a paycheck. He found one such guard and managed to get a word with him.

"Hey, buddy, I was wondering if you could help me out. I'm dying to meet Paulo Santos. I'm a big fan. You think maybe you could bring me backstage to meet him."

The guard looked half asleep. "Sorry. Fighters are off limits."

"I know you're trying to do your job, but it would mean a lot to me." Cotter took a roll of ten, one hundred dollar bills and handed it to the security guard.

The guard's attention suddenly perked up as he eyed the cash.

"Look," Cotter said, "I just want to say hi to him, shake his hand, then leave. What do you say?"

The security guard's eyes narrowed. "Follow me. You got two minutes with him, and you better not make any trouble."

Cotter had a big smile. "Thank you so much. I promise I won't give you any trouble."

Cotter had to check himself to make sure he wasn't being over the top. Trying to act like a fanboy, he didn't want to be too overt. This guard was a greedy bastard, but he probably had limits.

The security guard led him through the concourse to the level where the locker rooms were located. He waved and said hello to other workers while Cotter stayed close behind him. The guard used a key to open a double door, led him through a hallway, and knocked on a door.

The door to the locker room opened. Cotter walked inside, trying not to appear too eager.

The security guard said, "Mr. Santos, if you have a minute, I have someone who would like to say hi to you."

A very tanned young man turned around. The Brazilian spoke broken English that Cotter had a hard time understanding. "Oh, yeah. Sure, man. Not gonna be a problem."

"Paulo, it's great to meet you. I've seen all of your fights out of Brazil, and I'm a big fan." Cotter had never seen any of his fights, but knowing his ethnicity, he figured most of his fights probably had occurred in his home country.

"Oh, thanks, man."

"Hey, good luck in your fight tonight," Cotter said.

"I train real hard. I put on show for the fan. I do good fight tonight."

"Sure thing, buddy." Cotter extended his hand, and the Brazilian shook it. The moment they made contact, Cotter said the key words under his breath and transferred himself into Paulo Santos' body.

When Cotter broke contact with Stewey, the man wobbled and nearly fell to the ground.

The security guard caught him before he hit the floor. "Hey, you all right?"

Stewey's eyes had a vacant look, and he could barely stand. The security guard was exerting himself holding up Stewey.

Cotter had to stop himself from laughing. At least the guard was earning the money Cotter had given him.

After the guard led Stewey away, Cotter walked away when Santos' trainer began speaking to him in Portuguese. This would be a tricky business. To alleviate the situation, Cotter found an iPod on a table, turned it on, and shut everybody else out. Tonight, he would be getting a little payback with good ole' Jake.

***

Jake stood at the entrance to the walkway going toward the cage. He had been loose earlier but was now beyond tense. Sweat dripped from his brow. Just before leaving the locker room, Jake had vomited. Renken had expressed his concern, but Jake told him he was fine, just some pre-fight jitters.

Jake walked down the walkway on unsteady legs. Looking over his shoulder, he searched for Cotter in the audience. He was trying to spot the face of the man who had been driving the Corvette when Jake had last seen him, but it was pointless. With Cotter's ability to possess different bodies, he could be anybody.

The music reverberated in Jake's head. Paranoia crept into him as fans leaned over the railing to high-five him. Usually he was fan-friendly, but not tonight.

Perhaps it was just his overly active imagination, but the crowd seemed hostile, as if fueled by an insatiable blood lust. Jake closed his eyes and took a deep breath. He was driving himself crazy. He had to stay calm. Scanning the audience for

Kenna and June, he found them along with a few students from his class. June was waving frantically at him, while Kenna seemed tense.

Jake continued to make his way to the cage. The thunderous music overpowered most of the sound in the arena. His opponent was already inside the cage. Because Jake was the local favorite, he entered last.

Jake took one last look at the audience. Wherever Cotter was, it no longer mattered. He was about to engage in hand to hand combat with a highly skilled fighter. If he was not focused, he would get his ass handed to him.

Jake stepped inside the cage to the loud cheers from the crowd. The promoter of the event told him that he had built quite a following from his last fight. Jake had participated in an autograph signing session the previous day, which had drawn quite a few fans. Normally that type of fanfare would be enjoyable, but Cotter's looming presence put a damper on it.

Jake eyed Paulo Santos across the cage. He had met his opponent at the weigh-in, and the Brazilian seemed like a nice, affable fellow, but now he was staring at Jake with hatred in his eyes. Jake held his opponent's stare. Santos' newfound contempt was hardly a surprise. Most fighters he knew were entirely different people inside the cage.

Joe was giving Jake last second instructions, but Jake tuned him out.

Jake walked to the center of the cage to meet his foe. As the referee gave them their final rules for the bout, Paulo Santos spat in his face.

Chaos erupted. The referee turned to reprimand Santos. Joe was screaming from the side of the cage, while his opponent's corner men were shouting in Portuguese. Jake was too stunned to react.

Santos laughed and said, "You're going down, Jakey. Going down hard."

Jake froze. He had briefly spoken with Santos yesterday and could barely understand his broken English. Santos now spoke in perfect English and sounded just like Cotter.

Chapter XXXV

With trepidation, Jake walked to his corner. He wasn't sure what kind of games Cotter was playing. With all the training and preparation he had gone through for this fight, he now felt unprepared. Cotter was wild and unpredictable, liable to do anything.

From his corner, Joe said, "He's just trying to get in your head. Stick to the game plan."

Jake shook his head. His trainer had no clue what was happening.

Jake glared at Cotter across the cage. If he wanted a fight, Jake was going to give him one.

When the bell rang to signal the start of the bout, Jake moved forward. Normally at the beginning of the fight, he would touch gloves with his opponent as a sign of respect. Not tonight.

Cotter rushed at him winging wild punches. Jake raised his hands to block while stepping to the side. Cotter landed a shot to the side of Jake's head. The blow didn't have enough force to do damage. Jake popped Cotter with two jabs followed by a right cross. Cotter threw an overhand right so telegraphed Jake could have avoided it with his eyes closed. He countered with a straight right that sent Cotter to the canvas.

Instead of pouncing on him, Jake let him get back to his feet, wanting to give him the beating of his life.

"You're nothing, Jakey. I'm going to enjoy killing you, then I'm going to fuck your girlfriend."

Jake responded by giving Cotter a thudding kick to the thigh that made him step back. Cotter threw a couple of sloppy punches. Jake ducked them and landed a solid combination to Cotter's ribs, causing Cotter to wince.

"You like that?" Jake asked. "I've got more for you."

Jake feinted with a punch and came back with a roundhouse kick to Cotter's temple, which sent him crashing to the canvas once again.

Jake held his ground. He had never fought like this before inside of a cage, but this was not about winning or losing a match.

"Get up!" Jake shouted.

When Cotter got to his feet, he was laughing. The guy was just plain nuts. Maybe crossing over from the spirit world had made him lose his mind.

Cotter came forward and, instead of punching Jake, wrapped his arms around his waist. Before Jake could break free, Cotter head-butted him on the forehead.

Jake reeled backward, his orientation shot as his world spun around him. He dropped to his knees. In the background, Joe screamed at the referee. Jake looked up and found the referee reprimanding Cotter.

Fighting dizziness, Jake managed to stand.

The referee was holding Cotter's wrists. "I don't know what kind of crap you're trying to pull here, but I won't stand for it." He led Cotter to each of the judges at cage side and instructed them to deduct one point from him. Like Cotter gave a rat's ass about a point deduction.

The referee walked over to Jake. "Are you okay?"

Jake nodded.

"Let me have a doctor look at you," the referee said.

Jake shook his head. "I'm fine. Let's keep fighting."

The referee took a long look at him. "Are you sure?"

"Yeah. Let's start back up."

The referee restarted the fight. Still woozy, Jake had to remind himself Cotter couldn't hurt him conventionally since Jake's fighting ability was superior, which meant Cotter was going to resort to dirty tactics.

Jake pressed the action landing a jab-hook combination, followed by a round house kick to Cotter's ribs. Cotter threw a couple of punches Jake easily side-stepped. Jake landed a punch that cracked Cotter's jaw, sending him to the canvas once again. This time, Jake followed him to the ground. Jake landed a couple of punches before transitioning to the mount position, pinning Cotter to the ground.

He hammered Cotter with punches and elbows as Cotter's head thudded off the canvas. Jake continued to pound on him until Cotter reached up and thumbed Jake in the eye. Jake's eye began to water, and his vision blurred. Seizing the advantage,

Cotter got out from underneath Jake. The next thing Jake knew, a knee smashed the side of his head.

Immediately, the referee jumped in and stopped the action. "Eyepoke and an illegal knee to the head on a grounded opponent." He brought Cotter to the neutral corner. "I warned you before about these illegal tactics. I'm not going to tolerate it."

The people in Santos' corner began shouting in Portuguese. Jake had no idea if they were disputing the referee's claim or chastising their fighter.

Meanwhile, Joe seemed as if he was about to blow a gasket. Screaming at the top of his lungs, he grabbed the cage. "What the hell is this shit? What's this son of a bitch trying to pull?"

Using the cage, Jake pulled himself to his feet. The knee to the head had dazed him, but the thumb to the eye had inflicted more damage. He couldn't see at all out of his right eye. He could tell it was swelling shut. He staggered to his corner and stood in front of his trainer.

"I can't believe this." Spit flew from Joe's mouth. "This son of a bitch's a dirty fighter. A dirty fighter, I tell you."

Jake couldn't remember Joe ever being this enraged. He looked like he was ready to get inside of the cage and choke out Cotter.

"You okay, Jake?"

"I've felt better."

Joe shook his head. "He can't get away with this. The ref needs to disqualify this bastard."

"No way." This was his chance to dispose of Cotter. He couldn't let the referee end this fight yet. He knew there was crazy risk involved, both to himself if Cotter tried to gain control of him, as well as to Paulo Santos, a poor kid out of Brazil just trying to make a living in a rough sport who didn't ask for any of this, but he had to take the chance to eliminate Cotter.

Jake rushed over to the referee, who was conferring with a member of the New Jersey state athletic commission, discussing whether or not to disqualify Cotter.

Jake grabbed the referee's wrist. "You can't stop this fight."

The referee took a close look at his busted eye. "You need to be seen by the doctor, son. Your eye is in bad shape."

Jake shook his head. "I'm fine. Listen, don't stop this fight. I know Santos has been committing fouls. Let me decide the outcome. I'm begging you. Don't take this opportunity away from me."

The referee led him to the ringside physician.

Jake cursed under his breath. He couldn't tell how badly his eye looked externally, but he knew he could not see out of it. Under normal circumstances, he might be okay with a stoppage, but not tonight. Not against Cotter.

The ringside physician opened his right eye and shone a light in it. "Can you see?"

Jake knew that if he told the physician that he couldn't see, the referee would stop the fight. No questions asked. He couldn't allow that to happen. "No problems. The eye isn't bothering me at all."

The physician furrowed his brow. "Your eye can't open unless I force it to open. How can you see from it?"

"I can see with my other eye. My vision isn't great in my right eye anyway. My left eye is my good eye."

The physician continued to examine his damaged eye. "I'm going to let you go for now, but I'm going to take another close look at the end of the round. If I feel the damage is too severe, then I'm stopping the fight."

"Yeah, no problem." That gave him a couple of minutes to put a hurting on Cotter.

After conferring with the physician, the referee brought Jake and Cotter back to the center of the cage. He gave Cotter a stern look. "I won't tolerate another violation of the rules. You do anything else, and I'll disqualify you, and the commission will fine you. Do you understand?"

"Oh, yeah," Cotter said. "I understand perfectly."

The referee gave the signal to resume the match.

"Did you like that?" Cotter asked.

Jake landed two jabs and an inside leg kick. "I liked it just fine."

"I got some more tricks in my bag."

"So do I." Jake staggered his opponent with a front kick to his chin. He backed Cotter against the cage and grabbed the back of his neck in a Thai clinch. He landed knee after knee to Cotter's body and face, shattering Cotter's nose. Blood spurted down his face and onto his chest. He let go of Cotter, took a step back and landed a spinning back fist that sent Cotter sprawling to the canvas. The crowd was in a fever pitch, cheers resonating from the arena.

Amazingly, Cotter got up. Jake stared in amazement through his one good eye. The other eye was closed shut, rendering it useless. He had been landing just about every strike in his arsenal against Cotter, but nothing stopped him. For all his faults, Jake had to credit him for being a tough son of a bitch.

Jake pressed forward with a left, right combination to the head and a crescent kick that cracked Cotter's jaw, sending his mouth piece flying across the cage. Yet, he still stood. Cotter attempted another punch, which Jake ducked. He leaned inward, lowered his shoulder and executed a judo throw, slamming Cotter to the canvas.

From side control, Jake landed knees to Cotter's ribs, rearing back and putting all of his weight behind them. Cotter groaned, but Jake would not relent. He wanted to shatter Cotter's ribs. He continued to land knees, trying to make each strike more devastating than the previous one. The referee loomed over them. He looked as if he was ready to stop the fight.

Before the referee could stop the fight, the bell sounded signifying the end of the round. Amazingly, Cotter got to his feet and started to laugh. What the hell was wrong with the guy? Jake had unleashed hellfire on him, and he thought it was funny.

Jake sat on his stool in his corner, staring at Cotter on the other side of the cage. Jake might have one eye swollen shut, but Cotter was a mess. Blood flowed from his nose, and he had a gash above his left eye. His face looked puffy and both eyes were starting to discolor.

Joe applied an endswell to Jake's eye to keep the swelling down. Jake cringed as his trainer pressed hard with the endswell.

"You're doing great out there, Jake. This guy fights dirty, but you're landing everything you want on him. Keep up the pressure. You have some opportunities on the ground that you're passing up. Take him to the ground and pound him out."

The ringside physician came to look at Jake's eye. Jake tried to act as if it wasn't bothering him, but it was hard with the doctor poking around it. "How's your vision?"

"Perfect," Jake said. "Never better."

"Smart ass," the doctor muttered under his breath.

"Jake, listen to me," Joe said. "I want you take him down. Go for the double leg."

Jake shook his head. "The game plan is out the window."

"What are you talking about?" Joe asked.

"That's not Paulo Santos out there."

Joe scowled. "What do you mean that ain't Paulo Santos?"

Jake looked into his trainer's eyes. "I can't explain it to you, but that's not Santos. He's someone else."

Joe frowned. "Have you lost your marbles?"

This was the reason he couldn't tell his trainer about Cotter. Joe was too firmly rooted in reality to believe it. "Never mind."

Jake had a sudden thought. What if he rendered Cotter unconscious? Would that be enough to drive Cotter back to where he came from?

The bell sounded for the start of the second round. It was a three round fight, with each round five minutes long. Five minutes would give Jake plenty of time to execute his new plan.

Jake met Cotter at the center of the cage.

"I see you're still standing," Jake said.

Cotter nodded. "You didn't do shit to me. I got more tricks in store for you. I'm going to mess you up good."

Cotter came out swinging, punches Jake easily avoided.

"First, you have to catch me," Jake said.

Cotter missed with another wild punch. This time Jake popped him with a jab and a low leg kick, prompting Cotter to throw more punches. Jake got caught by one of those punches, which he shrugged off. He jabbed his way inside and wrapped his arms around Cotter's neck in a Thai clinch. Once inside the clinch, Jake drove repeated knees into his opponent's abdomen, eliciting a grunt from Cotter. Jake spun around and took Cotter's back. He wrapped his arms around Cotter's waist and locked his hands together. Wrenching Cotter off the ground, he slammed him to the mat with a German suplex. Cotter's back, neck, and head crashed onto the canvas with a thud. The crowd roared in appreciation.

Cotter was now underneath him, and Jake still had his arms wrapped around Cotter's waist. He punched the side of Cotter's face, then let go of his opponent's back, Jake spun around and drove him to the canvas, bringing his right hip down on Cotter's shoulder. Jake then reached his right hand between Cotter's head and shoulder and gripped his own triceps on the other side of Cotter's body. He triangled his arm and gripped high onto Cotter's back, forcing his left bicep into his opponent's neck. He dropped to his right hip while kicking his right leg under his left. Using the arm triangle grip, Jake torqued his upper body to the left, forcing his opponent to roll, completing the anaconda choke.

Cotter probably had no concept of what was happening, although he undoubtedly was gasping for breath. Cotter wouldn't be tapping out even though he was losing consciousness. Jake could only hope the referee would not stop the fight too soon. He held onto his grip, further sinking in his choke. The referee hovered closely over him. Underneath him, Cotter went limp. The referee reached for Cotter's hand and raised it but got no response. The ref called for the end of the fight and told Jake to release his choke, but Jake held on. He had to make sure Cotter was unconscious.

When the ref pulled him off, Jake finally let go of the choke. He got to his feet and stared down at Cotter, who was out cold.

The ref got in Jake's face. "When I tell you to break, you break. You're lucky I don't disqualify you, except your opponent did worse shit than you did in this fight."

Sportsmanship and rules didn't apply when dealing with Cotter.

Joe ran over and lifted him off the floor with a big bear hug. "Great job, Jake. You did it. You took all the crap he was giving you and still crushed him. Nice anaconda there."

Jake did not respond. He continued to stare at Cotter.

"What's wrong with you?" Joe asked. "That was the biggest victory of your career. Raise your hands. Show some emotion."

Half-heartedly, Jake raised his arms. He was trying to figure out if the man he was looking at was Cotter or Paulo Santos. He had a glassy-eyed look, which could mean it was Santos returning to the land of the living, or it could be Cotter reacting to having been choked unconscious.

As the announcer asked him questions in the post-fight interview, Jake gave short answers, barely paying attention to what the announcer was asking. All the while, his eyes followed his opponent as he left the cage.

Chapter XXXVI

Back at Jake's locker room, June and Kenna were waiting for him.

Upon seeing him, June cringed. She reached for his badly bruised eye. "What was going on out there? The other guy, he was like an animal."

"It was Cotter," Jake said.

Kenna's eyes went wide. "What?"

Jake glanced at Joe, making sure he was out of earshot. "Yeah, it was Cotter inside the guy's body. That's why he was fighting so out of control."

"How do you know it was him?" June asked.

"After he spit in my face, he told me as much. Trust me. It was Cotter."

"Well, now what?" June asked.

"I don't know. My plan was to choke him out and force him to leave his body and return to where he came from."

"What makes you think that would work?" Kenna asked.

Jake shrugged. "It seemed like a good plan at the time. I was also concerned that in those close quarters, he might take control of my body. Who knows? Maybe we'll get lucky."

"Maybe," June said. "I realize this may be a bad time, but Lawrence is throwing you an after-party to celebrate your victory. Most of our MMA class is going to be there. If you're not feeling up to it, I can tell them to cancel."

Jake waved his hand. "I'll take Kenna home and make an appearance."

"You sure?" June asked. "We can do something low-key instead."

Jake winked. "Maybe later." He put his arm around Kenna's shoulder. "How about you guys watch the rest of the show? I have something I need to take care of, then I'll come and get you."

"You sure you're okay?" Kenna asked. "You don't look so hot. Maybe you should go to a hospital."

"The physician at cage side looked at my eye at the end of the fight. I'll be all right. I can always get it checked out tomorrow. Right now, I need to take care of something. Okay?"

"Sure," Kenna said.

When they left, Joe examined his eye. It seemed as if everyone wanted to play amateur doctor tonight. "You'll be fine. You did good out there. There was a lot to like in that fight, despite all the dirty shit."

"I want to talk to Paulo Santos in his locker room."

Joe frowned. "The fight's over. I didn't like what he did either, but you have to let it go."

Jake shook his head. "It's not like that. I just want to talk to him."

"I don't know if this is such a good idea. Look, if that's what you want, I'll go with you."

Jake thought it over for a moment. "Okay."

They made their way to Santos' locker room, escorted by a member of the security staff.

The arena staff member knocked on the door to the locker room. They entered to shouting in Portuguese. Jake hung back until the shouting subsided, then made his way to his opponent.

Jake said, "Hey."

The first words came out in a thick Brazilian accent. "You must hit me real good, 'cause I no remember nothing."

Jake smiled. That clearly did not sound like Cotter. In fact, it sounded just like the person he had met at the weigh-ins. "Yeah. It was a tough fight."

"My trainer, he mad at me, say I no fight so nice out there, but I no remember nothing. I sorry. I no try fight dirty."

Jake patted his shoulder. "Don't sweat it. It wasn't your fault." The sad look on Paulo's face moved him. He went to Santos' trainer. "Hey, look, the stuff that went down tonight wasn't his fault. I said some nasty things to him during weigh-ins about his mama, and he lost it in the cage. If anything, it was my fault. Go easy on him. We all make mistakes." To further the point, he went over to Santos and hugged him. "Hey man, maybe we can fight again. I don't think you were yourself out there."

Santos smiled. "Yeah, I like that. You a good guy."

The trainer said something Jake could barely understand. He shook hands with everybody, hoping this would smooth things over.

As they were walking back to their own locker room, Joe put his hand on Jake's shoulder. "That was a classy move. You're growing up. Santos seems like a nice enough kid. I don't know what got into him out there. He was like a savage. What were you saying about him not being Paulo Santos?"

"It's just an expression. Like you said, he was like a savage out there."

When they got to the locker room, Joe undid the wrappings on Jake's hands.

Jake's visit to Santos' locker room gave him a ray of hope. Maybe, just maybe he had choked Cotter back to the spirit world.

***

Jake lingered by June's doorstep. They had just returned from the after-party Lawrence had thrown. Jake wanted to make an appearance but wound up staying for over an hour.

"What a crazy night," June said. "You know, being with you is never boring."

Jake grinned. "I try to keep it interesting."

"That you have. I had no idea you were fighting Cotter in that cage tonight. I guess, in retrospect, your victory isn't so impressive."

Jake frowned. "How do you figure? I beat down an evil spirit. How many people can say that?"

"Maybe so, but beating a quality professional fighter would be more impressive."

Jake shrugged. "Still counts as a win on my record. I feel bad for Santos. He doesn't have any idea what happened but has a lot of bruises to show for it, not to mention a loss on his record."

Jake stood for a minute staring at June, just content to be with her now that his adrenaline had wound down. He looked at his watch. It was past two in the morning and fatigue was setting in. "It's late. I should get going."

June yawned. "I suppose you're right. Well, it was certainly a night I won't forget."

Before he was able to give her a long kiss good night to remember him by, his cell phone rang. "What the hell? Who's calling me at two in the morning?" He looked at his caller ID and could not recognize the number. "Hmm." He clicked on his phone.

"You son of a bitch. You think you put one over on me, Jakey? You think you're hot shit with that cage fighting? That don't mean nothing. I'm gonna kill you. I'm gonna put a bullet in your gut and another in your brain and I'm gonna watch you die. Then I'm gonna kick your stinkin' carcass. You're gonna die, Jakey. Next time I come for you, I'm playing for keeps."

June's eyes were wide with apprehension. "What was that all about?"

"I guess my theory about finishing off Cotter by choking him out was wrong." Jake took a deep breath. "He's still out there and he's coming for me."

Chapter XXXVII

Jake hobbled to the living room where June and Kenna were waiting for him.

"You sure you want to do this?" June asked.

Jake nodded. "We have to. It can't wait."

"But you're still hurting," Kenna said.

Jake shrugged. Besides his right eye, which was blue and puffy, he had injured his right foot in the fight last night. His amateur estimation was that nothing was broken, but he may have sprained it. "Cotter sounded serious. I think this time he means to kill me. If Mia can help us, then we need to find out."

Kenna clutched the box holding the Ouija board and looked down. "I'm scared, Jake. I just want everything to go back to the way it had been."

Jake touched her cheek. "It's going to be okay. We'll stop him. We'll find a way."

June put her arm around Kenna's shoulder. "We're in this together, and we'll make it through together. You just have to be brave."

"I wish I could keep you out of this," Jake said, "but I'm going to need you to contact Mia." Not wanting to put Kenna's friends in danger, he had not allowed Kenna to invite them to Mark Saleski's office. It was bad enough that Kenna would be there. "Do you think it's going to matter that Ben won't be on the other end of the planchette?"

"It shouldn't. Cordy and I have contacted Mia before."

Kenna had expressed reservations earlier when Jake told her he wanted to contact Mia without her friends present, but he convinced her it made no sense to put them in danger since they were dealing with a supernatural homicidal maniac.

Jake said, "If it doesn't work, then we could always try it again tomorrow with Ben present."

June had volunteered to replace Ben. Originally, Jake was going to take the other end of the planchette, but when June offered, he readily agreed. She seemed to have more of a spiritual side to her than he had.

Mark offered to use his office. It would be empty on Sunday, and it would be hard to explain Mark's presence to his mom if they had used Jake's house.

They got in Jake's new Toyota and drove to Mark's office. His cover story to his mom was that they were going to the park for a picnic. Still early in the afternoon, the sky was overcast with a call for rain later that evening. The air felt crisp. Fall was about to give way to winter, which gave the air a certain gloominess. As he drove, Jake constantly looked in his rear-view mirror. He wasn't sure what he was looking for since Cotter could be anyone in any vehicle. After a few minutes, he gave up.

As they walked into the office building, Jake felt a sense of finality. He hardly knew what to expect, but one way or another, the situation with Cotter was coming to a head. The only thing he cared about was protecting those he cared about.

Mark, wearing a Hawaiian shirt and a pair of slacks, met them in the lobby. Jake could see his nervousness as he paced.

"Glad to see you guys again," Mark said. "I've been worried sick ever since my investigator told me Cotter had entered the arena last night. I certainly didn't think he would switch bodies with the guy you were fighting."

"You and me both," Jake said. "He's either a glutton for punishment or he's crazy. There's no way he could beat me in a cage fight."

"Maybe he has an ego the size of Texas," Mark said. "In which case that might be something we can exploit. Regardless, I'm glad things worked out for you. Based on that phone conversation you had with him, you may have rattled his cage."

"At least I won that round. I'm pretty sure he wasn't too happy about getting beat down by me last night. In our previous confrontation, he mentioned something about me thinking I'm some kind of tough guy. I guess in his world, people who look like me aren't that tough."

Mark motioned to the elevator. "Let's go to my office."

They followed him into the elevator up to his office. Once inside, Mark led them to a small table. Kenna removed the Ouija board from its case and laid it on the table. She put the planchette on the board.

"So how does this work?" Mark asked.

Kenna looked up at him. "It takes two people to make the connection. June and I will be the mediums. Are you ready?"

June nodded. "Jeez. I can't stop my hands from shaking."

Kenna held her hand. "It's really not that bad. It feels strange at first, but it's also kinda cool."

"What about us two?" Mark asked. "Should we do anything?"

"Just watch."

Kenna and June took chairs at opposite ends of the table. Kenna grabbed the planchette, and then reluctantly, June took hold of it. They moved it slowly around the board.

"Mia, are you there? It's Kenna. This time I have June with me instead of Ben."

They continued to rotate it around the board.

"How quickly does this happen?" June asked.

Kenna didn't remove her eyes from the board. "It depends. Sometimes it happens right away. There were a few times when we didn't get any response from Mia, and I thought we had lost our connection with her."

"Okay," June said.

"Mia, you have to answer us. It's really important. We need to talk to you now more than ever. Things have gotten dangerous with Cotter."

Jake folded his hands, squeezing them together. The tension in the room was thick. Mark had begun to perspire, and June's hands continued to tremble. Only Kenna seemed to be at ease.

"Mia, please answer us," Kenna said. "Cotter has been trying to kill my brother. Jake's here with me now. And so is Mark Saleski."

Jake felt a shimmer in the air. It was as if an electric current had swept through it. The hair on his arms and legs stood on end. He glanced at Mark, whose eyes had gone wide.

Mark mouthed, *Is it her*?

Jake nodded. This was how it felt the other time he had been present when they contacted Mia.

The planchette began to move, spelling IM HERE.

Mark gasped.

Jake put a hand on his shoulder. "Are you all right?"

Mark nodded. "I'll be damned. That really is her. I can feel it. It's like everything changed from one moment to the next. When it happened, I got this picture in my mind. It was a summer evening when we had gone to a carnival that had come to town. We were holding hands as we were about to enter the merry go round."

Kenna turned toward them. "Is he okay?"

Mark replied, "I'll be fine."

"Mia, Cotter tried to kill my brother a couple of times now. We need to know how to stop him."

I CAN.

June frowned. "You can? How?"

MUST BREAK THROUGH.

"Break through?" Kenna asked. "What are you talking about?"

The disk moved quickly now. Jake had a hard time keeping up with the letters. YOUR WORLD NEED GUIDE.

"You need to come into our world," June said. "That's how you can stop him, right?"

The planchette went to Yes.

"How are you going to enter our world?"

SAME WAY COTTER DID.

"You need us to say the same things we did that allowed Cotter to come into our world?" Kenna asked.

The planchette once more went to Yes.

"And you need a guide once you're here," June said. "You need to occupy someone's body in the same way that Cotter does."

Yes.

"What's going on?" Mark asked.

"In order to enter our world, Cotter made Kenna and her friends repeat some phrase," Jake said. "We have to do the same for her."

"You mean Mia's going to be here with us, back in the flesh?" Mark asked. "Holy shit. I don't think I'm prepared for that."

June stared at Jake. "In that case, you can use me as your vessel. You can enter my body and do what you need to do."

Jake frowned. "Are you sure? I've seen what happens to people when Cotter enters and exits them. You'll have no memory of what happened."

"I realize that, but I'm still the one best suited for this. If Mia is going to occupy someone's body, it has to be me."

Jake ground his teeth. He didn't want June to have to go face to face with Cotter, but it was the only logical thing to do. Kenna was just a kid, and he wouldn't permit her to endanger herself like that. Mark was an older guy who looked to be not in the best shape, not to mention his emotional state was questionable at this point. As for himself, Jake had to be ready to take out Cotter when the time came.

Jake nodded. "It has to be you. I just wish it could be somebody else."

"Don't worry." June smiled. "It's going to be okay. If Mia can stop Cotter, then it's worth the risk. Mia, I'll be your guide. If we manage to pull this off, then I want you to enter into me."

The disk spelled out, I WILL.

"When Cotter tricked us, he told us to say 'By the power of wind and fire, I give you passage. Eachlais'. Is that what we need to say?" Kenna asked.

Yes.

Kenna turned around. "We all have to say it."

June said, "Okay, Mia, are you ready for this?"

Mia answered Yes.

In unison, they said, "By the power of wind and fire, we give you passage. Eachlais." During the first five times they said the words, nothing happened. Then a wind blew through the office even though no windows were open. The next time they chanted, the wind grew stronger, blowing papers off Mark's desk. The wind continued to gust harder each time they repeated the phrase. A bright light flashed on one side of the room. A roaring flame rippled across the room, but it didn't seem like anything was actually burning other than the air itself. When the wind blew the flame toward them, Jake had to fight the urge to duck for cover.

"By the power of wind…" June stopped suddenly in mid-sentence. Her head snapped back, her momentum knocking her to the floor, where she landed with a thud.

"June!" Jake ran over to her. The turbulence that had been present subsided. He looked into her wide eyes. "June, are you okay?"

She blinked rapidly and shook her head. "I'm not June."

Jake backed up. Her voice no longer sounded like that of the June he knew. "Mia?"

She nodded. "Yes. I'm Mia. I—I managed to break through."

In the background, Mark's voice sounded like a croak. "Mia."

She began to rise, and Jake extended his hand to help her to her feet. "Mark? Is that you?"

He nodded.

A small smile crept onto Mia's face. "You look…different."

His cheeks were damp with tears. "Well, it has been a long time."

Mia nodded. "I suppose it has."

"God, I've missed you." He stepped forward, embraced her, and broke out into a full sob.

After a minute, Mia broke away from the embrace. "We have to deal with Cotter. Where is he?"

Jake shook his head. "We don't know. I fought against him in a cage last night, but now we don't know where he's at, who he's possessing, or anything else."

Mia frowned. "You fought him in a cage?"

"It's a long story," Jake said. "What I can tell you is that he's been killing people and committing other crimes, then switching bodies, all the while leaving others to pay the price for his crimes."

"That sounds just like Cotter," Mia said. "We have to stop him. It was an incredible ordeal to get here, and I need to bring Cotter back with me. First, we need to find him."

"That's not going to be easy," Jake said. "We have no idea where he is or even who he is. Mark has a private investigator trailing him, but after our fight last night, we lost his scent so to speak."

Jake looked at his phone when it chimed with a text. He gasped. The text came from his mom. It contained a photo with her tied to a chair. She wore a look of terror. The message read, *Stopped by your house Jakey. You weren't here but your mom was.*

Jake cried out, trying to fight the rising panic. "We have to go. Cotter's at my house and has my mom tied up."

Chapter XXXVIII

With the others in the car, he sped back to his house, his mind filled with dreadful possibilities. While they were talking, he tuned them out, praying his mom would not be harmed. He was hoping she could stay out of this mess, but now Cotter forced his hand. He was going to kill the son of a bitch.

When they arrived at his house, Jake ran to the front door, and the others followed closely. Jake opened the door and found Cotter. Rage coursed through his veins as he stared at his adversary.

Before Jake could think to do something, Mia stepped forward. "You don't belong here, Cotter. Your life extinguished years ago. This place is for the living."

Cotter sneered. "Fuck off, bitch. If you like that place so much, then why don't you go back? As for me, I was never down with the after-life. This is where I belong, right here with my good friends, Jake and Kenna."

Jake turned to Kenna. "Stay back! Find somewhere safe to hide."

"He can't hurt her," Mia said.

"What do you mean?" Jake asked.

"Kenna's his conduit. He entered the world through her, and therefore he cannot harm her. In fact, he must ensure that no harm comes to Kenna, just as I must ensure that no harm comes to June."

Cotter snarled. "Shut up, you stupid bitch."

"It seems as if I gave away his little secret."

That little nugget of information gave Jake relief, but Kenna could still get in the line of fire.

"Stay back, Kenna." Jake motioned with his hand. "Where's my mom?"

"Don't you worry about her," Cotter replied. "She's tucked away nice and safe."

"Leave my mom out of this," Kenna said.

Jake gritted his teeth. "Stay back. This is dangerous."

With obvious reluctance, Kenna took a few steps back and to the side. She still wasn't far away enough for Jake's liking, but he couldn't afford to take his eyes off Cotter.

"This is between you and me, Cotter. You obviously didn't come here for my sister. You don't know Mark and couldn't have been aware that we would be summoning Mia. I'm the one you want. Well, here I am. There's no need to involve anyone else."

Cotter smirked. "Yeah, I may not be able to do anything to Kenna, but I wouldn't mind taking out this fat lawyer or that skinny bitch from beyond the grave. I've killed almost a dozen people since I've been back including a cop just the other night. I'm having the fucking time of my life."

"Leave them alone." Jake took a couple of steps forward. "Let's settle this like men. I gave you a ridiculous beatdown last night. I know that must be eating away at you. You want revenge. Well, here I am. No cage. No referee. No rules. Just me and you."

"Yeah, that's all well and good, but I ain't playing your game." Cotter pulled out a gun from his jacket.

From behind him, Kenna screamed.

Cotter laughed. "You don't look so tough anymore. You think you're some kind of bad ass. Well, I told you I was going to put you six feet under. I may be many things, but I ain't a liar."

There was no time to think. It was all instinct and reaction. Still about ten feet away from Cotter, Jake charged at him like he was shooting in for a takedown. He dove left at the last moment, anticipating Cotter's reaction.

Cotter pulled the trigger just as Jake dove left. The bullet sailed past him. A moment later, he heard a scream. There was no time to look back. This time he shot in at Cotter's legs, grabbed both of them, and began to take him down. As Cotter was falling, he smashed Jake on the forehead with the butt of the gun. Things went momentarily black for Jake. He opened his eyes quickly, trying his damndest to not let consciousness ebb from him.

He continued to try to take Cotter down but got smashed once more by the butt of the gun. Blood flowed freely down his forehead and into his eyes and mouth. Despite that, he managed to drive Cotter to the ground.

Mia ran toward them and jumped on top of Cotter. She grabbed his gun, but he swatted her away with his free hand. Cotter pointed the weapon at Jake. Although Jake wasn't able to get the leverage he wanted, he punched Cotter's throat, causing him to gag and gasp for air.

Mia jumped on top of him once more and bit his hand.

Cotter screamed. "You fucking cunt."

Jake grabbed Cotter's throat with one hand and landed an elbow to the bridge of his nose.

Mia ripped the gun from his hand. It went flying and bounced off the ground. This created a mad scramble for the pistol. Cotter and Jake fought each other, trying to reach it. In the process, Cotter slammed Jake's face into the coffee table, the blow splitting his face open.

Dazed and bleeding like a slaughtered pig, Jake crawled toward the gun, but before he or Cotter could reach it, Mia clasped the gun. He wasn't sure what kind of experience Mia had with firearms, but she didn't seem confident in her grip of the weapon. Before she had a chance to fire it, Cotter punched her in the gut, causing Mia to double over. Cotter ripped the gun from her hand. He was about to turn the weapon on her, when Jake found his legs, lunged forward, and slugged Cotter in the jaw. A backhand from Cotter sent Jake reeling to the floor. Cotter fired the pistol. His reaction time slowed by the blows to the head, Jake could not escape the path of the bullet. Blinding pain seared through him as the bullet tore through his right shoulder.

He couldn't tell if it was a clean wound or if the bullet was still lodged in him. All he knew was that he never experienced pain this intense, including when he had appendicitis.

Jake found himself on the wrong end of the barrel of the gun as it stared straight at him. He tried to move, but his body wasn't in the mood to listen.

Out of nowhere, Kenna ran at Cotter and jumped on his back. Like a fury, she scratched at his eyes. Cotter flailed at her with his arms and eventually tossed her aside. Undeterred, Kenna jumped onto his back again. This time she pulled his hair. Blinded by pain, his vision blurred from all the blood, Jake had never been prouder of his sister. She was a fighter. No doubt about it.

Inspired by watching Kenna fight as if she was possessed, Jake shook his head, blood flying in all directions. He got to his feet, took two steps forward and landed a side kick to Cotter's head that knocked him off his feet. Kenna, who had still been pulling at Cotter's hair, went crashing to the floor. From his vantage point, his sister looked to take a hard fall. Cotter slid along the floor and knocked into Mark Saleski. It was the first that Jake had seen of Mark since the conflict began. Lying in a pool of blood, he must have been shot when Cotter fired his shot.

Mark was wincing in pain but still alive.

Jake went to get Cotter. The gun had fallen out of his hand. Jake had to capitalize on this momentary advantage. He grabbed

Cotter's shoulders. "You son of a bitch." He slugged him once, twice, three times in the face. He expected Cotter to fight back, but, instead, he just moaned. Something was wrong. Cotter never gave up. Even when he was taking a beating, he still had some smart retort to offer. Jake dropped him and turned around. That's when he saw an evil glint in Mark's eyes. Jake gritted his teeth. Cotter must have switched bodies when they made contact.

Cotter, now in Mark's body, went for the gun. Just as his hand clutched the weapon, Jake gave him a soccer kick to the abdomen. Cotter got to his feet, and Jake punched him twice in the face.

"Hold him, Jake," Mia shouted.

Jake did as instructed, grabbing him by the waist. Cotter tried to break free, but he had made a huge, calculated mistake. Having switched over to Mark's body, presumably to use the element of surprise against Jake, he took possession of a wounded man. Now that Jake had a good grip on him, he was not about to let Cotter get free.

Mia grabbed Cotter's hands and held them tight. "With the power of earth and water, set you free."

Cotter snarled. "What are you doing?" He tried to break away from Jake's grip, but Jake squeezed harder. There was no way in hell he was going to let him loose.

Mia stared into Cotter's eyes. "With the power of earth and water, set you free."

Cotter shook his head. "No!"

This time Jake repeated along with her, "With the power of earth and water, set you free."

Kenna stood alongside them and chanted, "With the power of earth and water, set you free."

A misty funnel formed in the office. It resembled a twister as it began sucking things into it. The surrounding air filled with mist. Anything that was loose began to swirl in this funnel.

Cotter gave a horrific moan. They continued to chant as the room became a chaotic scene. A loud boom sounded, and everything became still.

Cotter's head slumped forward. He no longer struggled. Still, Jake would not let go. Cotter was the master of trickery, and Jake wasn't about to be duped by him again.

"Is he gone?" Kenna asked. "And are you still Mia?"

Mia nodded. "Cotter's no longer here. Mark, it's Mia. Are you there?"

There was no response. Jake still held tight just in case.

"Mark, please come back to me. It's Mia."

Still nothing.

"I love you, Mark. I always have."

Mark raised his head. "Mia?"

Mia smiled. "Yes, it's me."

Jake finally felt confident enough to loosen his grip. Due to Mark's leg injury, Jake supported his weight.

"What's going on?" Mark had a look of wide-eyed confusion. "What happened?"

"Cotter took possession of you, but he's gone now," Mia said. "He's gone and he won't come back."

"Thank God." Mark took a deep breath. "Thank God. I've missed you, Mia." Mark's shoulders sagged. "I'm so sorry. I wasn't there for you back then. If I had been, things could have been different. For both of us. You wouldn't have died. We would have gotten married. All of it because I wasn't there for you."

Mia gently touched his face. "It's okay, Mark."

"I've been living with this ever since. Can you find it within yourself to forgive me?"

"There's nothing to forgive," Mia said. "But to set your soul at ease, I do forgive you. I have to leave. You and Jake need medical attention, not to mention that I don't belong here."

Mark nodded. "I know."

Mia gave Kenna a hug. "Thank you for being a friend to me when I needed one. And thank you for being brave in the face of danger."

Kenna began to sob. "I wish none of this had happened, but I'm glad I became your friend."

Mia moved over to Jake. Still supporting Mark, he felt as if he was going to pass out any moment now. The pain in his shoulder turned into numbness. His blood loss had been substantial. Still, he couldn't help but feel a sense of satisfaction.

"Jake, I owe you an eternal debt of gratitude. The courage you displayed today is beyond compare. You could have easily dismissed your sister's assertions as a child's imagination, but you stood by her. I see greatness in your future." Mia gave him a peck on the cheek. "And please express my gratitude to June for allowing me to use her body. I'm sure I would have liked her if I had the chance to get to know her."

Mia held Mark's hands and gently kissed his lips. It weirded Jake out since she was in June's body. He reminded himself that it wasn't June. It was Mia.

"I'll miss you, Mark." Mia slowly walked away. As she did, she chanted some words under her breath. Jake couldn't make out what she was saying. His eyes closed, and he swayed, having a hard time keeping himself standing.

Suddenly Mia stopped walking. She rapidly shook her head and blinked several times. She had a dazed look on her face.

"Mia?" Mark asked.

There was no response.

"June, is that you?" Jake asked.

When she did not respond, he was pretty certain it was June. Mark had come to quickly after Cotter left, but he had only been in Mark's body for about a minute. Mia had occupied June for much longer, so her recovery wouldn't be so quick.

"What's going on?" June mumbled incoherently

Kenna tugged at June's arm. "Mark and Jake both have both been shot. Everything's okay now. Cotter's gone for good. We need to get them to a hospital."

"Make sure she's okay." Jake raced out to look for his mom. He found her tied to a chair in the basement. He unbound and ungagged her.

His mom broke out into hysterics, so he did his best to calm her and tell her that the danger was over, and the situation was under control. He briefly tried to explain what had happened but didn't have time to answer all her questions. He had not heard any police arriving yet, but he couldn't count on that happening with the gun shots.

He returned with his mom upstairs. June was sitting on the sofa. She still looked dazed but more coherent than she had before.

Jake took out his cell phone and dialed 911, telling them two people had been shot.

Kenna filled June and her mom in on everything that had happened.

When Kenna finished, June said, "What are we going to do with this guy Cotter had been possessing? We're in no condition to get him out of here, and he won't know a thing about what happened?"

Jake shook his head. "There's nothing to do. Listen, before the police and ambulances arrive, this is our story..."

Chapter XXXIX

When the dust settled, Jake had managed to escape relatively unscathed. He had been treated for his bullet wound, and received thirty-two stitches on his head and face, but was able to leave the hospital a day later. He considered himself lucky. Things had gone much worse for Mark Saleski. Mark had spent twelve days in the hospital, part of the time in the intensive care unit. He was touch and go for a while. Besides the bullet wound to his leg and the loss of blood, he had developed an infection.

The story they went with to the police was that an unknown assailant, who turned out to be a man from the Mount Airy section of Philadelphia named Tom Wentworth, attacked them at Jake's home. They had no idea who this man was or why he attacked them. The reason they had been in Mark's office to begin with was to see if he would agree to represent Adam Fallon in his criminal trial. When they learned his mom was in danger, they rushed over to the house. The police had questioned why he had not called 911 when he received the text, and he told them he though the assailant might kill his mom if they had. The assailant had shot Jake and Mark before they were able to subdue him. Since they couldn't hustle Tom Wentworth out of the house, they had no choice but to let him take the fall. The truth was not an option. However, they declined to press charges against the man. Thus far, the case against Tom Wentworth was pending and the police had not decided whether or not to press charges against him.

There had been a fair bit of media attention to the story. Jake did his best to protect Kenna from it and tried to say as little as possible. Not that he was in any shape to fight, but Jake had been offered a half-dozen fight opportunities, including a couple from bigger organizations. Apparently, his beat down of a malevolent spirit, combined with the new fame he garnered, made him a hot commodity. He didn't care about those things. He just wanted to put this behind him, get back to training, and continue to explore his relationship with June. This whole ordeal had brought them closer. Now that she was a permanent fixture in his life, he couldn't be happier.

Today, Mark was finally being released from the hospital. Jake, June, and Kenna were going to be his welcoming committee. His kids apparently had other commitments and his soon to be ex-wife didn't want to have anything to do with him, all of which saddened Jake.

When they arrived at his hospital room, Mark was sporting a cane.

June smiled. "You look distinguished with that cane."

"I feel like a broken down old man. I have a lot of rehab ahead of me. Believe me, I plan on ditching this cane before long."

Jake patted his back. "Well, I'm doing rehab for my shoulder. We can work out together. Then when you're all mended, I can teach you how to fight in case Cotter ever comes back."

"Sorry I couldn't have been more help to you that day."

"Hey, man, you got shot in the leg," Jake said. "Trust me. You helped us plenty."

"Not to mention, we had an assist from the spirit world," June said. "Mia's something else. Too bad I never got a chance to meet her in person."

Mark nodded. "She was something. If there's such a thing as a soul mate, then she was mine. That's probably why none of my relationships have been able to work since then."

Kenna stared at Jake. "See. I told you so."

Mark frowned. "What are you guys talking about?"

Jake rolled his eyes. "Kenna has many theories about relationships that are beyond her years."

Mark nodded. "I see. Kenna's pretty sharp. She just might have things figured out. I would listen to her if I were you."

Jake smiled. "Yeah, she is pretty sharp."

"Well, at least something good has come out of this whole ordeal," Mark said.

"Oh, yeah?" Jake asked.

"I was inspired by the story you concocted when this all went down with the police. I decided to give Adam Fallon a call at the prison. After speaking to him on the phone, I will now be his attorney."

Jake's brows rose. "Really? You think you'll be able to get him off on those charges?"

"I can't promise anything," Mark said. "But without sounding immodest, I am pretty capable in the court room. I have a few tricks up my sleeve. Not to mention, based on what I know about the situation, I'll have a better chance of representing him than any other attorney he might go with. And I'll take his case free of charge. As far as Tom Wentworth goes, with none of us willing to testify against him, they won't have much of a case."

"That's great," Jake said. "Hopefully you can right some of the wrong that Cotter did. Unfortunately, we can't do anything about the people he killed, but these innocent people he possessed shouldn't be imprisoned because of what he did."

"It will give me something to look forward to as I do my rehab. I need something to give me purpose."

Kenna hugged Mark. "Thank you for agreeing to meet us that first time. When you saw we were a bunch of kids, you could have left, but you didn't. You're a good guy."

After the hospital staff discharged Mark, Jake drove him home. They walked Mark to his house.

"Thank you for being here for me." Mark lowered himself so that he was face to face with Kenna. "And the next time you talk to Mia, say hi for me."

"I will," Kenna said.

***

Later that evening, when Jake and June were together in her basement, he said, "This whole ordeal has taught me something."

"What's that, Mr. Introspective?" June asked.

"Always treasure what you value most in life and let those people know what you think of them because you never know if you might lose them. I love you, June."

June leaned in and kissed him tenderly on the lips. "And I love you. You know, we just might make a deep thinker of you yet."

"Don't count on it. Another thing I learned from all of this is that I'm a simple guy and I like my problems simple."

***

At the school playground, Kenna gave her friends a recap of picking up Mark at the hospital.

"I still can't believe you did all of this without us," Cordy said. "We should have been there."

"It was dangerous," Kenna said. "Jake and Mark got shot. That could have been one of you guys."

Ben put his hands in his pocket. "Well, we still should have been there for you. That's what friends do. I wish you had let us know."

Kenna put her arm around Ben's shoulder. "Next time I go up against a crazy, psychotic spirit, you'll be the first person I tell."

Ben rolled his eyes. "Thanks."

"So, are we going to contact Mia again?" Carlos asked.

"Of course," Kenna said. "Mia's our friend. If she needs someone to talk to, then we have to be there for her."

"But what if Cotter tries to sneak up on us?" Cordy asked.

"I know what it feels like when Mia is on the other end," Kenna said. "We have this connection, and I think meeting her in person will make it even stronger. If it's someone pretending to be her, I'll know. So far, she hasn't seen Cotter on the other side. Hopefully, it will stay that way. But as long as Mia needs us, we'll be there for her."

Thank you for taking the time to read my novel, *The Invocation*. I hope you enjoyed it. As an indie author, book reviews are vital. I would sincerely appreciate it if you could take a few minutes to post a review of this novel on Amazon.

Battle of the Soul

By Carl Alves

Andy Lorenzo has no family, few friends, poor social skills, and drinks and gambles far too much. But in a time when demons are becoming increasingly more brazen and powerful, he has one skill that makes demons cower in fear from him—he is the greatest exorcist the world has ever known.

In Battle of the Soul, a supernatural thriller that is a combination of Constantin and The Exorcist, since graduating high school Andy has left a long trail of demons in his wake while priests are dying while performing traditional rites of exorcism. Andy is the Church and society's ultimate weapon in combating this growing epidemic. He needs no bibles, prayers, or rituals. Andy is capable of going inside the person's soul where he engages in hand-to-hand combat using his superhuman abilities that only reside when he is in a person's soul. When eight-year-old Kate becomes possessed, Andy finds an elaborate trap waiting for him. He will do whatever it takes to win the most important fight of his life—the battle for Kate's soul.

"Ready for a lighthearted Battle of the Soul? Andy Lorenzo's got the requisite exorcism skills, but he's no single-minded zealot nor cynical bleak arts practitioner. He gets the biz done with a deft touch and a wink and a nod to family values. It's not John Constantine here but try Cary Grant in Monkey Business. Battle of the Soul is a fine, fun supernatural read!— Mort Castle, Bram Stoker Award Winning Author of The Strangers

Get your copy of Battle of the Soul on Amazon.

Conjesero

By Carl Alves

SAN Francisco homicide detective Kevin Russell has arrested serial rapists, murderers, and more sadistic thugs than he could remember. Nothing he has ever accomplished can prepare him for Conjesero, a supernatural serial killer who has been terrorizing the Americas for centuries. Conjesero—a creature with extraordinary intelligence and a vicious nature that has created a trail of bodies from Mexico to San Francisco—has always made law enforcement cower in fear and pretend that he doesn't exist. Only Kevin is willing to stand in its path. His desperation takes him on a journey inside the killer's twisted world. There is nothing that he is unwilling to do, even if it means making a deal with the devil, to stop Conjesero or die trying.

A well-rounded mix of mystery, action, and horror; the Conjesero is one of the most memorable and monstrous of evil killers written in years. — Eric J. Guignard, winner of the Bram Stoker Award and finalist for the International Thriller Writers Award

Get your copy of Conjesero on Amazon.

Blood Street

By Carl Alves

BLOOD Street is True Blood meets the Sopranos set in the streets of Philadelphia.

When vampires tangle with the Philadelphia mafia, one thing is certain - all hell is going to break loose.

Alexei chose the wrong neighborhood to claim his latest victim, a member of Enzo Salerno's crime syndicate. Now Philadelphia mob boss Enzo Salerno is determined to hunt down the man who killed his associate in such gruesome fashion in his South Philly row home and serve his own brand of old-fashioned Italian style vengeance.

Perplexed by this unnatural murder, Salerno uncovers clues that lead him to believe that this was not a mob hit, and that a vampire was responsible for this death. Magnus, the leader of Alexei's brood, must use all of his resources to save them from both the mafia and the FBI, sparking a bloody war that plays out in the streets of Philadelphia. Who will survive on Blood Street?

About the Author

Carl is the author of four published novels which span the horror, fantasy, and science fiction genres in no particular order. He lives in Central Pennsylvania with his wife and the two most awesome boys you have ever met. When not feverishly conjuring stories about monsters, aliens, and things that go bump in the night, he works as an engineer for a medical device company. Find out more about him by visiting his website at www.carlalves.com.

Printed in Great Britain
by Amazon

20210638R00195